E.S Andersson

William Silvercrona

and the magical goblet

Publisher: BoD · Books on Demand, Östermalmstorg 1, 114 42 Stockholm, bod@bod.se
Print: Libri Plureos GmbH, Friedensallee 273, 22763 Hamburg, Tyskland

ISBN: 978-91-8080-001-3

CHAPTER I
FLIGHT OVER THYRRIDEA

William looked out the glass window. Far away, through the gray morning haze, he glimpsed land.

"I can't believe we're almost home," dad said, hugging both William and Anne. The glass bubble floated peacefully through the air. William turned around and looked at the captain who was navigating the glass ship with a joystick on the black keyboard. He looked relaxed. The captain looked up and met William's eyes and said with a smile, "Would you like to try steering the ship?" He saw that William hesitated a little and added, "I will help you." William went over to the captain.

"What fun," Tim said, I'd love to watch.

Captain Nickodemus pointed at the keyboard and the different symbols on it. "You don't have to worry about them. You only need to use the joystick to steer the ship. If you pull it towards you, we'll rise, if you push it forward, we'll fly lower, if you point it to the left the ship turns to the left and if you point it to the right we'll turn right. It's not complicated at all." The captain handed the control table to William. William wrapped his right hand around the joystick and the captain put his hand over Williams and helped him to steer. "Now you can try to point the joystick half a centimeter to the left." William did as the captain said and he noticed how the glass bubble gently swung to the left.

"Now, push the joystick half a centimeter forward." The glass ship responded immediately and began gently to descend. William then straightened the joystick so that the ship leveled out. "You're really good at this," the captain said and gave him a pat on the shoulder. "You can continue to steer the ship straight ahead and I'll go and talk to your parents for a while. Let me know if you need any help."

Tim stood next to William. "Isn't it cool to steer the ship," he said with a smile.

"Mm," William answered and nodded, he was fully focused on steering. He looked out and saw how they were slowly approaching Thyrridea. After William had steered the ship for a few minutes and noticed how easy the glass ship was to steer, he began to relax. Tim was still standing next to him.

"Do you want to try?" William asked.

"Of course," Tim answered quickly. William handed over the joystick to Tim who continued to steer the ship straight ahead.

As they approached land the captain looked up. "You can continue to follow the coastline. I'll take over when we approach Libra."

"Ah yes," William said, "the capital is called Libra. I had almost forgotten that."

"I can fly a little lower so you can see more of the coast?" Tim said.

"Yes, please do," William replied.

The ship descended and William could clearly see the landscape beneath. The coastline of Thyrridea was surrounded by a rough and turbulent sea with waves crashing over the cliffs. The steep rock formations looked almost majestic as they rose up out of the dark blue sea. The wind picked up slightly and William watched as the waves splashed in over land. William noticed a white lighthouse at the far end of a small island off the mainland.

"That's the Lantern," Tim informed him, pointing to the lighthouse. "It has saved many ships from running aground. You see, the rocks are treacherous. It's really hard to navigate in this area," he said frowning. "Some rocks are barely visible and are located just below the surface of the water and you really have to watch out for them otherwise it's easy to run aground."

William was completely taken by the beautiful but dramatic landscape. "Is there anyone who lives out here?" William asked.

"Of course," Tim answered and pointed with his left hand. William saw that there was a small wooden cabin on one of the cliffs. "If you look a little further inland, you will see a farmhouse." William looked towards where Tim was pointing and saw that there was a farmhouse on a small island. In the center of the island was lush green grass that sheep grazed on. The island was surrounded on all sides by steep cliffs that plunged almost vertically into the water.

"It's very windy on the coast," Tim said. "The family has had to reinforce the house and they have wooden shutters to cover the windows so that they won't break in the strong wind that sometimes occur."

"How do they get food and how do the children get to school?" William wondered.

"Twice a week they get food and supplies by air transport and the children can choose whether they want to be taught remotely by computer or if they want to go to a boarding school. I think the younger children are taught from home while the older ones go to boarding school during the week." Tim said.

"Right." William said. Then they never have to go to school if they don't want to, William thought, but of course, it can get a bit lonely sometimes without friends to play with.

Tim interrupted William's thoughts. "But not many people live out by the cliffs. Most people live more inland. William continued to look out through the ship.

The glass ship continued over the coastline, passing the high cliffs. Beneath them, the land changed to what looked like a mixture of moorland and pebbles.

"For how long does this steppe spread out?" William wondered. "Probably for at least 4 kilometers," Tim answered, "But I'm not entirely sure, it could be longer." Mm, William thought, no wonder that there's little that can grow here, it seems to be a really windswept landscape. It looked desolated. "When do we reach the capital?" he asked.

"In about 20-30 minutes," Tim said.

"Tim, change course about 1 centimeter to the right!" the captain called out. Tim did as Nickodemus said and the ship steered gently to the right.

William saw that the landscape began to change character and below them lush meadows and hills began to spread out. The hills were low enough so that the landscape still gave a fairly flat impression. Here and there were a few groves of trees that provided shelter from the wind. But he still didn't see many houses. "How many people live in Thyrridea?"

"It's a pretty big country," Tim answered. "I believe it's about 20 million, but most people live in the three major cities of Laubery, Keansbridge and of course Libra which has about 7 million inhabitants."

20 million, about twice the size of Sweden, William mumbled.

"How are you feeling?" William's mother asked. "I'm really excited to see Libra," William answered, "but it'll be much larger than Sigtuna."

"That's right, William." I think we'll land in the middle of the city. There's an airport next to the school that you are going to go to." William's mother called out to the captain, wondering. "Are we going to land at West Clermont Lincoln University?"

"That's right," Nickodemus replied. "It's the nearest airport to your destination."

Below them, a mountain range began to spread out. "I'll take the controls now," the captain said, thanking Tim and William for their help. Nickodemus guided the vessel over the mountains and continued to fly over one mountain range after another. The ship was now high above the clouds and the wind increased significantly. The ship swayed violently in the wind. William sneaked a look at the captain as he steered the ship, but he seemed very calm.

"Please sit down in your seats and fasten your seat belts. This part of the flight is always a bit turbulent," the captain said calmly.

William and the others sat down and fastened their seat belts. Luckily, it was just in time because suddenly they hit a huge air pocket that almost took William's breath away.

"When the green light is turned on, you can remove your seat belts," the captain informed. After about 10 minutes of flight, the red light went off and the green light came on.

"Welcome to Libra! Nickodemus exclaimed solemnly. William quickly ran up to the window to look out. Below him, a huge city spread out. It was nestled in between several mountains. Tall buildings and clocktowers were visible everywhere. Several buildings were made of natural colored stone.

"Look there is the cathedral," William's father Henry said, pointing to a huge cathedral. The building was made of some kind of white sandstone, William thought. The cathedral was pointedly built and had large windows.

"We're going to visit it later on," dad continued.

One side of the city was open to the sea while the rest of the city was surrounded by mountains. When William looked down, he saw that the buildings were arranged in what looked like several small city centers on different islands within the city. There were several bridges over the river that snaked through the city. In some places the river was wider and some places it was narrower with a small footbridge over it.

"Libra is a city that is best explored from the water," Henry said.

"There is a boat trip I thought we should take so you can see the city," his mother filled in.

The city was built on slopes. Some areas were high up on the mountains while others were at sea level. William really liked what he saw. He liked the mixture of the high mountains with their steep cliffs and the proximity of the sea. "What a fantastic city!" he exclaimed.

Anne looked at him and gave him a hug. "I'm glad you like it."

"It's beautiful, almost majestic," William said, looking at the magnificent stone buildings. Some skyscrapers were built with glass, some shifted in a mixture of blue and gray while others shimmered in pearl and pale yellow. "I like the mix of the old stone buildings and the modern glass buildings," William said.

"Yes, it's beautiful," William's mother Anne sighed. They passed a large green area with several large leafy trees that almost formed a small forest. In the middle there was a lake. "It's the big park in Libra," Anne said. "This is where people go to have picnics, swim, run or relax. Sometimes we call it the lungs of Libra. You know photosynthesis and our need to breath in the fresh air of green vegetation and relax."

William nodded. The glass ship steered to the right and began to rise higher into the sky. I think we're getting closer to West Clermont Lincoln. William saw that they were flying over the older part of the city. There were no glass buildings here and most buildings were built of stone. The streets were a little narrower and the river only ran through it in a few places. The ship rose higher and the surrounding mountains were huge. There, almost in the middle of the city, he saw a gigantic building in light gray stone. The building lay on a hill that was covered with cobblestones. But the cobblestones were not as small as cobblestones usually are, instead they were much larger stones that were worn and slightly rounded and shiny from people walking on them through the years. William thought they almost looked smooth. An avenue with large oak trees along both sides led up to the entrance and a massive stone staircase led up to the two large green copper doors. At each side there were torches burning, placed in black wrought iron holders.

"Look to the right of the building William!" the captain shouted, "that's the airport." William looked to the right of the huge light gray stone building and in contrast to the old building, there was a large round black runway.

"You know William," the captain continued, "this ship doesn't need a long runway." To the left of the runway was a hangar where William glimpsed three aircrafts. A little further away was an air traffic control tower. Nickodemus steered the ship above the round runway and the ship landed softly. William saw that the huge building continued at a 90-degree angle behind the front. "Ladies and gentlemen, it's time to disembark." One of the doors in the ship was lowered and at the same time a staircase appeared from the lower part of the ship.

First out of the ship was the king of Thyrridea, Victor the first, with his two assistants, followed by William's mother and father, William and finally Tim. The captain saluted them all and wished them a pleasant stay in the country.

"I had forgotten how heavy my luggage was," William whispered to his mother.

"Oh, how hot it is!" William exclaimed loudly. It was really hot even though it was only morning. The temperature was over 25 degrees Celsius. "I really need to change into something lighter," William sighed and squinted in the sunlight.

"We will," Anne said. "Just wait a little while, I think the king wants to say something to you." William looked up. "Dear Mr. William. I want to thank you on behalf of the people of Thyrridea for your wise intervention. Without you the balance would not have been restored. Truly an excellent performance. Thank you!" The King cleared his throat again and looked at Tim. "Tim, I would also like to thank you for your efforts." The King then shook hands with William, Tim, Anne and Henry and then left in a brightly polished black car.

"Alright," Tim said, "I have to run to school and see what's on today's schedule. I'll see you around!"

"We will," William replied.

"Goodbye Mr. and Mrs. Silvercrona," Tim said and shook hands with William's parents. Tim started to walk towards the entrance. He turned to William and shouted "I would love to show you around the school but it's against the rules. It's decided that your mentors will do it."

"What a shame," William shouted back.

"I know" Tim called back and waved.

"It will be a few years before I start at West Clermont Lincoln University. I will have a few years of home school first so that I can get used to the country," William said.

"That sounds like a good idea," Tim said, "but we can stay in touch anyway."

"Of course!" William replied. He felt incredible happy that he already had a friend in Thyrridea.

CHAPTER 2
A TRIP BY BOAT ON THE WATER

"What do we do now?" William asked.

"Well," Henry said, "either we go home and change or we go on that boat trip we talked about."

"Let's take the boat trip," William said.

"All right, let's do it," Anne said. "We just need to figure out how to get there. It's a bit too far to walk. I wonder which bus route it could be?"

"We can take a boat taxi or an ordinary taxi," Henry filled in. William saw a black car with tinted windows pull up next to them. A window was rolled down.

"Excuse me, Silvercrona family? King Victor the first wanted me to tell you that this car is at your disposal all day." The driver explained.

William's mother shone up. "How thoughtful, please do express our thanks to the king. Let's get into the car," Anne said cheerfully. The driver got out of the car and opened the trunk and put in their luggage. He then opened the door for William who jumped into the backseat with his father and finally he opened the front door for Anne. William sank into the dark blue velvet plush seat and enjoyed the cool air from the AC. The driver got into the driver's seat, turned the key and the car drove off.

"I would like to welcome you to Thyrridea," he said with a smile. "Where do you want to go? I can take you anywhere you wish."

"We would like to go to King's Square and take the boat trip through part of the city."

"Yes, it's a perfect day with perfect weather for a boat trip," the driver nodded. "Yesterday it would not have been pleasant as the rain poured down, it was a real thunderstorm. Towards King's Square!"

William looked out the car's tinted windows while the car cruised through the traffic. William could see that Libra was a capital city. Everywhere he saw stressed people walking hurriedly and huge traffic jams.

"As you can see," the driver said, "we're driving through the old part of Libra." William had also noticed it. The buildings were relatively low and most of them were built of stone. The roads were not very wide and paved with cobblestones. They crossed several bridges that led over the city's waterways. William rolled down the window as they waited in a traffic jam and the warm air fanned through the car.

"It almost feels like vacation, William told his mother.

"That's right, dear."

"When does my homeschooling start?" William
wondered.
"Not for another three weeks, so take the opportunity to
enjoy," William's father said.
"This is how life should be! William said happily."
"We will soon arrive at King's Square," the driver
informed. "You can buy tickets on board the boat." The
car stopped and William and his parents got out.
"I'll wait here until you return," the driver said.
"How incredibly kind of you," Anne replied smiling.
"We'd better hurry. It looks like the boat is getting ready
to leave." William looked up at the boat on the quayside.

The boat blew it's horn once and William and his parents
ran towards the gangway.
"You're lucky," the skipper said smiling. "Three tickets I
assume? Would you like to sit on the upper deck?"
"Three tickets will be fine," William replied and turned to
his mother. "Mom, can we sit on the upper deck? We'll get
the best view of the city."
"You don't think it'll be too windy?" his mother
wondered.
"No, I don't think so," William said firmly.
"Three tickets to the upper deck then!" the skipper said.
"Perfect," William replied. They walked to the front of the
boat and then followed a narrow steel spiral staircase up
to the upper deck.

"What a tall boat," William noted as he walked up the spiral staircase.

"At least four floors," his father said breathlessly. "It'll be nice to sit down!" When they reached the upper deck, it was really windy. William and his parents had been given seats at the front of the boat. The boat blew it's horn again and a bell rang.

"Welcome to 'The Pearl' and to the grand tour of Libra. The tour will take about 1.5 hours. We will show you the most famous buildings in Libra and at the same time tell you a little about the history of Libra," the speaker voice continued. "If you are sitting on the upper deck and find it too windy, you can press the red button that is located at the end of each row at the boat's railing. If you press the button, a pane of glass will rise up through the floor and protect you from the wind." As soon as the speaker voice became silent William's mother quickly leaned over William's father, who sat the end of the row, to press the red button.

"That was quick," William joked as the glass pane went up through a slot in the floor. William thought it felt good to be out of the strong wind, but he didn't really want to admit it to his mother.

Looking around, William saw that most of the seats were empty. On the upper deck there were about 100 seats in many rows of transparent plastic chairs that were bolted to the floor. William leaned back to feel if the chair was comfortable and it was. It feels like I'm sitting on something, William thought. He stood up and saw that he was sitting on a fairly thin, flat white cushion. Ah, he said quietly to himself and sat down again. The boat began to slowly leave the quay and went out to sea.

"We're now leaving King's Square," the speaker voice said. "It's where the King of Thyrridea, King Victor the First, was crowned 10 years ago. He took over after his father Wilhelm the First, who hastily fell ill." William looked up at King's Square. It was huge, built almost like an amphitheater with rows of seats carved out in a semi-circle. At the bottom was a flat stone stage and in the middle of it was a marble statue representing a royal crown and a scepter. Both the crown and the scepter were covered in gold leaf.

William's mother leaned to William and whispered "Sometimes they have concerts at King's Square and it's great to sit and listen to music while looking at the water." Behind King's Square was a gray building with two large stone columns on each side. The boat slowly began to turn around so that William was looking directly at the sea. William stood up and saw how the blue water hit the boat. "Now we'll leave Kings Place and steer the boat towards the cathedral," the speaker voice informed. The boat picked up speed and headed straight out into the open sea.

"Wonderful!" William cried out.

When they reached the open sea, Anne nudged William in the side. "Do you see that island over there on the right?" She pointed at a gray dot far out in the sea."

"Not really," William answered, "but maybe when we get closer–" William was interrupted by the speaker voice which continued "We will now approach Gardon island. This island actually consists of a mountain range that has risen out of the sea. The mountain range contains a lot of caves, even underground caves. It is said that there is to be underground passages from the mainland, but it may well be a tall tale."

The boat approached the mountain island at high speed. William looked fascinated as the island came into clearer view. Such huge cliffs, he thought.

Henry leaned to William. "There is an old folklore that says that King Oscar, who lived hundreds of years ago, had to take refuge in the underground passages of Gardon. Many have since searched for these passages, but so far there is nothing to prove that they actually exist."

"Exciting," William mumbled as he enthusiastically continued to look at the island. The boat passed the island and then continued forward.

"Now we are approaching the All-seeing lighthouse. The reason it is called the All-seeing lighthouse is that it has saved many ships from sinking in these waters. However, when Thyrridea was invaded in the 2nd century AD, it sent out false signals that caused the destruction of several of the enemy's ships. That's why many sailors joke about it

and says 'Let's see if I've been nice today' when the lighthouse sends its signals. I assume that our skipper has been nice," the speaker voice said with a laugh.
William looked at the lighthouse. It was a large, sturdy stone lighthouse. It appeared that it had been repaired several times and William could well understand that it was very old. Exciting with a lighthouse that seems to have magical powers, he mused.

The boat passed the lighthouse and began to head inland. They passed several islands. Most consisted of rocks, but some had grass and other vegetation.
"We will soon approach the old parts of Libra, the speaker voice continued. The oldest parts of Libra are from 700 BC. In fact, Libra is the oldest city in Thyrridea. Its history has been both long and varied, but since about 1350 AD, the same family has ruled Thyrridea. Do you wonder who ruled Thyrridea before that? Yes, it's a good question and not so easy to answer. But what we do know is that different families fought for power and the rulers usually did not last very long on the throne."
The boat began to slow down and sailed slowly towards a paved square.
"This is the Celestial Square. Here, King Leopold, the first king of Thyrridea was proclaimed king."
The square was made of polished marble with large marble stones lying in a zigzag pattern. In the middle of the square was a statue.

"It's probably Leopold," William whispered to his mother. "Yes, Henry said who had overheard William's whisper. "That's right, William."
The boat steered into a canal that was to the right of the square.
"Awesome," William exclaimed, "that we can continue the tour inside Libra. It's almost a bit like Venice!"
"Mm," Henry said, "Libra has many canals and this is one of the biggest!"

They followed a relatively wide canal. On both sides of the canal, different shopping lanes ran.
"Look, they're waving to us," William whispered to his mother. "Yes, they do!"
William looked around and saw that other people sitting on the upper deck were laughing and waving back.
So nice people seem to be here, William thought as he smiled and waved back.
"Do you see mom? Even dad laughs and waves."
"Yes," Anne giggled, "even dad."
William saw a stone bridge a little further ahead.
"That's a low bridge. Can we really manage to pass under it?" Just when William asked the question, he heard the speaker voice say. "Now we will soon pass through one of the many bridges that exist in Libra. Hold on tight and don't stand up. It's a narrow fit." William swallowed and saw how the stone bridge got closer. When they were just under the bridge, William impulsively reached up with

his right hand to feel the stone of the bridge. He thought he felt something rough so he looked up. He saw how a luminous little text quickly was written *"Welcome to Libra, I'll see you soon/ A."* William quickly blinked to see if he really had seen it but the text remained. "What fun!" William mumbled. A new text appeared *"Relax and enjoy the boat trip."* William almost began to giggle. He nodded and the text disappeared. Imagine, how cool it is that Arild can communicate with me here, William thought and felt light in his heart.

The boat passed under the bridge and a little further ahead William saw a huge stone church on an island. At the top of the church there was a tall tower with a large brass bell.

"Ahead you'll see the Cathedral of Libra. If you look up under the bell tower, you'll see a carillon, or as it's also called, a glockenspiel," the speaker voice enlightened them. William looked up, he had to put his hand in front of his eyes to be able to see because the strong sunlight almost blinded him. He squinted at the bell tower and saw small finely made marble figures that appeared to represent seven men in different costumes. Several of them had long caftans. He just began to think about what the seven different figures represented when the speaker's voice continued

"The carillon shows the seven men watching over Libra. According to legend, they stand for the balance of the country. It plays a tune twice a day. Seven o'clock in the morning and at midnight. The figures move in a circle and bless the land by looking out at the city while bowing their heads. As they pass each other, they bow to show the other respect and prosperity. The carillon rotates 3 turns and if you have the opportunity to listen to it during your visit, I think it is well worth the time. In popular speech, the bells are usually called the heavenly chimes because of their clean and delicate sound."

The boat rounded the cathedral and the speaker voice continued
"If you look at the left side of the cathedral, you will see a huge glass wall. The wall was built to let the first rays of the morning sun in and provide a magnificent light inside the church." William looked up at the formidable wall of glass mosaic that shifted in different bluish-purple tones.
"How beautiful!" William exclaimed.
"Yes, it sure is," his father replied. "Just wait until you have graduations at West Clermont School."
"Oh," William answered, "will all the school graduations be here?"
"Yes, Christmas and summer."
"Exciting, what a magnificent end to the semester," William said cheerfully while trying to imagine himself inside the cathedral.

"You will be able to visit the cathedral many times William," Anne said. "You will even have lessons in the cathedral if you choose that topic in your study plan."

"What?" William said surprised, "can I already choose which subjects I would like to study in school? That wasn't possible in Sigtuna."

"Yes," William's mother replied. "That's right, but not all subjects. Most subjects are still mandatory for you but there will be some optional subjects. One of these optional subjects is about significant churches and historical facts, but you'll find out more on your introductory day when it's time for you to go to the West Clermont school."

William, who had always liked history, was delighted.

"Do you remember, Mom, when I was little, I wanted to become an archaeologist?"

"Of course, I do!" Anne smiled and stroked his hair.

The boat passed by the western side of the cathedral and continued slowly through the old parts of Libra. There were well-maintained old stone houses with small windows and shutters everywhere.

"If you look to the left, you'll see Libra's main shopping street. It leads straight to a large shopping mall filled with shops and restaurants and even a library. Speaking of libraries," the voice continued, "I want you to look to the right at the big mountain top. If you use the binoculars attached to a pocket under your chairs, you can see Libra's oldest library located almost at the top of the mountain. In the past, you had to walk along a specific marked trail to get to the library and, as you can imagine, it took several days. Nowadays, there is a cable car that quickly takes you safely to the library."

William struggled to get the lens caps off the lenses of the binoculars, which were unfortunately a bit stuck.

"What the..." he said impatiently, but just then the lens caps came off and William could finally look at the mountain through his binoculars. William zoomed in and saw that on a cliff, just as the voice had said not far from the top lay something that almost looked like a fortress.

"But it looks more like a castle than a library." William whispered to his mother.

"You're right," his mother answered. "The library holds some of the most valuable books in the history of Libra, so the library was built as a fortress to defend against attackers, and believe me, many have tried to take over the library."

"Did anyone succeed?" William wondered.

"Yes, I'm afraid so. I think it has happened three times in the history of Thyrridea. Is that right?" Anne said wondering to Henry.

"Yes, that's right," William's father answered, "but it was nearly a fourth time, but it was repelled just before we moved to Sigtuna."

"Yes, I remember that," Anne said shivering. "I'm glad they didn't succeed."

"Security at the library is rigorous and every visitor has to identify themselves before entering the library's various rooms. The area is patrolled by guards both day and night and the surveillance systems are numerous and advanced. If you as a tourist want to visit the library and have forgotten your ID-card at home, you can get a temporary one at the nearest police station," the speaker voice informed.

William zoomed in on the library a little closer. The fortress was really impressive. Around it there was a moat filled with water. The fortress had four powerful towers and the walls seemed to be at least several meters thick and made of gray carved stone blocks. A stone bridge led across the moat to the two wooden gates. There were no windows but here and there on the fortress there were small openings. William wasn't sure if they were there to let daylight in or if they had some other function. William found it hard to take his eyes off the library and only when the boat turned into another canal did he put down his binoculars.

The speaker voice continued
"Straight ahead you can see the huge glass tower in Libra. If you, during your visit, want to get an overview of the city I recommend that you go up in the tower. From there you have a fantastic view of the whole city. You can also take the opportunity to have something to eat or drink in

one of the restaurants up in the tower. I can really recommend this and especially in the evening when most of our large buildings are illuminated in different colors. It is almost magically beautiful." the speaker voice said and sighed dreamily. "And speaking of beautiful, if you are interested in space I recommend that you also plan a visit to our observatory. You can see it on your right side." William looked to the right but saw only a department store.

"I need to clarify myself," the speaker voice continued, "you need to look up to the right." William did as the voice said and now he saw a high platform. The platform was like a 30 meter high cylinder and on top of it was the observatory. The observatory was a gigantic round glass building that shifted in a faint gray-blue shade.

"Wow," William said.

"We have to visit it," Henry whispered.

Anne and William nodded.

The voice continued; "The observatory opens at eight in the evening and at half past ten they have tour."

"Why do they open at eight when the tour is not until half past ten?" William heard a child whisper behind him.

The child almost immediately received a reply from the speaker voice. "At eight o'clock the film screening begins and you also have the opportunity to visit the space museum. At the Space Museum there is an opportunity to test what life is like inside a spaceship. This is usually a very popular attraction so make sure to get tickets in good time."

The boat passed the observatory and William immediately saw that a canal was closed. He took out his binoculars and read the sign, *No unauthorized access.* How strange, William thought, but he did not have time to think much about it because the speaker voice interrupted his thoughts.
"Now we will head out on one of the major canals and visit what is commonly referred to as the Lungs of Libra, which is the great park in Libra. "

The boat turned into a large wide canal and it was not long before a park spread out on both sides of the canal.
"Now we have arrived at Libra's largest park. It is over 2,3 square kilometers in size and contains several ponds as well as swimming facilities along one side of the canal. The park is carefully landscaped with an herb garden, a tropical garden and a ZOO. Of course, there are also a number of restaurants and cafés for those who so desire. The park was first built by King Leopold, but has been expanded over time. It is safe to say that the park is one of Libra's most popular destinations."
The boat passed through a part of the park and then turned west.

"We are probably on our way to the modern part of Libra," William's mother whispered. "I think you're really going to like that part of town."

The boat moved forward and William noticed that the houses began to change. There were still the cobbled streets, but instead of the lower stone houses, various large glass buildings could be seen.

"As you can see," the speaker voice said, "we are now in the modern part of Libra. It was built a hundred and fifty years ago and is a manifesto of glass, innovation and modernity. Several of these high-rise buildings are office buildings but there are also buildings that are dedicated to advanced research and contains many top-secret laboratories."

William saw a large atomic ball made up of small glass triangles and that shifted in all colors.

"The atom, or glass ball as it is called in popular speech, was built for the opening of the big research week held here in Libra two years ago. The atom symbolizes the beginning and the end of research, meaning that all research leads us to the beginning of the creation of all things. We will now go out into the sea again and then return to King's Square." The boat guide informed.

The boat entered one of the large canals and then out onto the open water. The boat increased speed and the wind picked up. William stood up and looked out over the dark blue water. Wonderful, William mused to himself. I can't believe I will live in this beautiful and exciting city. Although he had enjoyed living in Sigtuna very much and liked the small scale there, this was a more exciting and a considerably larger city that had more to offer. Libra is much larger than Stockholm, which is Sweden's largest city, William thought. If I miss them at home, I can always visit them. William felt happy and he liked the way the wind ruffled his hair. The boat went fast and made big waves in the water. William felt a rush of happiness in his stomach. This is really a new chapter in my life, he thought. William began to understand why his parents were so excited about moving back here. He stood in the bow of the boat for a long time and enjoyed being out at sea. What William had liked at home in Sigtuna was the proximity to water and here he also got to live in a town that was right next to the sea, he noted with satisfaction.

"We are approaching King's Square and I must therefore ask you to prepare to disembark." The speaker voice said. William saw King's Square in the distance. "We who work onboard the boat wishes to thank you for your interest during the tour and wishes you a pleasant day to stroll around in our beautiful city. Please watch out for signs that say *'private'* or *'No unauthorized access'*, these areas are off limits and you should absolutely not enter. Having said that, I hope you will have a pleasant afternoon." The guide fell silent and the people began to stand up.

CHAPTER 3
ROSENDAHLS STREET NO. 7

When William and his parents got off the boat and stood on the quayside, they saw the black car waiting for them. The driver got out of the car. "Did you have a pleasant boat trip?" he asked.

"It was incredible. It was really amazing to see the city again," William's mother answered with a smile.

"You are welcome into the coolness of the car," the driver said while he opened the door to Anne. William and his father took the opportunity to open the back doors themselves.

"Where do you want to go now?" the driver wondered when they sat down in the comfortable seats."

"I think it's time for us to go home to grandma and grandpa," Anne replied.

"Perfect," William said, who longed for his grandparents. He was also curious to see the house they were going to live in.

"Let me find the address. Where is it now?" William's mother said while rummaging around in her bag. "Here it

is!" Anne picked up a folded piece of paper and read it aloud. "Rosendahls street no. 7." The driver entered the address into the GPS and started driving.
"I think it'll take about half an hour to get there. It depends on how heavy the traffic is and whether we get stuck in any queues." the driver informed. William made himself comfortable in his seat and looked out the tinted window.

The car cruised through the traffic. Several roads were multi-lane and William thought there were cars coming from many different directions. William couldn't help but admire the driver and his driving style. He drove smoothly while fast. He almost floats through the traffic, William mused. William looked out at the dramatic surroundings with the high mountains all around. A little further away, he saw a large bridge that stretched between the mountains. In one place, the bridge was very long. It was a bit rounded and had bridge railings and poles that stretched high above the roadway. Under the bridge and between the two mountains was a deep ravine. From a distance the cars that drove on the bridge looked like little toy cars crawling along. Imagine how big the bridge really is, he thought. It must be gigantic. The driver changed lane and direction and William saw that they were heading towards the older parts of Libra. They continued through the older parts and the road started to go upwards. The Traffic began to thin out. The driver turned left and into a street where the street sign said *Rosendahls street*. He drove to the end of the street and stopped in front of a large black wrought iron gate. He rolled down the window pressed a button on the gate post and announced that they had arrived. The gate opened and he drove into the gravel driveway. The driver drove around a small grass circle in the gravel driveway and parked in front of the house.

William looked out at the lawn and the lush garden. It was obvious that it was an old garden that was well settled and lush. Towards the road there were tall bushes that gave the garden privacy. William could make out a high black wrought iron fence that stretched around the plot. The house was large brown brick house with bay windows and a shiny black roof.
"What a house!" William exclaimed, "it looks like an ambassador's house. (Houses where ambassadors live tend to be large houses that give a powerful impression).
"Yes, it really does, and they have maintained the house very well while we have been away!" William's father said happily. On each side of the front door of the house were two black bronze lions. William thought they were very impressive and ran up and patted the lions.
"Are you the ones who are going to protect me and the house?" He said laughing. There really was something different with the bronze lions, William thought. They looked almost alive.

That's all William had time to think as the dark brown massive oak door opened and William's grandmother and grandfather came out. William threw himself into grandpa's arms.

"Oh grandpa, I've missed you! It's been so long."

"Haven't you missed grandma then?" William's grandmother asked jokingly.

"Of course I have," William answered quickly. William's grandmother Ruth was a cheerful, plump and very kind woman in her 70s. She had light brown, slightly curled hair that ended just before her shoulders.

"I've missed my kind grandmother," William said and gave her a big hug. William immediately noticed that his grandmother was pleased.

"It's nice to finally see you again," William's mother cried out and jumped up and gave first her mother and then her father a big hug.

"Come in, come in," grandmother Ruth urged. William and his parents thanked the driver who then returned to the car.

"I want to check out the house," William shouted.

"You may do that. Grandpa and I were thinking that you would have the top two floors and we'll take the ground floor. Your moving boxes and furniture have already arrived and we took the liberty of unpacking them for you."

"How sweet of you," William's mother said.

"Thank you very much, Mr. and Mrs. Silvercrona!" William's father added. "I can't believe you did it all on your own."

"Well, not really all by ourselves," William's grandfather Fritz said while clearing his throat.

"Can you imagine," Grandma Ruth filled in, "the same day that your furniture arrived, five movers came and told us that they had been instructed by Captain Nickodemus to help us to unpack all the boxes and furniture so that it would be ready when you arrived."

"That's amazing," Anne said sighing with satisfaction. "It feels good to not have to unpack all the moving boxes and screw together the furniture. We can just enjoy and relax."

"You'll have to see if you think the furniture is in the right place, else we can always move them around," Ruth said. "William, we have put your furniture and things in two rooms so you can choose which room you want to sleep in. I think we've chosen the right room," Grandpa Fritz said, winking.

"You are absolutely wonderful," William's father said and gave both of his in-laws a hug. "What a lovely house this is! I have a feeling we're going to love it here. "

William quickly ran up the large oak staircase that led up to the upper floor. When he reached the top, he looked around. Straight ahead was a large sitting room. At the far end, by the bay window, was their dark brown Chesterfield group, which consisted of two leather sofas and matching armchairs. On the left wall was a large glossy dark wooden bookcase that was full of various books. Next to the bookcase was a recliner with a reading lamp. In the room there was a dark green tiled stove with various ornaments at the top. The room led on the right side to a smaller room which had a billiard table to the left and straight ahead there was a large flat-screen TV in the middle of the wall. Below the TV there were three black shelves where there were different forms of TV and computer games, a computer, an x-box and a playstation console. In front of the TV was a large dark green carpet that looked really soft. On each side were two dark brown wooden shelves that were full of different movies and series. In front of the TV stood a solid dark wooden table and a dark gray plush sofa with lots of cushions. The sofa was made up of three sections joined together. It made the sofa look like a U with straight corners. It looks really cozy, William thought. I can sit here and watch movies and play video games.

"Ah, you've found the media room," Ruth said who had snuck up behind him and was now standing in the doorway. "We kept all your movies and series even though most of them are available to stream these days." Ruth smiled. "You know, I had to convince your parents that it a media room was an absolute necessity, his grandmother said winking. "Sometimes you need to relax and not think, I was about to say a single sensible thought, but you know what I mean?"

"Yes, thank you." William said smiling.

"Come on, I'll show you the rest of the house." William followed his grandmother. "Here you have a bathroom," Ruth said and pointed to a room on the left. William peeked in and saw a bathroom that was all white marble with a bubble bath on the far right. William had not seen the two guest rooms to the left of the stairs when he came up. Grandma pointed to the rooms and said, "In case you want some friends to stay overnight." The rooms were typical boys' rooms in different dark blue and dark green colors. Each room had a dark brown English desk and on the desk there was a laptop.

William turned around and walked over to the large windows by the sofa group. When he looked out, he was stunned. Outside he saw cliffs and the sea. To the right was a large wooden bridge. On the lawn were several old trees and rose bushes. When he looked to the right, he saw a low building that was also made of bricks.

"It's the relaxation area," his grandmother informed him. "You can sit and relax there in the jacuzzi and look out over the water and the sunset, or you can take a bath in the indoor pool or soften your joints in one of the massage chairs. You can also use the sauna and then go out on to the jetty for a cool dip."

"How wonderful!" William exclaimed. "I always wanted my own swimming pool." Ruth ruffled his hair.

"I'm glad you've got one now."

"Let's go upstairs and look at the third floor," grandmother said. William ran ahead up the stairs and Ruth followed. The third floor differed from the slightly dull colors of the second floor. Here the décor went in beige, white and light yellow. At the far end of the room, William saw a large glazed in balcony with white mullioned windows. William immediately walked over to it. There were two cream-colored fabric sofas facing each other and an armchair. In the middle was a square braided tin table. Some beige plaids lay over the sofas. Mom will like this, William thought, who knew that she was weak for bright colors. In the corner were three silver candlesticks.

"It must be wonderful to sit here and look out at the sea or to crawl up on the sofa and read a book," William said.

"Over here you have mom and dad's study." William went to his grandmother who was standing by a door to the right. He peeked into the room and saw that the room also went in bright colors. There were two white desks and two beige leather chairs on black wheels.

"You never know," Ruth said, "sometimes your parents might need to work a little from home and then it can be good to have a workplace and a computer each to write or email on." William nodded. William turned around and looked again at the large middle room. Their large white Gustavian table stood in the middle of the large room and above it hung their crystal chandelier.

"If you open the door to the right, you will see your library where we have collected all our own books and some of your books that we thought were important in some way." William looked in and to his amazement he saw a large room that certainly was about 70 square meters. There were books on every wall. Some bookshelves stood in a row one after the other. On a bookshelf were lots of newspapers and several different scientific journals.

"You have to keep up to date," grandma said, winking at William. William quickly noted that a lot of the books looked very old. Their spines were leather and slightly worn. On the right side was a large white tiled stove. Around the tiled stove stood seven white leather armchairs. Next to each leather armchair was a brass reading lamp.

"The room is huge, William whispered

"Mm, Grandmother said, and it continues.

"What do you mean, continues?" William asked.

"Come on, I'll show you," she replied.

William went after Ruth and where William thought the room ended, he saw that it instead continued at an angle to the left.

"Now we are in the left flank," Ruth said. Everywhere there were dark brown wooden bookshelves.

"You really have a lot of books," William said.

"Yes, we have collected quite a few over the years," she replied. "I think you will find several of them useful.
William noticed that there was not a single window in the library, the light came from built-in spotlights in the ceiling.
"Where's my room?" William wondered.
"Over there is your parents' bedroom," Ruth said and pointed at a brown wooden door. The door next to it is one of your rooms."

William immediately ran over to the door. He opened the door and peeked in. He immediately recognized his desk, computer and chair that stood by the big window. The room felt bright and airy. The walls were white and the curtains were also white. William didn't see a bed in the room. Strange, he thought to himself. Where the bed should have been, there was a dark square wooden table. Around the table were eight black desk chairs. On the wooden floor was a thick white carpet
"I thought that if you have group work at school you might need a bigger table to sit and work at," his grandmother said who saw that William looked questioning.
"Where's my bed?" William wondered.
"Oh we put your bed in your bedroom," Ruth said cheerfully.
"Where is it?" William asked. Ruth pointed to a door on the right side of the room. The door looked a little

different from the other doors in the house and looked a little like the door to Longtails tower room. It was a thick old oak door with a large brass key in the lock.

"Sometimes you might need to lock the door," she said. Ruth opened the door and William saw that there was another wooden staircase, though this was narrower than the others he had seen earlier in the house. The staircase was about a meter wide. When William came up the stairs, he saw his white bed standing in the middle of a square tower room. There were four large windows and the view was magnificent. William took a deep breath.

"Wow, what a room!" he exclaimed. William saw his stargazer and two other binoculars standing in front of one of the windows. When William looked up, he saw that the ceiling was made of glass, almost like a glass pyramid.

"That's awesome! Now I can sleep under the open sky and look at the stars before I fall asleep."

"If you want it dark just turn this knob, his grandmother said. When she did, a dark blue thick blackout curtain appeared that ran on a rail around the room and began to cover the windows. "To remove the curtain, turn the knob in the opposite direction."

"That's clever," William said.

"If you don't want to look at the stars when you're sleeping or if you're disturbed by rain dropping on the glass ceiling, turn this knob," she said and pointed to another knob that was sitting next to the other. "You can try it if you want?" William walked up to the button and to his surprise he saw that a thin wooden roof began to move upward along the four corners of the pyramid on the outside of the glass. One for each side

"Cool," William said. William saw a wooden ladder standing at the door. The wooden ladder didn't seem to lead anywhere.

"Why is there a wooden ladder by my bed?" he wondered.

"Oh, I forgot to show you. It's grandpa who's had a little fun," she said giggling. "Let's see if I remember. Where did I put the remote?"

"What does it look like?" William asked and he immediately helped her with the search. "Is it this one? he asked and showed her a black remote control.

"No, that one is for your TV," Ruth replied. "I think the one we're looking for is in silver. There, I think I see it," she said and pointed at William's desk. William quickly went to get it.

"Let's see. There are two features on this one. If I remember correctly," his grandmother said and pressed a button on the remote. William saw that above the wooden ladder a part of the wall went down a bit and behind it an opening appeared. "It's a secret path that leads to a shelter and from there you can take an underground passage either to the West Clermont School or to the Cathedral. Sometimes you may need to go somewhere without being seen or if you just want to get to safety," she explained. William nodded shivering.

"The other button, what is it for?" William asked.

"It's for hiding and closing the hatch," she said.

"Mm," William said.

"If you use the stick here, you can pull down different star charts, which are rolled up on the ceiling. They can be important to you when studying the night sky," grandmother said while pointing to a metal bar with a small hook at the end.

Yes, William thought, this room was unlike any room he had ever seen before. How cool that it's mine. He felt that he could hardly wait until it was dark and he could look at the stars and celestial bodies from his own bedroom. William felt somehow strangely connected with the universe and its powers. It must be because I have the compass inside me, he thought.

"The room is absolutely perfect," he said aloud and gave his grandmother a quick hug.

"Thank you dear." Ruth answered.

"Now I think it's time that we go down to the ground floor." Grandmother Ruth walked down the wooden stairs. Outside the wooden door leading up to William's bedroom William saw that there was another wider wooden staircase leading downstairs. "It would have been a bother if we had to go through all the other rooms to go downstairs again," she explained. They passed the second floor and came down to the ground floor where his grandparents lived. They came into the kitchen and what a kitchen it was. William looked around. Straight ahead was a large glass wall. Outside the glass wall, William saw that there was a large wooden deck with outdoor furniture. William walked up to the glass wall and discovered a glass door leading out to the wooden terrace. "I just have to go outside." William opened the door and came out on the sun-warmed deck. It was pleasantly warm under his feet. "

"There are slippers in the shoe shelf on the wall," his grandmother shouted and pointed to a wooden shelf just inside the door.

"It's all right. I'll be fine," William replied. He looked out over the water. The wooden terrace was high up. All around there was a sloping lawn, some old trees and cliffs. It looks just like a postcard, William thought to himself. As he looked closely, he saw that the wooden terrace ran in three different levels down the slope. On the wooden terrace there were terracotta pots that were filled with different plants. He saw two lemon trees some orange trees and what looked like an olive tree. A wooden staircase led between the different levels of the terrace. William went down to the ground-level of the terrace. He had the sea right in front of him and to the right was the jetty. William saw that he didn't need to walk on the grass to get to the jetty. Grandma and Grandpa had built a small wooden pathway that led to the jetty and to the relaxation area, which was a building in white brick and glass. On the white brick walls there was what William thought was ivy climbing up the walls.

"Isn't it lovely!" William's father said behind him.

"Mm," William replied. "Just look at the big lawn where we can play football."

"Yes, this house really has it all," William mumbled. When William looked around, he saw that the black wrought iron fence went all the way down to the water. When he looked up at the house, he saw that the house was shaped like an L. He also saw the glass pyramid going up above the ceiling.

"I can't believe I'm going to live here."

"Yes, it's wonderful," his father said and put his arm around him. "What do you think, shall we go up to the others now?"

"Well, I think I'd rather sit out on the jetty and relax a bit." William said.

"You do that," his father said and gave him a light hug. William went out to the end of the jetty while Henry went up to the house. William rolled up his trousers and sat down at the edge. The water reached up to just below his knees. I can't believe how good it feels. William moved his feet back and forth in the water. Far away he saw a big ship moving closer towards land. Maybe it's the Princess, he mused. If I had my binoculars, I would have been able to see if it is. William pulled his feet out of the water to go and get his binoculars. When he stood up, he noticed a pair of binoculars hanging on a hook on the edge of the bridge.

"It's unbelievable," he said. "Someone hung binoculars here. It's something I could have done," He picked up the binoculars and adjusted its sight. William saw the large glass ship clearly.

"It's the Princess," he shouted out loud. William was incredibly happy to see the ship. It almost felt like seeing an old friend. He came quickly to think of Longtail, Mr. Owen and The FairyTale Forest. He got up and started gesticulating and shouting. "My friends, here I am!" He picked up the binoculars again to look for some kind of sign that they had seen him. William didn't have time to think long before he heard the boat blow its horn twice in response. William started to laugh straight out.

"I can't believe that someone on the ships bridge saw me," he giggled. William sat down on the jetty again and put his feet in the water. I'm glad it's summer. He lay down on the jetty and looked up at the sky. Far away, he heard some seagulls.

Days went past and weeks turned into years. William enjoyed life in Thyrridea and enjoyed the homeschooling that was divided between his parents and grandparents. William felt that a certain holiday feeling remained with him. Maybe because his lessons were not very long and on top of that he was motivated and it was easy for him to learn new things which made studying much more fun.

William sat out on the jetty and relaxed after the morning lessons. A lot had happened in the years gone past and now everything felt so natural, almost as if he had always lived in Thyrridea. William was dozing on the jetty when a seagull's cry woke him up. What was that? he wondered and sat up. On the jetty, a seagull stood and watched him. "You're really not afraid of people," William said kindly and put his hand gently towards the seagull. The seagull saw William's hand and walked calmly up to his hand and to William's surprise, the seagull put his head in William's hand and looked at William. The seagull must be sick, William thought. The seagull walked closer to William and lay down right next to him. William didn't really know what to do. Instead, he patted the bird and whispered "it will be alright, I promise you. I'm going to take you to a vet and you'll be fine soon. But what's that, something hard?" It felt almost like a small capsule. William lifted the seagull's wing and indeed there was a capsule. William carefully removed it. Immediately the seagull stood up, nodded his head and flew away. That was amazing. His heart pounded hard as he unscrewed the lid of the capsule and a white piece of paper fell out. William read the rolled-up paper.

Hey W, hope you're all right. I'll see you soon! Take care// A

William felt a rush of joy, perhaps a new adventure, how exciting! He quickly got up from the jetty. He tore the message into small, small pieces that he scattered in the water and went inside.

CHAPTER 4
THE UNKNOWN GRAVE/MAGICAL SHORTCUTS

He went quickly up the stairs and into his room. Now let's see, he said quietly to himself. Where did I put Longtail's book? He thought for a moment. Yes of course, in my yellow-brown bag. William took the bag and opened the wooden door and went up to his bedroom. He sat on the bed with the bag on his lap. He opened the zipper and took out the book. It's beautiful. William hadn't had time to study it closely before but now he had. He looked and felt the thick light brown leather with his fingers. It is very well preserved to be several hundred years old, he thought. He traced the gold inscription on the front with his index finger. *The knowledge of origin, its magic and power.* He turned the book over and saw the same round mark on the back of the book as on the front cover. It was a golden symbol that was oval with three waves meeting. How privileged I am to have Arild as teacher and that I could borrow the book from Longtail, William thought. I have to practice the three formulas that Arild taught me. William repeated the formulas quietly to himself. I wonder if there is anything special that has happened or if Arild just wants to go through with me how he intends to organize my teaching?

William thought for a long time. Eventually, he put the book down on his bed and started to flip through the pages. The book had two parts. Out of curiosity, William closed the book and then opened it on a randomly selected page. It's exciting to see which side I end up on, he mused. The page that turned up was light blue and with squiggly silver letters it was written: *How to discover hidden tunnels in a room.* William laughed out loud. That was odd, he thought. I wonder if there are hidden tunnels in my room. But shouldn't grandmother have known? I'll go and ask her. William sat up. But his eyes fell on another line of text. *Bedrooms are personal, always explore secret passages when you're alone in your room.*
"That's strange," William muttered. "I could swear that sentence wasn't there before." "Well," he said out loud, "I'll have to do it myself then." Before William read the spell on the page, he quickly spoke the spell that Arild had taught him so that no one else could read his mind or see where he was. Then William read the spell on the page aloud. When he uttered the last word, he was amazed because the whole room began to sparkle in silver and everywhere in his room there were silver-clad doors. Next to each door hung a small blackboard with something

written in silver. William walked up to the door that was next to his desk. On the blackboard it said: *Knock three times on the gate. This path leads to the cathedral.* William knocked three times and the door slowly slid open. William thought it would be a dark pathway, but instead it was lit with a silvery white glow. William took the book under his arm and walked through the door. William thought the door would close itself behind him, but it didn't. Maybe that's why I was supposed to be by myself? he thought. Both sides of the path were covered with old brick tiles. On the ceiling shone what can best be described as, several silver balls. That's where the silvery glow comes from, William noted, and continued into the pathway.

It was a high and wide pathway, which allowed William to walk upright. After walking for a while, he came to a large magnificent stone staircase that was long, wide and led straight downwards. The stone was all white. It must be marble, he mumbled. William stood at the top of the staircase and looked down.

"What a huge staircase!" he exclaimed. It was grand and had large stone columns that held up the white forged railing on each side of the stairs. William began to walk down the stairs and with every step that he took a loud echo followed. Suddenly William had the urge to shout test the echo. "My name is William," he shouted! The sound bounced back "My name is William, my name is

William, name is William," it sounded throughout the place. "Amazing acoustics!" William shouted "Amazing acoustics, Amazing acoustics, acoustics," the sound lingered on.

William, now light at heart, continued down the stairs. I wonder if it's a long way to the cathedral? When he finally reached the bottom of the stairs, William stopped, turned around and looked back up at it. The stairs must really have belonged to a castle or similar, he reasoned. Why else would you build a big staircase like this? William took a few more steps back and admired the staircase. It creaked when he put his right foot down. What's going on? William thought just as the stone columns slowly began to move downwards and the whole staircase swung around. "What!" William exclaimed. On the back of the stone staircase there was another staircase that led even further down. It was not nearly as large and magnificent as the stone staircase. Instead, it was a narrow oak staircase. William hesitated for a second but then he decided to see where the staircase led. Maybe it'll lead to the cathedral as well. It was dark and the silvery light did not reach down the stairs. I simply need to walk carefully, he noted and held one hand against the cold stone wall and took one careful step at the time.

"Oops, the steps must be at least 25 centimeters high." He went further and further down. He felt with his hand that there were different inscriptions in the stone wall, but in the dark he could not see what they said or looked like.

William continued to follow the stairs down. The old oak staircase creaked with every step he took. At last, when he once again stretched out his right leg to take a new step, he felt that his foot touched a stone floor.

"Finally, that's the end of the stairs." he said out loud. "I wonder where I am now?" He instinctively felt along the stone wall to find something to light up the dark with. He took another step into the room and as he did, a number of torches were lit high up on the ceiling.
"Wow, it's a vault." William looked up at the huge stone columns that went from the four corners of the room and connected in the middle of the ceiling like an arch. When he looked at the stone walls, he saw that there were different signs in some kind of dark green and red writing. Around the stone columns were various decorations of leaves and flowers. How strange that the floor is shining clean, William thought. The vault led into another room. William had to crouch slightly to get through the opening to the next room. When he entered, the room opened up. What looked like a small, almost insignificant opening from the outside hid a magnificent and large room. This room also had a vaulted ceiling but the roof was much more ornate than in the previous room. Some kind of glass mosaic covered most of the ceiling. William quickly realized that the ceiling mosaic represented the sea. He could clearly see the waves and how the sun was reflected in the water. The light in the room seemed to come from

the ceiling mosaic that shimmered in blue, green, and gold. In the middle of the room was a large tomb that was carved out of stone. The stone tomb stood on a podium. William walked up the stone steps and looked at the stone tomb. It looked like a large rectangular boulder. What surprised William was that there were very little decorations on the tomb itself. Actually, there were no ornaments at all. William searched carefully for any inscription that revealed who was buried in the stone tomb but he found nothing.

"That's strange," he said quietly to himself. "There is usually some inscription of who is buried in a tomb, but there is nothing here that reveals who it is. That's weird." William searched again. He made a thorough search and felt with his hands on top of the stone lid, but he found nothing. Very strange. Why is there a stone tomb like this in this beautiful room? Something is not right. I'll have to see if I can find any information in the books when I get home. William walked out of the tomb, through the vault and began to walk up the stairs. As soon as he put his foot on the stairs, the torches in the room were extinguished and it became dark again. He walked quickly up the wooden stairs towards the silvery light which he could faintly see far above.

Once he got to the top of the oak stairs he ran to the spot on the floor where he thought the button should be and indeed, a "click" was heard and the huge stone staircase spun around to its original position. What a relief! William felt a great deal of stress. He had a feeling about the unmarked tomb that he couldn't quite shake. He ran up the stone stairs, which was quite a feat considering how long it was. What was an unmarked tomb doing in such a beautiful burial chamber? Who was in the grave? William pondered on it as he hurried through the pathway back to his room. Once William reached his room and walked through the opening, he saw that all the silver-clad doors were gone and that his room looked normal again.

What a good spell, it knows when I have returned to my room, he thought. He turned around to see if the silver-clad door to the cathedral was gone as well, and it was, and there was no trace of it on the wall.

"That's good," he said half aloud to himself. "Then I don't have to think of anything to finish the spell."

William sat down on the bed to think. I have to try to find out more about the unmarked tomb. Where can I find such information? William had learned that in Sweden, the churches had a register of who was buried where. I wonder if there is any similar register here? Oh, how I wish Arild was here. Then I could have asked him. After William had thought about it for a while, he came to a decision. I'll go to the cathedral and see if they have any books there or if I can find a churchwarden that I can ask. William locked the magic book that he had borrowed from Longtail in his desk and ran down the stairs.

"Grandpa, grandpa!" William shouted. "Grandpa, where are you?"

Fritz came out of his study. "What is it, William? Has something happened?"

"No, I'm all right," William said. "I'd just like to know the fastest way to the cathedral?"

"Mm, it's a very nice building. It is well worth a visit," William's grandfather continued. "The easiest way to get to the cathedral is simply to take bus route 1 from the bus stop outside our house. It stops almost right in front of the cathedral and the trip takes about 10 minutes."

"Then I'll do it," William said. "Can you tell mom, dad and grandma that I I'll be back around nine or half past nine?"

"I'll do that, go and have fun now," William's grandfather said as he put on his reading glasses and went back to his study."

William threw on his jacket, grabbed his notepad, wallet and pens and put in a backpack and ran outside. When he reached the gravel path, he stopped. Why am I running? The man in the unmarked tomb has probably been there for at least 100 years. So why am I in such a hurry? William forced himself to take three deep breaths and relax. Then he continued in a more moderate pace towards the street and the bus stop. If there was one thing William didn't like, it was waiting for buses. He sat down on the bench at the bus stop and waited. But William didn't have to wait long until a black bus with a 1 on the sign showed up. William bought a ticket to the cathedral and went to the back of the bus and sat down. William quickly realized that there were not many passengers on the bus. William looked out the window as the bus drove past one quiet road after another, with tidy villas and high walls or hedges. The bus then began to approach the city and William saw many cars and people hurrying past. Again, it struck him what a huge city Libra was. On every stop people got on and off the bus. William, as you already know, has a really good sense of location so his hand was already on the stop button when the speaker voice in the bus called out that the next stop was the cathedral. William pushed his way to the bus door and was very happy when he got off the bus. It was now getting dark outside and the cathedral was illuminated with bright spotlights.

"Wow, how big it is!" he gasped. William suddenly felt a lot younger than his 14 years. What should I say if I get hold of a priest or churchwarden? he thought. I can't say that I've walked in a secret tunnel and saw an unmarked tomb. No, I just can't. I need to figure out something else. William walked on the cobblestones that led up to the cathedral.

That big door must be the main entrance, he mused. William had realized that the cathedral would be magnificent, but he was still not prepared for what met him. This was the most magnificent thing he had ever seen. The cathedral was enormous. William had never in his life seen a cathedral with this much space inside. The ceiling was incredibly high. To the right was the older part of the cathedral. It was fitted with rows of ornate benches, covered in gold and above a balcony with seven rows of seats that looked to be almost on top of each other. Wow, William thought, this cathedral can hold a lot of people. To the left was a newer extension in a more modern style. The modern part was all white, with white walls. The only things that were ornate were the pulpit and the altar, which were also covered in gold. Behind the pulpit and the altar was the enormous glass wall that William had seen on the boat trip. The glass wall let the dark of the evening outside with all the lights from lampposts to shine right into the cathedral. William heard footsteps approaching on the stone floor.

"Young man, if it is a tour that you want you will have to return tomorrow at 11 o'clock. The cathedral is now closed and intended only for quiet prayer and meditation." William cleared his throat. "You see," he said. "I'm looking for someone who can tell me who's buried in the cathedral."

"I don't think anyone who works here can tell you that without consulting our records. We keep records of who is baptized, married and buried here." The man looked at his watch. "I think our priests have gone home for the day, but I'll check with our churchwarden if he can help you. Please come with me."

They passed through the older part of the church. William couldn't help but reach out and touch one of the gold benches as they passed by them.
"Is it pure gold?" William asked.
The man nodded as an answer. They went further and further into the church.
"We're heading over there and through that dark oak door," the man said and pointed.
William could see that there were many rows of benches as they walked past. He couldn't help but try to figure out how many people the cathedral could hold. William lost count when he happened to look to the right and saw several magnificent graves in a long row on the right side. Several were fenced off with various forms of ornate fencing, some were black wrought iron fences, while others were in gold and greenish copper. At the graves there were usually several rows of benches. The benches were dressed in various velvet fabrics, dark green, dark blue, red and gold. On the floor were several marble candlesticks with large white candles that were lit. William saw that there were large oil paintings by the graves depicting the person buried there as well as various landscape motifs or motifs of different buildings. He also saw that on the walls sat stone tablets with a text that briefly described the fate of the buried persons.

"We're almost there," the man said and held the door open to William. "We just have to go up the spiral staircase."

William had never seen such an old wooden spiral staircase.

"We're going up to the third floor," the man informed, "and then the first door on the left."

William found that the wooden staircase creaked considerably with each step they took and he exhaled with relief as they reached the final step on the third floor.

CHAPTER 5
MEETING WITH FATHER ORMUND AND THE CATACOMBS

William walked in through the doorway and saw a very large library in front of him. The walls were lined with dark bookshelves, which in turn were full of books on every shelf. The whole room felt old and the air was stale. It was as it hadn't been cleaned for at least 30 years.

"There is rarely anyone here," the man explained, "but still we do not want to throw away the old books, they somehow belong to the cathedral. Wait here and I'll go and get the churchwarden. Maybe he can help you." William nodded. The man pressed a light switch and a large brass lamp was lit on the ceiling and then he left the room.

William now saw that it was indeed true that the room was rarely used. There were thick layers of dust on the bookshelves and here and there large cobwebs covered some of the books. But the wooden floor seemed to have been cleaned recently. He walked up to two of the small windows that let in the light from the stars. When William stood on his toes, he could just reach up to the window frame. He looked down and saw the water below. We're probably pretty high up, he thought, but then he was interrupted in his thoughts by someone who cleared his throat.

"I understand that you want to have a look at our church register."

William turned around and saw a white-haired old man. His back was slightly bent and he looked as if he needed a proper haircut and a shave. William saw that the man was wearing a clerical collar.

"Are you really the churchwarden? William asked?

"Of course I am, when I retired as a priest, I got an offer to work part-time as a churchwarden and one of my duties is to take care of the old books. When my wife died, I felt incredibly lonely so now I brighten my days working as a churchwarden. But I pretty much only do what I can and want to do, nothing more. If I understood it correctly, you are you looking for a record that shows who is buried in this cathedral, is that right?"

"Yes, that's right, by the way, my name is William," said William and held out his hand.

"My name is Father Ormund," the churchwarden replied. "It was certainly a long time since someone requested to see our old records, but it will be fun to show them to you. However, I must warn you, our record is vast and it's a lot of books to go through. Is it anyone special that you are looking for or does it concern any particular period in time?"

William didn't really know how to answer the question.

"Hmmm, I don't really know, but I am most interested if there is any record of those who are buried inside the cathedral."

Father Ormund froze. "You mean the ones you passed on the way here?"

"No, not really. I have read that in several churches people were buried under the churches in special vaults," William said.

"I see, now I understand what you mean," Ormund said. "There are not very many who are buried under our cathedral, but I will gladly take you down to our catacombs so you can see for yourself. I think I know pretty well who's buried there."

William felt himself getting excited. Maybe he would finally find out who's buried in the strange vault.

"Do you think you can show me?"

"Now?" Ormund said with surprise. "Most people don't like to go down there during the evening, but if you want to, why not? Then let us go down. The entrance to the catacombs is behind the altar."

William and Ormund went down the stairs and towards the altar. Ormund went first and William right after him. Then the former priest went to the right behind the altar.

"You see, William," Ormund said, "these graves were hidden from grave robbers, that's why the entrance to the catacombs is hidden. I must ask you to turn around until I tell you." William did as he was told. It took a little while until Ormund told him that he could turn around. William now saw that a large stone in the floor had been opened. "I'm afraid there's no light down there. You'll have to take this flashlight," Ormund informed and handed him a big black flashlight. William directed the beam down. The stone staircase was steep and narrow.

"Stay to the right," Ormund said, "there are hooks in the stone wall at regular intervals. You can hold on to them." William did as he was told and moved the flashlight to his left hand. The hooks were made of iron that hadn't rusted.

"The air is very dry down here which means that they do not rust," Ormund explained.

William cautiously looked down on his left side and was very happy that he was holding the hook tightly. There was a drop of about 20 meters down.

"Oh," William said out loud.

"I know. It's quite a drop but you get used to it." Ormund said who walked with quick steps down the stairs.

"How secure are these hooks really?" William wondered and pulled hard in one of them.

"They are properly secured," Ormund replied calmly. Soon William picked up his pace and now he was only three steps behind Ormund.

"Now we are approaching the catacombs. You should know it's like a maze down here. There are passageways everywhere.

"How many do you think are buried here?" William asked.

"I don't know exactly, but I would guess there are about 100 or so," Ormund answered.

When they came down, Ormund bent over and picked up a candelabra. He turned off his flashlight and lit the candles with a match and said "Now we're ready".

"Why did you turn off your flashlight? Doesn't it give better light than the candles?" William wondered.

"Yes, it does," Ormund said, "but you have to respect the dead and it feels more dignified to walk around by candlelight than with artificial light."

"Ah, I see, but is it ok if I bring my flashlight with me just in case?" William wondered.

"It's ok." Ormund answered. "Which one of the graves are you interested in?"

William didn't really know what to say. He was afraid to say too much and said quickly.

"No one special. I would love to see them all."

"Well," Ormund said, "that's not possible. The catacombs are several miles long, but they are divided into different sections by time period. Do you have any idea what era you're interested in?"

William thought so hard that it almost creaked then he said. "I'd like to see the oldest graves."

"Ok," Ormund said, "they are several thousand years old. I just need to remember the best way to go to them."

"No, I've changed my mind," William said quickly and tried to figure out how old the tomb could be. Maybe it's a few hundred years old but I wonder if it could be several thousand years old. I don't really think so.

"I think I am most interested in graves that are 600 years old and younger."

Ormund scratched his head, then he replied. "We have a section containing burial sites for various significant people ranging from royalty to famous scientists. Maybe you'd like to see them?"

"Yes, I'd love to," William said and shone up.

I hope the tomb is there, William thought quietly to himself. The tomb that I saw was really special so it's certainly an important person buried there. Perhaps the person in question wanted to be anonymous and that is perhaps why no name was engraved on the tomb, William pondered further.

"As you saw earlier, some of the prominent people are buried inside the church on the right, but these are not the graves you want to see?"

William shook his head.

"Then I have to think about it," Father Ormund said. He stood still for a while and muttered a little to himself then he said out loud "Now I know where we should go. You see, the more famous or the more important a person was, the more complicated the route is just to confuse grave robbers. Mr. Rossoe, who designed the maze, was a clever and intelligent man. When the catacombs were completed, he burned the drawings and he was the only one who had memorized the layout of the maze. Shortly before his death, he told a priest and then the map was passed down through generations of priests but was never written down."

"But those who carried down the coffins and made the graves, they had to know where to put them?" William asked.

"Well, that's the thing. Those who worked with the graves had to wear special blindfolds. They had no chance to neither see nor memorize the way. To make sure, the priest that led them down did never go the quickest way but led them on different detours on the way."

"When was the last time someone was buried in the catacombs?" William asked.

"It must probably be about two to three hundred years ago. Today, there are other cemeteries where people are buried. The most famous one that most tourists like to visit is the Cemetery of Light. It is beautifully located on the outskirts of the city at the foot of a mountain where you also can see the sea. There are also other smaller cemeteries.

"Does everyone in Thyrridea have a church funeral?" William asked as he came to think of Lord Theodorus.

"No," Ormund replied and became silent. Then he said diplomatically. "There are different factions and thus different ceremonies, but now it is best that we start walking."

William understood that Ormund did not want to discuss the matter further and followed him.

"How come I don't have to wear a blindfold?"

Ormund stopped and looked at William in surprise. "But you're the compass. Your reputation has already reached Thyrridea. A lot of people talk about you and how you found a part of the Stone of Origin and thus restored the balance between the stars."

William became completely speechless. He had not thought that the rumor about him would have reached Thyrridea. Somehow William had thought that what happened on the ship also stayed on the ship. William didn't know what to say. There was a moment of silence. William really didn't want anyone to know anything about him and especially not to think that he was some kind of remarkable person.

"I don't think there's anything special about me." William said neutrally. "I certainly did what everyone would have done if they had been faced with the same thing."

Ormund looked at him intensely.

"You're probably right," he finally said, "and if you want me to pretend as if it's nothing, we'll forget everything I've said."

"If you want to do so I would appreciate it," William mumbled.

"As you can see, the aisles are dark and narrow and several of the aisles cross each other. It's all done to make it extra difficult to memorize the way." William felt like they were walking around in circles. Everywhere they went he saw how aisles split to the right, to the left and several times they passed intersections of many different aisles.

After they had walked for a while, Ormund said.

"We're almost there."

William saw that they were standing in front of a tomb.

"You can borrow my candelabra and go in and have a look. I'll wait outside," Ormund said.

William took the candelabra, crouched through the entrance and when he finally could stand straight again, he felt a cold gust of wind. Quickly, William protected the candelabra with his right hand. Strange that there is a breeze in here. There must be some kind of cavity that extends all the way to the surface, he figured.

The room was square and relatively large. On the right side were large stone coffins and the same in front of and to the left of William. He had believed that prominent persons would have plenty of gold and precious stones on their coffins. But there was no such thing on any of them. Instead, the stone coffins looked almost insignificant. I must read what is written on them, William thought.

William began reading on the coffins to his right. They contained ancient rulers of Thyrridea, a bishop and three scientists specializing in space. It's just as Ormund said, William thought, there are really important people buried here. William continued to read on the coffins that stood straight ahead of him. They also contained different scientists, a king and then there was a smaller coffin. The lid read, *William, a 17-year-old boy of noble birth and noble mind who fought for good to the last.* William got goosebumps all over his body.

"His name is the same as mine and we're almost the same age," William exclaimed. "That's scary."

William felt visibly affected by standing beside a grave almost as big as he was. The boy who had died while fighting evil was only a few years older than me. Ormund, who thought it had taken William a little too long inside the tomb had gone in to see what was going on.

"Horrible to die at such an early age," William said aloud.

"Yes, he was a real fighter," Ormund replied. "Those who met him testified to his great courage and wisdom. He defeated evil on several occasions. I think I could say that he is the person who has meant the most to the development of Thyrridea. Without him, it is unclear if the country would have remained free and independent. You see, age doesn't always bring wisdom and courage. It's something you're born with to some extent. Sometimes the mind of a young person is clearer and more uncorrupted than that of an older person." Ormund said and then murmured quietly to himself, "So true, so true." immersed in his own thoughts.

William felt noticeably drawn to the coffin and he felt the compass on his wrist heat up a bit. I have to learn more about who he was, William thought to himself as he ran his hand over the mark on his wrist. I must check with Arild when I see him. William walked up to the small coffin and couldn't help but to touch the lid.
"I'll be back" he whispered.
"Thank you for showing me these graves," William said and turned to Ormund, who was still immersed in his own thoughts.
"Oh, you'll have to excuse me. I was standing here dreaming away. Do you want us to go back?" He wondered.
"Yes, I think it's time to do that," William replied.
William noticed that they took a different route back. They followed a slightly wider aisle. Suddenly William stopped. Not far away there was a skeleton.
"Who's that?" William asked.
"Oh, it's probably a grave robber who got lost in here a long time ago."
William swallowed as he passed the skeleton. The aisle narrowed a little bit. I really hope he remembers the way back, he thought. They passed many different aisles and went into several smaller side tunnels. William noticed how the floor began to slope upwards. Then we're

probably on the right track, he thought. The candles had almost burned out on the five-armed candelabra.

"We're almost there. Over there you see the stairs," Ormund said and pointed.

They went up the stairs and when they reached the exit Ormund blew out the candles. William then saw a very faint streak of light shining through the opening.

"Now you have to turn around," Ormund said. William heard the boulder moving. "You can come now."

William turned around again and walked through the opening.

"Now I'll close the entrance," Ormund whispered. "Quiet," Ormund held a finger over his mouth to indicate to William that he should stand still. William didn't move but listened. He heard footsteps that were moving away from them. Ormund moved the boulder back and they snuck silently towards a large stone column and hid behind it until the footsteps disappeared.

"We were lucky there," Ormund mumbled while he exhaled. If we had arrived a little earlier, the people might have discovered the path down to the catacombs. They snuck through the church. All the lights were off and the only thing that let in a shimmer of light was the large glass wall. Shadows formed everywhere and William was glad to have Ormund by his side.

"How are you going to get home?" Ormund wondered.
"I think I'll take the bus." William answered.

"If you want, I can come with you to the bus stop and wait with you until the bus arrives?" Ormund said.

"You don't have to," William replied. "How are you going to get home?"

"I usually walk," Ormund said.

William looked at his watch. Oh, it's already 20 minutes past midnight. Ormund opened a wooden door and William realized it was the staff exit. William thought it was nice to get out into the fresh air. The water around the cathedral was still and the moonlight shimmered in the black water. William picked up his cell phone and called his mother. She answered right away.

"Where are you, William? Do you need any help?"

"I'm outside the cathedral with Ormund."

"Who's Ormund?"

"He's a priest and churchwarden," William replied.

"Wait there and we'll come and get you. Does Father Ormund want a ride home, too?" his mother wondered.

"My parents will come and pick me up and if you want, we can drive you home as well?"

"Yes, but I don't want to bother you," Ormund said, "but of course, I'm usually not out this late, so it would be kind of you."

"Sounds good," William said and turned to his mother on the phone.

"When do you think you'll be here?"

"In about 10 minutes," his mother replied. "I'll see you soon." William hung up and put the phone in his pocket.

William couldn't stop thinking about William in the grave. I wonder how he died? William didn't really know if he should ask Ormund about it. But considering that it would take time until he would meet Arild again and William didn't like to wait for answers, he asked Ormund anyway.

"How did William die?"

Ormund was quiet for a little while then he said. "No one can say for sure. Some writings say that he was stabbed while he was asleep, but you see, William was very skilled with magic and spells, so I would be very surprised if it was true. Other writings suggest that he was poisoned. Who knows," Ormund sighed softly. "It could have been a combination. Maybe he was poisoned first and then someone stuck a knife in him.

William shuddered. "Did they find the culprit who did it?" William wondered worried.

"No, they first arrested a member of the Arona family, an old man with a rather dubious reputation, but they had to release him as he had an alibi, so the murder was never solved. I think he was the one who murdered him, but he couldn't have acted alone, the deed must have been planned by someone higher up the hierarchy. At least that's what I think," Ormund murmured.

He was quiet for a while then Ormund added. "And can you imagine that for a while, William's body was missing and then found in a cave out on the island of Gardon."

"Ugh," William said aloud. "Who would want to take a person's body?"

"Well, you never know. It depends on what the purpose is," Ormund answered, "but it sure is terrible, all of it," he sighed.

Just then, two headlights flashed. "It's mom," William exclaimed with relief. Ormund and William crossed the footbridge to the car. William jumped into the backseat and Ormund sat down in the front passenger seat.

"Let me introduce myself," Ormund said and reached out his hand.

"A pleasure, my name is Anne," William's mother said and greeted him.

"It's very kind of you to drive me home," Ormund said.

"You're welcome," Anne replied. "Where would you like me to drop you of?"

"I live on Old Church Street no. 12 in the older part of Libra."

"Then I think I know pretty well how to get there," William's mother said and drove off. William felt how tired he was. He had a hard time to stay awake. He heard how Ormund guided mom through the city. After a while, they stopped in front of an old red brick building.

"Here it is," Ormund said. William looked out and saw that the whole house was dark. Ormund thanked them and got out of the car, then he stuck his head back in again and said "Goodbye William, I'll leave you my card with my email and phone number in case you want to get in touch with me."

"Thank you very much," William said and took the card. Ormund closed the car door and walked towards the entrance of his house. Mom didn't drive of right away.

"We'll wait until we see that he's safely in the house." Ormund opened the red door and waved to the two of them, then he closed the door behind him.

"Now we can leave. How was your day? And how late it is," William's mother said.

"I've been down in the catacombs of the cathedral, William answered. I found a grave where a 17-year-old boy was buried. It felt very strange. His name was also William. Mom, do you think it was a coincidence that I saw that particular grave?" William hoped that his mother would say it was pure coincidence, instead he was a little disheartened when his mother quickly answered.

"No, I don't think so, William. Life is rarely a coincidence. We can talk more about it when we get home."

William immediately felt a sense of discomfort. He wished it had been a coincidence, but deep down he knew his mother was right. William's fatigue was gone. Instead, he sat and looked thoughtfully into the night.

"What are you thinking about?" his mother asked.

"You know that, Mom," William answered.

"Yes, I probably do," his mother mumbled. "We'll talk about it more when we get home."

CHAPTER 6
SEARCHING FOR INFORMATION

The tires crunched against the gravel as the car drove up the driveway. They parked in the garage and then they went inside. William saw that the lights were on in several rooms on the ground floor so he realized that at least one of his grandparents was still awake. He opened the door carefully so as not to wake anyone. Fritz immediately came out of the kitchen. "Are you alright, William? I was getting a little worried. Come on, let's go into the kitchen and have some supper. Grandma and your dad are asleep." Just after Fritz said that, William heard steps from the stairs.

"Sleeping who said I was sleeping?" William's father said as he stepped into the kitchen and shortly afterwards William's grandmother also came in.

"How's my favorite boy?" she said and gave him a hug.

"We're about to eat, William's grandfather said. "Would you like a sandwich and some hot chocolate or tea?"

"Tea will be fine for me," William's mother said. William went and sat down on the kitchen sofa. When he looked out the window, he saw that there were black wrought iron lanterns placed in the garden. They lit up the dark night and the dark water outside the house.

"Tell me what happened," Fritz said.

William closed his eyes and began to tell his story. He told them about the tomb he had seen. He didn't tell them how he had found it, only that he had seen a tomb. Then he told them about Ormund and the catacombs and about the chamber that had contained the grave of one named William, who was only a few years older than himself.

"It was really creepy," William said. "It was almost like seeing my own grave. I can't explain it any better than that."

Everyone sat silent in thoughts.

"This is not good," Fritz said.

"No, it's not," William' mother agreed.

"I think I'll check with some of the brothers in my order if they know more about that William." Fritz said. "I'm going to a meeting with the order tomorrow."

"But," William said, "you can't tell them anything about the catacombs or anything of what I've said."

Fritz looked at William. "What is said in the family stays in the family," he replied quietly.

"I think," William's father said, "that we should go through and maybe increase the security of the house and also the security around you, William."

"Now I think it's time to go to sleep," William's mother said.

When William was on his way up the stairs to his room, William's mother came to him.

"Your dad and I have been talking and we think I should sleep on a mattress in your room tonight, William. It'll be kind of like when you were little and had nightmares. Do you remember that?"

"Of course, I remember," William said. He felt that it would be really good to have his mother sleep in his room. She was always calm and secure. They walked up the stairs. Grandma picked up a folding bed from a closet and William's mother came with a mattress.

"Do you need help?" William's dad asked.

"You can go and get a duvet, pillow and a sheet for me, please," Anne answered. They quickly made the bed. Then William went and washed up, put on his pajamas and brushed his teeth. When he came back to his room, his mother was already in the folding bed next to his and was reading an interior design magazine. William knew that his mother often needed to unwind before she went to sleep, and that she usually read a magazine to disperse her thoughts. William lay down in his bed.

"Mom, I'm incredibly glad that I have you."

"And I am extremely happy that I have such a wonderful son." Then she was quiet for a while before she continued.

"William, do you think you can sleep or do you want to talk about the other William?"

William thought about it.

"Yes, I think I can sleep, but it was very scary, like seeing my own grave."

"I understand that, William, but you have me, dad, grandmother and grandpa and we are here with you. And William, it wasn't your own grave you saw, remember that."

William knew his mother was right, but it still felt that way somehow.

"I know," William answered quietly.

Then William's mother turned off the light. "Good night my treasure."

"Good night mom. I love you," William said.

"And I love you very much. I can hardly believe that I have such a good, wise and intelligent son," mom answered and gave him a quick hug. There was a light knock on the bedroom door and dad, grandma and grandpa came in.

"Good night to you and dream about the angels," Fritz said. William smiled back and remembered that his grandfather used to always say that to his mother before she went to sleep.

"We have secured the house and the alarm system is on so you should be able to sleep well."

"If you need anything, just wake me up," William's father said. They waved and then they closed the door behind them as they left the room.

"Mom, I don't really know if I'll be able to sleep tonight."

"I understand that," Anne said.

"My mind is full of many different thoughts."

"Just let your thoughts float away, do not try to stop them," his mother said.

William did as she said and thought about everything he had experienced during the day. He thought there was something frightening and threatening about it all. I'm glad I'm home, he thought and looked at his mother. Before falling asleep, he quietly read the protective spell that Arild had taught him. When William's mother heard that William had fallen asleep, she put her magazine on the floor. She looked at her son with a worried expression. I can't believe it's already begun. I thought we would have at least a few quiet years in Thyrridea before the battle. It is clear that a lot has changed since we left Thyrridea and that it's difficult times. I really hope that William is protected. William's mother clasped her hands and then she fell asleep.

Fritz closed the door and said good night to Henry. He told Ruth that he would work some more in the study and that wasn't a lie. Fritz really did go to his study. It was just that when he got to the study, he didn't go to his desk and started to work. No, instead he stood by the window. This is really not good, he said quietly to himself. He sat down at his desk and took out his ink pen and started writing on a white sheet of paper. When he had finished, he folded the paper, took out red wax and put a stamp on the letter.

He carefully opened the window, whistled softly, and handed the letter to a large gray pigeon that landed on the windowsill. Fritz patted the pigeon on its chest and whispered, "Fly quickly now, the message is urgent." Fritz stood for a while and watched as the pigeon flew away then he carefully closed the window.

"That's it," he said before sitting down at his desk again and started to work. After about half an hour, he heard a gentle pecking on the window. He opened the window and gently took the paper from the pigeon's mouth. Fritz quickly read the message. "That's good," he said quietly to himself. He then put the paper in the ashtray, lit a match and watched the message burn. Fritz closed the window and then he went to bed.

Both William's mother and William slept uneasily during the night. William had nightmares that he was wandering around in the catacombs and once again standing at William's grave and that the compass mark burned while hearing a boy's voice echoing in the vault: *You are me, William. Don't you understand? Be careful and hurry.* William woke up with a jolt. To his delight, he saw that the first light of dawn had already found its way into the room. Beside him, his mother still slept soundly. William lay down and after a while he fell asleep again. When he woke up, he was alone in the room. He pressed the button and the curtains opened from the windows. Outside, the weather was beautiful. The sun shone from a clear blue sky. It's probably around noon, William thought. He still felt tired in his arms and legs. It had been a restless night and he still heard the other boy's voice echoing in his head. What am I supposed to understand and why should I hurry? William wondered. It seems that he wants to warn me of a danger. I wonder if it's the same danger he was exposed to? William tried to shake off the unpleasant thoughts. I have to figure out what this is all about. William sat down at the computer and googled the words "William young boy dead" but got no hits. He then went to the library in the house. He looked at all the shelves that were full of books.

"Where should I start?" he said out loud to himself.

"You mean where should you start looking for information about William?" Fritz said who had just entered the room.

"Mm," William replied.

"I'm afraid we don't have a book that can help us find out more about the circumstances surrounding William's death. But I'm going to a meeting with my order tonight and I'll see if I can get some information about William, who he was and what happened to him. If anyone knows anything, it's my brothers in the order. Come on, let's go down stairs and have breakfast, or maybe we should call it brunch as it's already half past eleven." William followed his grandfather down to the kitchen.

"Where are the others?" William asked.

"Your mom and dad had some errands in town and grandma is at water gymnastics. They'll be home soon." Fritz prepared cereals, yogurt, bread, milk and various kinds of cold cuts and cheese.

"Do you want some sea buckthorn juice, it's good for you," Fritz said. William nodded.

"I don't understand why I'm so exhausted. It feels like I've been on a training camp. My whole body aches," William said.

"You know your body and mind is as one. When you have experienced something that is very hard on your mind, it is common that it also affects the body. If you rest for a while, you'll see that you will soon get your strength back. Today I think it would be good if you took it easy so that both your body and mind have time to recover. When you've finished your brunch, take a book and lie down in one of the lounge chairs outside on the terrace and relax. William finished his meal and helped clear the table.

"Wait," grandpa said suddenly. "I think I have a book that you would like. Come on, let's go up to the library." They went upstairs and grandpa went to the history section. He took out an old book that described the different kings and queens of Thyrridea. This is an encyclopedia where you will find information about different rulers, if there is any particular person who attracts your interest you can then search for more information. I seem to remember that you like history."

William shone up and gave him a hug. "I'll take the book with me outside." William took the black book and went outside and sat down under a parasol. There was a pleasant light breeze from the sea. In the background, he could hear some seagulls. He opened the first page of the book and there was a list of all the rulers of Thyrridea. The first king was Leopold who assumed the throne in 200 BC. Before that, the country had been ruled by different field lords who fought over the territory. The field lords were men who came from rich families who had their own armies. When William looked at the list, he saw that King Wilhelm was the last king. Well, William thought, the book is older than ten years because the current ruler is not on the list.

William flipped distractedly through the book. He looked at the pictures of various kings and queens. Some looked friendly while others looked very determined and had hard look in their eyes. William recalled from history lessons that kings and queens were usually depicted a little from below or riding on a horse to make them look powerful. William noted that usually it was the eldest son who had inherited the crown when the father died, but if the King had no son, sometimes his daughter had inherited the throne but it was very rare. William found that this had happened on only two occasions. Instead, it was more common that one of the king's brothers took over the rule. William found that the kings usually had many children and that several died early in life from diseases. You didn't grow as old as you do today, William thought, likely because they lived a harder life back then and that medical care wasn't as advanced as it is today. William only flipped through half of the book. His thoughts were still set on the other William. He wished that it would be evening soon so that grandpa could get information from his brothers of the order. William felt restless, like there was something he should do, but he didn't know what. He got up and went down to one of the rocks and sat down and looked out at the water.

What could the other boy mean by that I was like him? William picked up a stone and threw it into the water. I don't get it. And what is the explanation for the unmarked tomb? Why did he find it when he took the shortcut to the cathedral but not when he was in the catacombs? What if I could talk to Arild, maybe he could have helped me. William tried to get himself together, but he couldn't. He got up and walked along the cliffs. William felt like something crept in his body.

"There must be something I can do," he murmured quietly. "What could it be?"

"William. William!" He recognized his mother's voice and turned around. Up on the terrace his mother was calling out to him while she gesticulated that he should come.

"I'm coming," he shouted back. William walked with quick steps up to the lowest terrace then he walked up the wooden stairs that connected the different levels of terrace that were built along the slope.

"There's a phone call for you," his mother shouted.

When he reached his mother, she handed over the phone while whispering that it was Ormund on the phone.

"Hi, it's Ormund." William barely heard what he said because he was whispering very low. "I can't speak louder than this because I'm worried someone is eavesdropping. I've found something interesting that I need to tell you. Can you meet me in half an hour in the cathedral?"

"I'm on my way," William answered and hung up the phone.

"What did he want?" William's mother Anne wondered.

"I don't really know, but he wanted to see me in half an hour. He said he had found something that might be of interesting for me."

"Do you want me to drive you there?"

"If you have the time, I'd like that, but I can take the bus as well," William said diplomatically.

"I'll drive," William's mother said firmly. When they were in the car, Anne suddenly said. "Now I want you to promise me to be careful, William. If you feel the slightest discomfort or that something feels wrong, you need to call me or dad right away. Promise me that."

"I promise," William said. "But I'm only going to see Ormund."

"I know," William's mother said, "but I still want you to promise me."

The car ride went quickly and William's mother dropped him off at the cathedral. William walked up the walkway to the cathedral and quickly entered through the large entrance. As usual, there was an aura of tranquility in the cathedral as it often is in most churches that you visit. Almost a little as time stands still, he thought. William noticed he was ten minutes early. He sat down on a bench at the very back of the cathedral, behind one of the great pillars and closed his eyes. His thoughts wandered. What if it was just his brain that played tricks on him? It was clearly a bit scary to see a grave with your own name on it but does it have to mean anything? He thought about Arild. If there was one thing Arild had taught him, it was to trust himself. If Arild had been here, he would have said that I should trust my intuition, which in this case means that William and I are very similar and that William is trying to warn me. William's thoughts were interrupted by a voice.

"Psst, over here behind the pillar." William stood up but it was impossible to see who it was that had called for his attention. It must be Ormund.

William walked towards the big pillar and indeed it was Ormund who was waiting for him.

"I think it's best if we talk in my study." he said quietly. "The cathedral is usually quite empty at this time of day so not many people will see us together." Ormund and William moved quickly up the spiral staircase and when they were almost at the top of the stairs, Ormund pointed at a door. "It's in here. Here we can talk in private." William followed Ormund in.

"What happened here?" William cried out. The whole room was in a mess. Bookshelves were overturned, the desk was a mess and there were books everywhere.

"What happened?" William whispered low.

"I wonder that too," Ormund said with tight lips in a thin voice. "William," he said seriously. "I hope you take this the right way, but if anything should happen to me before I have had time to inform the next priest about the map over the catacombs, I would like to pass this information to you here and now." William got all giddy.

"You see, I know the map by heart, but it is also written down, something that very few people know about, but I always carry that map with me." He looked under his priest's robe and gave William a rolled-up parchment.

"Learn this by heart," he whispered. "I have thought a lot about who would want to desecrate a church and a priest's belongings, but it is difficult to understand. I'll have to think about it more when I've calmed down. I don't think very well when I'm upset."

There was silence. Then William took the parchment and put it in the inner pocket of his jacket.

"Promise me," Ormund said, "that you'll not tell anyone that you've got this map. Not even your parents. Promise me, because I don't want to see you get hurt."

"Not even to your successor," William wondered with a low voice.

"No, he hasn't been appointed yet, but not even to him. Promise me that." William promised. Again, the room fell silent.

"I might as well tell you how to get into the catacombs." Father Ormund whispered in a barely audible voice how to open the entrance and William carefully memorized Ormund's instructions.

"I'd like to ask you something," William said. "What do you really know about William's grave? Do you have any theory of your own as to who might have killed him or who had an interest in stealing his body?"

Ormund looked William deep in the eye. "I almost sensed that you would ask me about that," Ormund said with concern. "But I want you to remember that this is only my theory. It doesn't have to be true and there are a lot of missing pieces in the puzzle. As I understand, William lived about 1500 AD. There is very little information about his origin in the books that I have researched. It's clear that he belonged to the Silverstar family, which was a very powerful family at the time. Some say William fell victim of thieves who assaulted and murdered him with a knife. But from what I have learned William was a very physically strong person who could handle his sword expertly and he was also very good with magic spells, including protection spells. There were rumors that he had been poisoned and because of that he was weakened. "But who would want to kill a boy?" William wondered.

"Yes, it's a good question," Father Ormund said. "But you must realize that we didn't live back in those days so we don't know what was in the mind of the perpetrators. I don't think he fell victim to random thieves. Instead, I think his murder was extremely well planned. But as I said it is only my theory. It doesn't have to be true, remember that, William."

William pondered, finally he said. "Yes, I agree, I don't think he was randomly murdered. Promise me you won't tell anyone that we've been down in the catacombs or that I've been asking questions about William."

"I promise," Ormund answered, "but now you have to get out of here quickly so that no one sees you."

William walked quickly out of the room and down the stairs. He looked around the whole time to make sure that no one saw him. In the cathedral it was very quiet and peaceful. I'll sit down on a bench and pretend to rest for a while in case anyone has seen me. After a little while, he got an idea. Wouldn't it look better if I pretend to admire the cathedral? He got up and walked around. William, who has a very good hearing, heard steps that approached him from behind. He pretended like nothing, until he heard someone clear his throat. William turned his head slowly around. It was the priest he had met last time he was in the cathedral.

"Nice painting, isn't it?"

"Yes, it's beautiful," William replied sincerely.

"This image of Christ was painted by a well-known artist named Artholus." The priest said.

"Incredibly beautiful," William replied.

"Could Ormund help you with books about the burial chambers?" the priest asked.

"I was in his library, but it was hard to find the right books, so I ignored it," William replied.

"Yes, he has many books our father Ormund," the priest chuckled.

"Yeah, that's true," William said.

"But isn't it a beautiful cathedral."

"Yes, it really is," William answered truthfully.

The priest and William talked a little in general about the cathedral then the priest departed as he needed to prepare for a service. William remained for a while before he left the cathedral. When he came out, the sun shone brightly, but the large trees around the cathedral gave cool shade. Everything That Ormund had said swirled around in Williams' head. Yes, of course, I must hurry to contact Grandpa. He can't tell anyone at his order that I have been down in the catacombs and he must be extremely careful with his questions about William the Elder. William found his grandfather's phone number on his phone and called. It rang and rang but no one answered. William was just about to hang up when he heard his grandfather's voice.

"Hello, is that you, William?"

"Yes, it is, wait a second." William looked around to make sure he was alone on the bridge. "Grandpa, I'm going to ask you something, don't ask me why."

"I understand," William's grandfather replied quietly.

"I don't want you to mention to anyone at the order that I've been down in the catacombs. I want you to be very carefully when asking about William. Now that I think about it, I don't want you to mention him at all."

William's grandfather became completely silent.

"Promise me that," William said.

"Yes, I promise," his grandfather answered. "Is it ok if I do some research on my own?"

"Mm," William said, "but you have to be discreet. No one can know. Not even your closest friend."

"I promise, but then I may not get any new information."

"No, but I'll solve it some other way."

"I'll see you when you get home. Take the opportunity to go for a stroll around the city and get to know Libra a bit on your own," Fritz said.

"Maybe I will. Now I have to hang up." William saw a family a little further away on the bridge.

"I'll see you tonight."

"We will," William replied and then he hung up the phone and put it back in his pocket. Maybe I should take a stroll around the city anyway, William thought. Maybe there is a bookstore that has something interesting.

CHAPTER 7
FRITZ

Fritz was really concerned. He frowned unconsciously and stared down at the floor of the study. What kind of trouble is William in and what can I do to help him? This was much worse than he could have imagined, nor could he confide in or ask anyone for help, and he was certainly not allowed to do anything that could draw any unwanted attention to him. Fritz walked back and forth in his study. He had already contacted the Grand master of his order. He had not said what it was about, but the Grand master would understand that it was important as the order's pigeons were never used to convey ordinary messages between the members of the order, or brothers as they called themselves. Fritz had known the Grand master since school, although of course he was not grand master back then, just an ordinary boy. Fritz felt that he could trust him, but at the same time he had promised William not to mention anything to anyone. Fritz lit his pipe, blew out a cloud of smoke and thought. If only he could introduce William to the Grand master, then surely

William would feel the same confidence for him as he did. "But they don't have time to meet," he said in a low voice to himself. The brothers were supposed to meet in their building at 8:00 pm tonight. "Oh, that's not possible! he said resignedly. He sighed loudly and took a deep puff from his pipe. He looked at the gold watch on his desk and realized that it was 6:30 pm already.

"No Fritz," he said to himself. "Now you have to hurry up and find a solution." He drummed with his fingers against the armrests of the armchair when it suddenly hit him.
"Of course," he said out loud. "Of course I will do that!" He sat back and felt satisfied with himself. The time never goes as fast as when you shut your eyes for a moment and that was exactly what Fritz had done.
"Oh my god, look at the time!" He walked quickly up to the wardrobe where his black suit hung, looking as fresh and clean as usual. Ruth is really good at ironing, he noted contentedly. He took the suit and the accompanying white shirt and put them on, then he reached for his brown briefcase. "Finally ready!" He put on his overcoat at the front door and went out to the car. Outside, dusk had already begun to settle.
"You can see that it's near the end of summer," he said when he drove in the light drizzle. He started humming a little tune while he was driving. It's all very strange, he thought. I'm always in a good mood when I meet my brothers. The car turned up onto a large gravel driveway

with high black iron gates in front of it. Fritz put in the secret code on the display and the iron gate slid up.

"Welcome brother," a voice said in a speaker within the display. Many of the brothers have already arrived, Fritz thought a bit stressed as he saw all the cars that was already parked in the parking lot near the house. He brought his briefcase and knocked discreetly on the big oak door.

"May I take your coat?" the butler asked politely.

"Of course," Fritz replied hurriedly and gave him the overcoat. He took his briefcase and entered the next room, where a black velvet curtain hung by the door frame. He closed the curtain, opened his briefcase and put on his ceremonial cape. It was made of a relatively thick but smooth material that allowed the cape to be folded four times in the bag without becoming wrinkled. He quickly put on the cape and attached it with a silver brooch by his neck and put the hood over his head. He left the briefcase to the butler and walked quickly across the black-and-white checkered marble floor to the main hall.

The hall was almost full. At the front were three thrones, one larger in the middle and two smaller on each side of the larger throne on which the Grand master sat. Along the sides of the hall there were two rows of chairs that were fitted with velvet cushions in dark blue. Fritz sat on the smaller throne to the right of the Grand master. The Grand master nodded and the ceremony began with the brothers swearing allegiance to their country and their king. Fritz felt that he relaxed. It felt good to be with his like-minded brothers.

Normally Fritz used to pay close attention to the ceremonies and follow the rites with a relaxed calm. He recognized the symbols and knew what they meant, but tonight he found himself repeatedly being out of focus. Instead, he thought of his grandson. I really hope nothing happens to William, he muttered quietly. It was not until the ceremony came to an end and the cup of wine was passed between the brothers that he was truly there. The ceremony ended with the cup being carried out of the room and the Grand master nodded first at Fritz and then at the brother on his left. Everyone got up and left the hall in a decided order, with the Grand master first. The Grand master lowered his hood and led the way to the dining room, where a three-course meal was served. Fritz ate quite fast, excused himself and took his coffee cup and entered the order's library. Oh, how he liked this library! Dark brown bookshelves filled with books. The ceiling was painted like a night sky, with stars shining with the help of small lamps. Marble that went in shades of blue covered the floor and created the feeling of walking on an ocean. On the walls hung images of mathematical formulas such as the Pythagorean Theorem, Michelangelo's golden ratio and other valuable symbols and images. Fritz walked around in the library with the coffee cup in his hand. He heard the door being opened and closed and then a discreet cough. Fritz turned around and looked right into the Grand master's green eyes.

"I came as soon as I could. However, I was a little detained by brother Sauluson."

"I understand," Fritz said with a smile, "he always likes to talk a lot."

"Now you have to tell me what has happened. I understand that it's something serious. It is very rare that you use our pigeons."

"Yes, I am concerned," Fritz said. My daughter, son-in-law and grandson is here in Libra. I didn't want to say anything to you earlier but before my grandson William arrived in Thyrridea, he was involved in a controversy with Lord Theodorus."

The Grand master became completely silent, after a short while he said slowly and thoughtfully. "It's extremely serious Fritz."

"Yes, I know, but the worst part is that I think our house is being watched."

"It's certainly possible," the Grand master replied with concern.

"I would like that a protective barrier was established around our house, just as it is established around the order house." Fritz continued,

"A complete protective barrier with all that it means? the Grand master wondered.

"Yes," Fritz answered briefly.

"I will ensure that it is done with utmost discretion," the Grand master said.

"Thank you," Fritz said with relief.

"Now, my old friend, why don't we join with the others, wouldn't it taste good with a glass of whiskey?"

"Of course," Fritz replied smiling.

The two gentlemen walked chuckling out of the library and sat down in the small drawing room where the smoke of cigars already had begun to fill the room. Fritz relaxed and talked about everything under the sun with his brothers. They discussed books, history and everything that had happened and was happening in the community. No subject was too big or too small to be discussed. Fritz thought that it felt good to divert his thoughts, albeit only for a little while.

"Are you staying the night like you always do?" the Grand master wondered.

"Yes, I think so."

"I have arranged for delivery of your "water treatment" tomorrow at 10 am."

"Thank you, it will be perfect," Fritz said. Fritz suddenly felt tired. "You'll have to excuse me, gentlemen, but it's been a long day. I'm going to go to bed, good night."

"Good night, good night," he heard the others mumble amongst the smoke of cigars. They will probably stay up for many hours, Fritz thought when he headed towards the guest room. Suddenly he heard the library door close and he saw the back of a man, dressed in a suit, who quickly left the room. Fritz is usually very good at recognizing people. We all have different talents and this is one of Fritz's talents. Strange, Fritz thought, the person who left the library didn't look like any of the order brothers. He could tell from the posture and way the man moved that it didn't look like anyone Fritz knew. Never mind, I'm just tired and imagining things, he told himself. He took a few steps towards the guest room but then he stopped. No, I have to look into it, he thought. Silently, he moved to see where the man went. Fritz walked as fast as he could without making a sound, but it was too late. The man was gone.

"What a fast mover he was, Fritz murmured and turned towards the guest room, but when he passed the library, he stopped. As I'm wide awake I might as well go inside and see if I can find any clues as to what that man was doing in the library.

Fritz opened the door and turned on the light. The library looked as usual. I think I'll check the bookshelves just to see if I see something that's out of place. Said and done, Fritz walked slowly back and forth between the rows of books. All the while he looked carefully at the books to see if any book was placed a little carelessly.

"Everything seems in order," he whispered quietly to himself. But then he came to the section of bookshelves that were in the far end of the room. There was something about the second shelf from the bottom of a bookcase that caught his attention. It wasn't that any book was carelessly placed. No, it was something else. Fritz felt with his hand on the back of each book and indeed, two of the books leaned a little more towards each other than the other books. When he put in one finger between them, it became clear that a very thin book was missing. Usually when the brothers borrow a book from the library, which happens regularly, they fill out a note with the title of the book and who borrowed it and a return date then they put the note in a plastic pocket that stands out so that the others easily can see that a book is missing on the bookshelf. Fritz rubbed his beard. There's no note here and there's a book missing. He read on the titles next to the missing book to get an idea of what kind of book that was missing. "The priesthood and its rituals" it said on a book, "Burial Sites and its placements" it said on another book. A third book was named "The Cathedral and its secrets." Fritz froze. The missing book probably had something to do with burial sites. He immediately got to think of the burial site that William had told him about. He took the book "The Cathedral and its secrets" from the bookshelf and looked up its registry. He brought his index finger like you usually do when you're looking for a special word in a register. "C," he read out loud to himself, then he continued, "cantor, there we have it, the catacombs page 136," he mumbled. He turned to page 136 of the book but was surprised to discover that the page had been torn out.

"What!" Fritz exclaimed. He quickly slammed the book shut and put it back on the bookshelf.

He looked around anxiously to make sure no one had seen him. He walked over to a bookcase at the very end of the room and pulled out the seventh book on the seventh row and the bookcase opened up. He went in and closed the bookcase behind him with a button on the wall to his left. The button switched on the light in the room at the same time. He was now in a room that was so secret that only the Grand master, Fritz and the counselor who sat to the left of the Grand master at the ceremony knew about it. The room had a marble floor that went in several different shades of brown that symbolized soil. The walls and the furniture, which consisted of a few bookshelves, a glass cabinet and a desk, were painted in a gold color that symbolized fire. Fritz walked up to the glass cabinet and knocked lightly three times on the glass with his right index finger and a lock appeared. He took out a key from the left pocket of his jacket and unlocked the cabinet.
"Now, let's see," he said out loud. Fritz's brain worked fast. He remembered that William had told him about a priest who had shown him the catacombs, the same priest perhaps knew something about the other William's tomb that William had seen. It was important that he quickly made contact with the priest, Fritz realized. To ask him if he had any more information about William's grave. Maybe he even knew where it was. In addition, it was

extremely important to warn the priest that he would probably have an uninvited visit because he was the only one who knew the layout of the catacombs and he could be in great danger.

Fritz bit his lips. I really have to hurry. He felt gently at the top of the glass cabinet and there it was. He exhaled with relief. It was an extremely small lever, so incredibly small that if you didn't know it existed, you'd just think there was a slight bulge in the wood in the cupboard. He pushed the small lever to the right and waited tensely. It squeaked and the glass cabinet began to laboriously move downwards. Hurry up, Fritz thought tensely. The Grand master or the counselor could come in at any moment. At last, the cabinet had finished moving and had exposed an illuminated tunnel. He hurried into the tunnel and as he stepped on the first step of five, a creaking sound was heard as the glass cabinet went up again and hid the tunnel. What a relief that it worked, Fritz thought and exhaled. He had been told by the former Grand master that there was a secret tunnel to the cathedral from the glass cabinet when the former Grand master felt too weak to be Grand Master and therefore had summoned Fritz with the desire that he would be the next Grand master. However, Fritz had felt that he could not undertake such an important assignment. He had thought long and well before he declined. The old Grand master had been disappointed but had decided to summon Fritz once more. This time Fritz received some books about magic, clergy and the importance of all the rituals, as well as a lot of other secrets. Among other things, he had told Fritz about this tunnel. Then the old Grand master had taken his hand and said, "To me, you are the rightful Grand master. Now I've given you all the knowledge I have to give. Keep it safe and use your knowledge wisely. I hope to see you again." Fritz remembered it as if it had happened yesterday. He had held the old Grand master's hand for a long time and promised that he would return tomorrow. It was just that tomorrow never came. At nine o'clock in the morning they had called from the order's office and announced the sad news that the Grand master had died. Fritz shook his head. "No, I can't think about it anymore," he murmured. "I need to act quickly."

The tunnel was not that high and Fritz had to bend forward to be able to walk. On the walls hung cobwebs and Fritz heard rattle from the tunnels. Rats, Fritz thought with disgust. Gradually, the tunnel got a little higher and he could almost walk upright. It's a good thing he remembered the directions. *"When the tunnel divides, hold to the right four times and then to the left 3 times."* The old Grand master had told him that when the tunnel was built 1,000 years ago, it was designed so that you could easily get lost in it. Most of the aisles ended with a wall at the end of the tunnel. Pretty nasty, Fritz thought as he walked, but certainly very effective. Fritz followed the instructions carefully and at the last left turn there was a short staircase with about five steps up. When he set foot on the last step, a clicking sound was heard and the door opened. The rays of the moon flowed in and shone on him. Fritz silently stepped into the cathedral. "I wonder where in the cathedral I am?" he thought. He looked around. "Oh my, I'm next to the big organ! I have to hurry I have no time to lose." At this very moment, it hit him. It's the middle of the night, it's not at all certain that the priest is here. Maybe he's home sleeping. Well, there's nothing I can do about it now. In worst case, I guess I'll just have to wait until morning.

Fritz had met Father Ormund a few times before. They had never spoken directly to each other, but mostly exchanged polite phrases. Fritz had also attended some of Father Ormund's services. Fritz knew that his room was almost at the top of one of the towers of the cathedral, so he hurried to it.

It was dark in the narrow staircase and Fritz was very careful where he put his feet. "How lucky I am," Fritz thought. "He's actually here." He slowly pushed up the half-open door.
"Father Ormund," he called with a low voice as the door slid open. Strange, the light is off, Fritz noted and searched for the light switch and found it on the right side of the door and turned it on. Fritz was shocked by what he

saw. The whole room was in a mess. Desk drawers were pulled out and lay tossed on the floor. Bookshelves and books were in a mess.

"What in the world," Fritz exclaimed. "I'm too late," he said tightly. Fritz composed himself and then methodically went through the room to check that Father Ormund was not trapped below one of the bookshelves. Fritz routinely felt so that he had his pocketknife in his left jacket pocket. If he pressed a button on the shaft of the knife, the blade folded out. You can never be too careful, Fritz thought. He did one last round in the room and then left silently. I was too late, he thought annoyed. There was nothing else he could do now but to quickly get back to the order house. I'll have to go back to the cathedral tomorrow and see what they have to say. Fritz hurried through the tunnel and quickly followed the directions backwards, that is, where he had gone left before, he now went to the right and vice versa and it was not long before he was inside the secret room again. Fritz was on edge until the glass cabinet was in place, then he sat down in an armchair and exhaled. He was tired, sweaty and ill-tempered. Fritz rested for a while then he made sure his clothes and hair was in order. He looked in the mirror and found that he looked presentable, then he slowly walked out into the library. The library was lit but Fritz could not see anyone and soon the bookshelf had swung back into place. What Fritz did not know was that there were motion detectors that did not allow the bookcase to be opened from the secret room if someone was within three meters of the bookshelf in the library. Fritz walked slowly between the lines of books and pulled out some books and pretended to read the titles before putting them back on the bookshelf again. Finally, he borrowed a book on gardens, put in the plastic card showing that he had borrowed the book and was on his way to the exit when he heard a discreet cough. Fritz tuned around slowly.

"Did you find anything good to read for tonight?" Brother Harel smiled?

"Yes, as a matter of fact I have," Fritz answered casually. "It's nice to have a book to read before you go to sleep. What about you? is it the same with you?"

"That's right, and I have to say that the library has a calming effect on me."

Fritz nodded in agreement. "Good night, maybe I'll see you at breakfast?"

"Maybe we'll do," Brother Harel replied.

Fritz hurried to the guest room. He noted that his briefcase stood inside the door. Good service, he noted pleased. Fritz turned on the reading light. He had a routine to always think about the events of the day before he went to sleep. I wonder what they've done to Father Ormund? he thought before he fell asleep.

Fritz had a very restless sleep. He kept turning in bed all night. He dreamed that someone had taken William and that William was calling for help. Panicked Fritz rushed through dark tunnels and into old rooms where cobwebs hung over the furniture. But William was nowhere to be found. Fritz tossed and turned anxiously in the dark. Finally, he woke up with a jolt and sat up in the bed.

"This is worse than I thought," he said softly. Fritz threw off his blanket and went out of bed. He peeked out through the curtain and to his relief it had begun to light up outside. "What is the time?" he thought. He picked up his wristwatch from the nightstand. "Half past four," he muttered. "Not many hours of sleep last night," he thought to himself while he sighed. I have to make up a plan. I need, just like William, to try to solve this with the other William's grave. Whenever Fritz tried to solve something, he started with what he knew about his opponent. Then it was a matter of anticipating his or her next move and trying to counter them without attracting attention. Fritz pondered. William had been shown a very special grave. It is no coincidence that William did find that grave, Fritz reasoned. Very little in this world is a coincidence really. It was a truth that Fritz always assumed and that was true in the vast majority of cases. There is the missing Father Ormund, who had shown William another grave. It can't be a coincidence either. Then I find that someone has stolen a book or books about graves in our library. "It just has to be about the other William's grave," Fritz said resolutely.

Then it hit him like a lightning bolt from above. Of course, no wonder William didn't want me to tell anyone. I have to be extremely discreet. He quickly made up his mind. I have to go through the books and objects that the old Grand master gave me. Maybe there is something that can give me a clue to William's grave. Fritz felt the tension in his body release. I really think I need to get some more sleep. Something tells me that I'm going to need it. Fritz went back to bed and fell asleep peacefully. He didn't wake up until his cell phone rang at ten past eight in the morning. He quickly got up, showered and had breakfast in the dining room. When he returned to his room, he folded his cape, took the briefcase and headed home. When he got home, he went straight to his study. He took off his suit and changed clothes.

"Now we shall see," he said while he closed all the curtains and locked the door. As they will soon arrive and do the new security installation, I better lock the door with the second lock as well. Fritz locked the second lock with the key to the glass cabinet. After he had locked it, he went to an inconspicuous painting with a lonely flower on the wall. He pushed the painting aside and put in the number "1244" on the display that was hidden behind the painting. A humming sound was heard and armor plated doors slowly folded up until they covered both the door and the windows. Now it's only one step left, Fritz whispered as he closed his eyes and pronounced a spell that the old Grand master had taught him and a large ball of fire formed in the middle of the room, fifty seconds later the fireball had split up and covered walls and ceiling.

"That's it," Fritz said contentedly. "No one can get into the room, nor can anyone detect what is going on in here. Yes, you really have to protect yourself these days." Fritz quickly corrected himself and said, "protection was of course needed in the past as well" while he walked up to the center of the room and reached for one arm of the chandelier with both hands and turned one of the candle holders. While he did this, he looked at the glass cabinet in the room.

The glass in the glass cabinet suddenly changed shape and instead of showing porcelain objects, such as bowls and cups instead a gold goblet with diamonds and emeralds and shelves with books became visible. One of the books was large and thick with hardcover in leather. On the other shelves there were rolled up maps, more books and various more or less recognizable objects in gold and silver. Fritz did not know the secrets of the various objects, but he was sure that they contained powerful magic. On one shelf there was a single letter. It was the letter that the old Grand master had written to him before he died. Fritz took the letter. He had read it several times before, but he figured it was best to read it once more. Maybe he had missed something. *"From Grand master to Fritz."* it was written at the top of the letter, a little further down the page the text continued. *"Dear Fritz. It saddens my heart that you do not want to take my place as Grand master. However, I respect your decision. But that still doesn't change my firm and full belief that you're the rightful Grand master. That's why I'm handing over all the secrets that were given to me by the former Grand master to you. These are objects and books with a tremendous knowledge and magic that you have to keep safe and of course use during your lifetime. When you, like me, are in the autumn of age, I want you to respect my will and hand these items over to the brother of the order whom you consider to be the rightful Grand master. Fritz, do always remember that the true light always gives you the truth as light and darkness never can be mixed, they are like oil and water."*

Fritz folded the letter and sat in silence for a while. He knew that light and darkness never can unite, as well as it is never possible to mix a truth with a lie. Things have to be separated. Fritz rubbed his beard like he always did when he pondered. Was there anything else the old Grand master had meant? Did he mean anything special with these lines? Fritz sat with the letter in his hand for a long time. Then a thought appeared in his head. It's simple, he thought, but it's worth trying. Said and done he walked up to his desk and lit the candle that stood there and held up the letter against the light. Fritz drew a breath in amazement when he saw that the text in the letter disappeared. Instead, another text appeared written with silvery letters with dense line spacing. *"Fritz"* it said. *"As you already know, there will always be a struggle between good and evil, between light and darkness and between truth and lie. In this glass cabinet there are a lot of objects that can help you in this fight. At the top left is a gold goblet. This goblet has been used in many different ways. The special thing about it is that it tells the whole fate of every person who has brought it to his or her mouth. To see if it has been touched by a person you are looking for, turn the foot of the goblet and spell the name of the one you are looking for, to see if that person's lips have touched the goblet."*

The text continued to describe all the objects in the glass cabinet. Fritz carefully but quickly read through the text until he halted when he came to a description of a map in the cabinet. *"In the cabinet there is also a map. It is not a complete map, but it marks where the tombs of all former Grand masters are located in the catacombs beneath the cathedral. The map also tells you how to get down to the catacombs. If you intend to go down in the catacombs, you have to be careful not to get lost."* What should I do now? Fritz thought. He looked at the gold goblet that shone in the cupboard. Fritz had always thought there was something special about the goblet. It wasn't big or beautifully designed. No on the contrary, it was fairly small, only 15 centimeters high and the gems that were placed in a ring around the goblet were not exactly spectacular but seemed insignificant and small. What made the goblet stand out were all the words that were engraved on it and at the bottom of the foot all the letters of the alphabet were engraved. I need to learn more about William. He took the goblet in his hands and slowly twisted its foot while spelling out William's name, W,I,L,L,I,A,M.

Odd, nothing happened. Then William did not touch the goblet, Fritz thought disappointed. He was just about to put the goblet back in the cupboard, when a powerful beam of light shone straight up from the goblet and it became hot as lava.

"Ouch!" Fritz yelled and instinctively let go of the goblet. At the same time, the whole room became dark and the candle on the desk was blown out. The goblet hovered around the room instead of falling to the floor. A muffled voice began to speak while the image of a seventeen-year-old boy was projected onto the wall. *"William"* the voice began, *"is a boy who was born in the year 1505, Mother and father unknown. He grew up with the Silverstar family. William developed early on a strong sense of right and wrong. He also had a great interest in magic and already at the age of 8 he was able to perform magic that no one had ever seen before. He carried the mark of the compass. It was a great loss when he was killed in the year 1522. The body was lost and then found and then lost again. His death was a tremendous loss in the struggle for good and a great sorrow for the land of Thyrridea. The goblet has never since been in the hands of such a significant person, neither before nor after his death."*

Fritz looked at William's picture that had appeared in the beam of light. You could really tell he'd been through a lot. The gray-blue eyes seemed to stare back at Fritz. Fritz was filled with a tremendous sadness. William must have been very lonely. He walked up to the picture of William and touched his face gently with his index finger while he whispered. "I wish I could have protected you. I wish it with all my heart."

Suddenly the picture of William opened his mouth. "You can help me. Use the goblet. Ask the goblet to bring you to me." William repeated the same sentences twice. The light from the goblet disappeared and Fritz just managed to catch the goblet before it fell to the floor.

"I will, William I promise," Fritz said quietly.

Fritz stood silently with the goblet in hand for a long time after the image of William had disappeared. Finally, he shook himself. No, get hold of yourself Fritz, he said out loud to himself. He took the goblet and spelled *"Take me to William."* Once again, the goblet began to soar.

"Oh, I almost forgot. I have to bring the map of the catacombs if the goblet brings me to the cathedral."

The goblet started talking. It was the same voice that gave Fritz the brief information about William. It was still the same voice but this time it was not the same mechanical speech but instead the goblet chattered on. Fritz was very surprised

"Oh, what fun," the goblet said. "William has instructed me to bring you to him. It's amazingly exciting. You see, I haven't spoken to anyone since I met William, except for briefly giving information about different life stories to others, and that's… let's see." The goblet was quiet for a short while and then continued, "almost five hundred years ago." The goblet became silent again. "Five hundred years is a very long time, as you may understand, I'm very old."

"I understand," Fritz said, who really didn't know how to relate to the fact that the goblet could speak.

"It was William who enabled me to speak, you could say that he made me aware of everything that is going on around me. But of course, when I just stand in the glass cabinet I sleep. It will be fun to get to soar a bit and go on adventures. Isn't it amazing, Mr.? By the way, what did you say your name is?"

"My name is Fritz Smith and I'm very pleased to meet you."

"Yes, I'm pleased to meet you too. William has taught me to only talk to people he has somehow given me ok to talk to. You never know how people are."

"You're so right," Fritz replied with a smile. Fritz understood that behind the glossy shell of the goblet was a really strong will and a good intellect.

"What's your name?" Fritz asked politely.

"William named me Goblet. Now we shall see," Goblet continued and hovered next to Fritz's bookshelves on the short side of the study. Goblet mumbled some spells while it bent a little forward and Fritz saw how smoke came out of the goblet. Goblet quickly blew the smoke over one of the bookshelves.

"That's it, I've created a shortcut."

And indeed, a dark hole had appeared in the bookshelf. Fritz was impressed,

"How did you do that?" he wondered.

"William taught it to me and we practiced long and hard on the spell and I am incredibly proud that I managed it. You see, I haven't done anything like this since William. Imagine how proud he'd be of me now."

"Yes, I'm sure he would be!" Fritz replied.

"Follow me," Goblet said, hovering towards the opening. "Let's see." He uttered another spell and a warm red glow spread from the goblet. "There, now we can see as well."

Fritz looked around but he only saw black walls and black floors and ceilings.

"How does this actually work?" he wondered.

"We have created a shortcut that did not exist before. We simply use the air around us to create an air bridge."

"But its black walls, floors and ceilings," Fritz said.

"That's right. When we create an air bridge through other matter, no light comes through, that's why it looks like black walls and ceilings. But in this way, we can go everywhere without anyone noticing, do you understand?"

"That's clever," Fritz said, "really clever!"

"Yes, William was very resourceful!" Goblet answered.

"I understand," Fritz said cheerfully.

Goblet shone with its red light on the floor of the tunnel and Fritz could see that the floor was really black.

It's really exciting that light can bend like that.

"Yes," Goblet chattered on. "William taught me a lot about that kind of thing. He was very interested in the laws of physics."

"Yes, it's really exciting. There are many things you can learn from them," Fritz said. "If I understand it correctly, when we walk in this tunnel we do not know where we are or what rooms we have walked past and not even if we are already in the catacombs."

"Exactly, we know nothing," Goblet answered and continued. "Oh how I love adventures like this."

Goblet floated in front of Fritz, illuminating the tunnel with its red-light beam that made the tunnel shimmer in a light red color.

"What happens if we go through a room and someone is in that room and that person passes our tunnel?" Fritz wondered.

"He, He," Goblet giggled. "That's the funniest part. Those in the room don't feel a thing. But if they pass us right in the place that we're in, in the tunnel, oh I hope, hope!

Then you will feel that someone is going through you and it tickles something terrible much. It's awfully funny," Goblet giggled. "But I'm sure we won't have that kind of luck today." Goblet soared in front of Fritz and hummed happily on a tune while he hovered slowly on.

Fritz quickly noticed that the tunnel always stretched two meters ahead of them and two meters behind them. It was kind of like a worm that kept moving.

"Oh, I had many fun adventures with William," Goblet sighed longingly. "When an adventure was over, we could sit for hours and just chat with each other. It was great times!" Goblet giggled and sighed happily. Suddenly, Goblet stopped and swayed back and forth while making a sniffing sound.

"Is something wrong?" Fritz wondered. Goblet did not respond and continued to sniff.

"Don't move!" he shouted to Fritz. "I smell danger."

"Do you smell danger?" Fritz asked nervously. Fritz had never exactly liked tunnels and not being able to see what's around him either. It felt a little like being trapped.

"Don't move," Goblet whispered. "Don't even blink." Fritz stopped immediately and froze just like a stone statue. Fritz had learned that if you were to stand perfectly still, you first have to start by relaxing your whole body, and then freeze your posture at the moment of relaxation. Fritz heard footsteps approaching and two voices talking in old Thyrrian. Fritz had never heard anyone speak in old

Thyrrian, but he had read some books written in the old language. Yet he found it difficult to fully understand what the voices were saying.

"Just think that the moment is near, finally I'm going to get the boy and put him where he's supposed to be."

"Yes, but if you don't succeed, I have to," a dark voice replied. "But you need to be careful. He has received tremendous powers."

"I know all of his powers. Don't forget that I've been close to him for a long time now," the other voice replied short.

"I know, I know," the dark voice replied. "It has been difficult for you, but now he must be stopped."

"He will be removed," the other voice replied dryly.

"Phew!" Goblet sighed when the voices had passed.

"Who were they? Can we stop them?" Fritz said agitated. "I have to stop them!" Fritz felt the blood pulsating throughout his body. If it's a fight they want they'll get it. He remembered William's eyes and if it was that they had ended up in a time loop of some kind he would do anything to stop them no matter what Goblet said.

"Unfortunately," Goblet sighed, "we can't change the past. Sometimes when using these shortcuts the light also binds the sound from a long time ago. What you heard, you could say, was as if someone had recorded a conversation with an old tape recorder. The conversation belonged to something that happened about 500 years ago," Goblet said and then he became completely silent for a while before he continued. "But, as William used to say, Life must go on." Goblet stood silent for a few moments and then he shook himself and stopped shaking with a laugh. "Come on Fritz, we have an adventure ahead of us and I want to enjoy every second, you never know how many hundred years I have to sleep after this adventure before it's time for another!"

"You really know the art of living in the present," Fritz sighed, who was still a bit shocked after hearing the voices. Fritz thought on, but it's certainly something that everyone may need to learn more about. He corrected his watch and checked that his knife was in its place.

"All right, let's go!" Fritz exclaimed and increased his pace. The shortcut decided where they would go. For a while, it felt like they were going very steeply upwards.

"I wonder if we're going up a mountain or something?" Fritz gasped. Even Goblet seemed a bit tired and could not continue at the same fast pace as before.

"You know what?" Goblet gasped. "I think we should take a look."

"Can we?" Fritz wondered.

"Actually, I don't know. William taught me a spell, but you can only use it three times during a shortcut. Let's see if I remember it."

Fritz thought it sounded like Goblet said "Ostende mihi ubi sumus" but he was not sure because Goblet uttered the words very softly. Suddenly, a round pane of glass formed in the tunnel. The glass pane was very foggy so

Fritz took out his handkerchief that he had in his jacket and wiped the fog from the glass.

"But look at where we are," Fritz exclaimed. Fritz didn't like heights so it was really no wonder he didn't like what he saw. They were walking almost 100 meters right up in the air.

"How amazingly strange! It's like an airlift!" Fritz exclaimed. Beneath them lay Libra with all its buildings. The houses looked like small Lego houses. Everything looked very picturesque when you saw it from high above. Suddenly they heard a loud thunder. "Oh, I think we're in a thunderstorm." Goblet repeated the words "Claudere visum" and the round glass pane disappeared.

"Let's hurry up. It definitely can't be good to be high up in the air when it thunders," Fritz said quickly. Fritz walked and Goblet hoovered as fast as they could.

Soon the climb upwards leveled out and they could take it a little easier and recover their breath. The thunderstorm finally ended. But as Fritz rightly remarked, it could be because they might be indoors, where they couldn't hear the thunder.

"What is that?" Goblet exclaimed. Fritz, who had been in his own thoughts for a while, looked up and stopped.

"We can't go any further," Goblet said surprised.

"We can't? How strange," Fritz said. "Are we already there?"

"No, no," Goblet said, "when we arrive, the shortcut opens up so that we easily can get out. But here is a dead end."

And it really was a dead end. Fritz felt with his hand at the end of the tunnel and it was just like a big dark wall.

"Well, I don't think it's by force that we are supposed to open up that wall," Fritz said. "So what could it be that would open it up? Did William ever tell you anything about how to possibly open the shortcut in case it's closed?"

Goblet thought long and well. "No," he said thoughtfully. "I'm fairly sure he never told me."

"There must be a way through the wall," Fritz said out loud. "If you take and shine on one side of the wall and I'll see if I can feel anything on the other side, then maybe we can find something that we can open it with," Fritz instructed.

Fritz and Goblet worked calmly and methodically. Goblet focused his light on every centimeter of the wall and Fritz did the same with his hands. Eventually they met in the middle and they looked resigned at each other.

"Hmm," Fritz said, "that didn't work."

"You're right," Goblet said gloomily. They were silent for a long time.

"No, this is not good enough," Goblet said and hoovered up. "This just has to work!"

"I've thought about it," Fritz said, "can you let me read all the words that are engraved on you. Maybe I can find some kind of clue as to how to open the wall?"

"Of course, you can," Goblet answered in a posh tone of voice. Then he added in a more ordinary tone of voice, "Unfortunately I do not know what is engraved on me. They were engraved on me before William created a consciousness in me and in all honesty, I may have slept a few times even after William created consciousness in me."

"I understand," Fritz said.

"But you are not allowed to pick on me when you read. I hate it when people pick on me."

"I promise," Fritz said.

And Fritz began to read. In some places there were only loose words engraved on the goblet, while in other there were long sentences engraved. All of it was very difficult to decipher, partly because it was engraved with squiggly and lower case letters and partly because the sentences and words seemed to be written in different languages. Some of the languages were probably extinct a long time ago, Fritz guessed.

"No, I can't find anything that might be of any help to open that wall," Fritz sighed. Even he was getting a little discouraged. "Do you think I may see what's at the bottom of you? In case something is written there? It's not likely, but then we've ruled out that possibility as well."

"Yes, go ahead," Goblet said. "By the way, you can hold me upside down as long as you do it gently and remember that I have a high blood pressure. I cannot stand on my head for very long because then all the blood runs to my head and that gives me an insane headache."

"I promise," Fritz said while he had to bite his lip to not start giggling. "You're a little dirty. Is it ok if I remove the dirt with my handkerchief?"

"Maybe you should clean the glass cabinet better," Goblet answered dryly

"I'm sorry, I will do it better in the future." Fritz said. There was a moment of silence but in the end, Goblet accepted Fritz's apology.

"Ok then," Goblet said, "I'll allow it this time."

I have to hurry up so that he doesn't change his mind, Fritz thought and quickly picked up his handkerchief and with a gentle touch he removed the dirt from under the goblet. Fritz flinched. "There is actually something written here. It says *A to W cat*. I don't know what A stands for, but W may stand for William and cat may be short for catacombs." Fritz repeated the words slowly "A to W cat" and the whole wall began to tremble. Not in an unpleasant way but more like a gentle shake. The wall broke a part and large pieces of dark material fell on the floor of the tunnel. At the other end there was a warm reddish glow.

"What happens to me?" Goblet exclaimed. Fritz saw that Goblet had begun to shake and then it became completely silent. A voice came from inside Goblet. It was not the dark voice that Goblet had when he was to tell about the fate of different people, this was a different voice. It sounded like it came from a young boy. However, it was not William's voice. It sounded like the voice came from an old scratched vinyl record.

"I really hope it works. I really hope I'm recording." The voice cleared its throat and continued. "Welcome to William's grave. Here lies the greatest magician who has ever lived. He was a boy with a very big heart and brain that had an extraordinary sense of right and wrong. Unfortunately, he was probably betrayed by someone who was very close to him and thus also close to me, Alexander. I have therefore brought William to his final resting place. I have put strong protective magic over his resting place so that only those with a pure heart and who wants William well can enter. If not, you're going to die. William taught me a lot about magic. But you should know, only the very few with the purest of hearts will be allowed to enter this place. If you cannot enter, I want to wish you good luck in life and that you will continue your work for what is true and right in life. Continue to live in the Spirit of William as I like to call it. In order for you to be able to enter, insert your left index finger in the scanner to the left on the wall and press." A reddish display appeared on the left side of the wall.

The voice fell silent. Goblet didn't move for a few minutes. Then it shrugged. "What happened? I have such a terrible headache," Goblet said sourly. "Did you hold me upside down for too long?"

"No, I did not. A promise is a promise," Fritz answered. Fritz briefly explained to Goblet what had happened.

"Oh, that's good," Goblet laughed. "That's good news! I've been thinking a lot about who it was that betrayed William. Good to hear that it wasn't Alexander as he was the only one in Williams own age that William could confide in. That is certainly good news."

Goblet took a leap towards the red display and put his foot on it. The foot was scanned with an infrared glow.

"Welcome Goblet," Alexander's recorded voice said, with the difference that the recording didn't sound scratchy at all anymore. Now it was Fritz's turn. Fritz felt a little nervous. Not because he doubted himself, but more because he really hoped it would work. Fritz put his left index finger on the display. His index finger was scanned and once again Alexander's voice was heard. "Welcome Grand master!" But I'm not a Grand master, Fritz thought and was about to open his mouth and object.

"Don't say anything," Goblet whispered. "I think the scanner reads your real identity, but it doesn't mean you have to be in that position in life." Fritz shut his mouth again. It was true what Goblet had said.

"You may now pass, one at the time," Alexander's voice enlightened them.

Goblet went through the opening first. An infrared beam scanned him from top to bottom and then up again. Then it was Fritz's turn. The infrared beam also scanned him from top to bottom and then up again. Then he, too, was able to pass through the opening.

They stood by a stone staircase that was illuminated by a reddish glow. Within three seconds the staircase swung around and exposed a small oak staircase down.

"That's beautiful!" Fritz exclaimed. "That's incredibly beautiful. This must be the grave William told me about." At the end of the oak staircase, Fritz and Goblet came to a room of stone in which all four sides were illuminated by torches. There were huge stone columns that went from the four corners of the room and were tied together in the middle like an arch. Fritz saw that there were different signs in dark green and red writing on the stone walls. Around the stone columns, various ornaments of leaves and flowers meandered. The floor was covered in dust and gravel.

"Look Fritz," Goblet cried out. The vault led into another room. "Come on, hurry up!" Fritz had to crouch slightly to get through the opening to the next room. When he came into the other room, the room opened up. What from the outside looked like a small, insignificant opening hid a grand and large room. This room also had a vaulted ceiling but the ceiling was much more ornate than the previous one. Some kind of glass mosaic covered most of the ceiling. Fritz quickly realized that the mosaic represented the sea. He clearly saw the waves and how the sun reflected itself in the water. The light in the room seemed to come from the ceiling mosaic that shimmered in blue, green, and gold. In the middle of the room there was a large tomb carved out of stone. The stone tomb was on a podium. Goblet just stood there devoutly and drew his breath. After a few minutes when Goblet finally opened his mouth, Fritz thought he would say something really nice and devotional to his friend William, so Fritz was very surprised when Goblet instead opened his mouth and shouted "Hey, William, we're finally here, Fritz and I. What I've missed you and how much fun we've had. What adventures!"

It was a little strange was that the sound didn't bounce back, but rather it seemed that the walls were sucking up all the sound. Goblet continued. "You cannot imagine how much I've been longing for you! And now my dreams have finally come true. But I have to say in earnest that I would have liked us to have had a little more time together. But now William, I want to introduce you to Fritz. Say hello Fritz," Goblet yelled.

Fritz didn't really know what to say. He had always been taught to be respectful when visiting a grave.

"Say hello now, don't be so picky. You know William was never very much for proper manners and things like that. He wasn't much for frills and stuff like that at all. Say hello now, right away," Goblet said a bit annoyed to Fritz.

Fritz opened his mouth, he didn't know where all the words came from, but he felt he wanted to tell William about everything that had happened. Fritz told of his anger that he had not been able to change William's fate and that he wished he had been able to stop what had happened. He told about the old Grand master and about the man in the library. He told about his grandson William, whom he cared a lot about and wanted to protect. In short, Fritz told the whole story. When he was done, it felt like a big rock had been lifted from his chest.

"And William, I want you to know that even though I've never met you in real life, I feel incredibly close to you and I wish I could have helped you there and then. I want you to know that not all grown men are deceitful and false," he continued quietly.

Goblet was baffled. "I just thought you'd introduce yourself, but this was really something. Would you like a hug?"

"I think so," Fritz said, who felt close to tears.

"Well, I can't really give you a hug, but this is what I did to William when he felt sad." Goblet floated up to Fritz's cheek, tipped himself a little towards him, and out of the goblet blew a warm wind. The wind swirled towards

Fritz's cheek and it was as if millions of tender feather-light pats touched his cheek. Fritz closed his eyes.

"Better?" Goblet wondered.

"Much better," Fritz answered gratefully.

"Let's see," Goblet continued. "William said in his video message to you that you would help him. I think there's something in this tomb that William wants us to find. Why don't we start searching?"

Fritz and Goblet started looking around. It was a little hard to search for a clue that could help them find out who killed William when they didn't know what the clue would look like. They searched for a long time but found nothing.

Eventually Fritz said. "Maybe we should stop our search and start over. What do we really know?"

Fritz and Goblet sat down and rested their backs against one of the stone walls. Fritz was a man who was extremely structured and always wanted to paint a picture of the situation and it was especially important to him in those situations in life where you did not really know what the right answer was.

"Let's see," Fritz said. "We have the message that I received from William, in which he said that he needed help and that I should find him. And now we've actually found him. Then there are those two voices that we heard in the shortcut. At least it seemed like one of them knew William very well. Did you recognize any of the voices?"

Goblet bowed its head.

"No, I didn't. It's quite likely that the light is refracted in a shortcut and thus maybe sound as well may be distorted so that you do not recognize voices."

"Off course you're right," Fritz replied thoughtfully.

"Then I have to say," Goblet continued, "William almost never used to talk about the people he met or what relationships he had with them. What I know is that William had a teacher named Agerlini at the school and that he used to teach William in magic, but I never met him. Then, of course, I knew Alexander, son of a high-ranking nobleman, he was the same age as William. I met him a few times. William also used to talk about a few other confidants but who they were I never found out and I didn't want to ask William either. With all that has happened, of course I should have asked him. But William could be very private."

"I understand," Fritz said. "If we're to summarize what we know, it's that we're looking for something that might give us a clue as to who killed William and why he was killed."

"Don't you think he was murdered because he was too powerful?" Goblet wondered.

"Could be," Fritz said. "But if I've understood you correctly, not many people knew about his knowledge and he seems to be a person who kept a lot to himself. And how can anyone murder a boy? It seems unbelievable. But we can't rule out that he was murdered because he had become too powerful, but I think there's something more behind it," Fritz said thoughtfully.

Goblet was quiet for a while. Fritz felt it was difficult for Goblet to try to think about the killer's motives.
"I think we should look for clues in the first room," Fritz said. "William wanted us to find him, and we've done that now."
"It sounds like a good idea," Goblet answered, who still couldn't quite shake off his discomfort.
It's always hard to find something you're looking for, Fritz thought, and it's even harder to find something when you don't know what you're looking for. Fritz and Goblet tried to keep their eyes sharp and their mind open. They shone with their light and felt gently on all stones they could see. If a stone stood out, was loose or otherwise attracted their attention they searched it. Fritz caught himself staring at three stones at the foot of one of the stone walls. There was something about the three stones that made Fritz want to take a closer look. There's nothing special about them, but still. Fritz looked at the other three walls where they met the floor and none of them ended with three smaller stones, instead there was relatively large boulders at the bottom of the walls. Fritz hesitated, he didn't want to ruin anything in the tomb if there was nothing behind the stones. Goblet saw Fritz hesitate and looked at the stones.

"You know, William wouldn't mind at all if you took those stones out," Goblet stated.

"Do you really think he wouldn't have minded? Fritz asked.

"No, I really don't think so," Goblet answered. "William wasn't a person who cared much about material things." Fritz felt relieved. He quickly got down on his knees, pulled out his knife and began trying to remove the stones from the wall. Fritz was methodical about it and small pebbles and gravel fell to the floor, but the stones didn't move. In the end after about 15 minutes with the knife around the stones, which to Fritz felt a whole lot longer, the first stone finally came loose. Soon after that the second and then the third stone came loose.

"There's a hidden compartment here," Fritz shouted excitedly to Goblet.

"How exciting!" Goblet shouted back while jumping up and down in the air.

Fritz slowly felt with his hand in the compartment and gently grabbed a package which he slowly pulled out. It was a book wrapped in several layers of protective leather.

"Oh, my God!" Goblet shouted as he jumped up and down. "Open it!" "I will," Fritz laughed, he was extremely relieved that there really was something behind the stones. He gently folded away the leather and uncovered a black leather book. Fritz carefully opened up the first page of the book. In blue ink and with neat handwriting it was written on the brown paper: *"Hey Fritz."* Fritz's mouth opened wide in sheer amazement. But how...? he thought? *"I, who write this to you, is called Alexander and I was a school friend of William's. As I think you have understood, we were also close friends. I don't know if you know about it yet, but I think you suspect William's death wasn't due to the fact that he was murdered during a robbery as has been announced. No, William's death was thoroughly planned and could only have been done by someone who knew him very well. His immediate circle consisted of six or seven people. I, Goblet, his magic teacher Master Agerlini, Father Orfius a priest in the church, Mr. Bergial, a high nobleman and Mr. Glowney, Grand master of the South Star Order"*

But that is my order, Fritz thought. The letter continued *"These are the people I know William met and with whom he had more or less close contact. Of these, I have only met Goblet, the priest, the magic teacher and the Grand master. One or perhaps several of them must have been involved in William's murder. I've been trying to find out more about William's death, but it's been hard. After William died, the new king gained more influence over the West Clermont Lincoln university. It felt like a tough time at the university with more control and limitations on what was allowed to be taught in the field of magic. Shortly after William's death, I was the victim of an assassination attempt. It was when I was about to eat my porridge in the morning. I have always been sensitive to smells and there was something that did not smell right with the porridge so I had the porridge analyzed and it contained a large amount of arsenic.*

That's when I decided to disappear. Father Orfius helped me and together we constructed my death. My official grave is in the catacombs, along with William's false grave. Since my 'death', I have been able to research who murdered William and I have been able to move around freely using an invisibility spell that I found in one of William's magic books. I and Father Orfius took care of William and buried him in this chapel. In connection with his funeral, we decided to manage the magic and knowledge that William had left us and to try to solve the mystery of why William was murdered and who was responsible for it. William once told me that there would be a namesake for him in about 480-500 years and that his namesake would also be a bearer of the compass mark. The compass is a tremendous force and I don't know if the younger William has had time to figure out the power of the compass yet. The compass is the unifying link that balances and uses the power of light, darkness, fire, water and earth. We have collected all the items and books that we have been able to find that William owned and used and they have been stored by Father Orfius. If you put your hand on the sun in the roof of William's chapel, a path will open to the room where the objects and books are stored. Use the objects wisely and pass the knowledge on to the younger William. Our William would have liked that." The page was signed "/ AA".

Fritz sat quietly for a long time and he was angry. I can't believe that back then two boys had been allowed to be so badly hurt. One murdered and the other had to disappear from sight. Fritz clenched his teeth hard. If only I'd been there, he thought.

CHAPTER 8
WILLIAM AND LIBRAS OLDEST BOOK AND ANTIQUARIAN BOOKSTORE

I think I will do what Grandpa said on the phone and get to know a bit more about Libra, William thought. William walked aimlessly around looking for a bookstore. He passed old houses and several small bridges. Some bridges were built of stone while others were built of wood. William strolled around and enjoyed the busy life of the streets. William didn't really know where he was going, but wandered on in his own thoughts. He came to a dark little square. When he looked straight up towards the mountains, he saw the great highway winding up into the mountains. A large part of the road was built on large concrete pillars that rose from the valley and high up on the mountain. It must be a powerful feeling to drive in your car that high up and look down on the city, William thought. A section of the road was built as a large oval circle, supported by several concrete columns that were at least 100 meters high. William let his eyes wander of the high bridges and instead he focused on the square. There was a small café to the side of the square. Around the square grew large chestnut trees. As William looked down, he saw that the ground in the middle of the square was made of marble. As he got closer, he saw that it was richly decorated with ornaments in different shades of green. In the center of the square there was a fountain depicting a boy reading a book. William sat down on the edge of the fountain and looked at the water and at the boy. Beneath there was a small stone sign on which moss had grown. William tried to read what it said but he concluded that he believed the text was written in Latin. He took out his phone and looked up a translation of the text. *"He who seeks knowledge finds answers"* I hope so, William said to himself. He looked at the boy and guessed he was seven or eight years old. William thought there was something tranquilizing about listening to the pouring water. He looked straight ahead and suddenly felt calm.

After a while he rose and walked on aimlessly. He went further into the narrow alleyways that became narrower and narrower the further in he walked. The cobblestone was worn and the houses looked a little run down. The color of the facades flaked and stones had fallen off the walls in several places. The balconies he saw also looked old and in need of repairs. On some of the balconies, laundry hung on ropes and on several there were ceramic pots with plants that bloomed in various red and pink colors.

"I think it's different kind of Pelargoniums," he said half high to himself.

"Books and antiquarian, the oldest in Libra," he read on a sign that hung a little askew in front of a shop window. William felt an irresistible urge to go in there. He had always liked books and there was something very special about older books, almost a bit like secret knowledge. Before he opened the glass door, he instinctively checked his inner pocket and, to his relief, felt that the map was still there. He opened the glass door that squeaked and an old-fashioned bell hanging above the door pinged.

William came into a dark, shady room. There were things from floor to ceiling. Mostly books stacked in several brown painted and worn bookshelves.

"Hello, anyone here?" William didn't get an answer. "Hello!" he called out again. On the front of the counter there was a brass bell that he rang. William had expected a bright sound from the bell but instead it gave out a dull sound. He put the bell back on the counter and waited. William was about to ring the bell again when he heard a shuffling sound. From a back door, a very old man emerged. His hair was white and ruffled. He was wearing a pair of glasses that sat crooked over his nose. He had a beige roughly knitted cardigan with several holes in it. His pants were light grey and wrinkled.

"What can I do for you young Sir?" He wondered and looked at William.

"I really don't know," William answered truthfully.

"Oh," the old man replied while looking at him with his shrewd eyes. "Maybe I can help you find what you're looking for. Is it old objects or is it books that you are interested in?"

"I really don't know," William said.

"Hmm, come with me and we'll see what we can find for you."

William followed the man into another room where there were things stacked everywhere. There were used old bowls, glasses, cups, saucepans, watches, jewelry, ladles, flower pots, towels, vases, cutlery, paintings, almost anything you could think of. Along the walls were worn bookshelves. William looked around and wondered how the man could find anything among all the things.

"I believe you're wondering how I can keep track on all my objects, but you don't have to worry, I know where everything is. I have it safely stored in here," he said, and pointed with his index finger at his forehead. "This isn't the only room, follow me and I'll show you."

The old man showed William around in two more rooms. One room was straight ahead from the room they were in and the next room was to the left and then they were back in the entrance room.

"Now we've walked around my little shop," the man said. "I think I'll look around for a while."

"Just tell me if you need my help," the white-haired man said and pushed up his glasses.

William reached for a book and saw that the man was looking at the arm where the compass mark was. The mark was very faint right now and you really had to make an effort to see it.

"Uhm," the old man coughed. "I see I have a prominent visitor today. Come on, let's sit down and have a cup of coffee."

"I'd love to but I don't drink coffee," William replied politely, "but if you have something else I can drink I'd appreciate it."

"I'll arrange something else. Come with me, my friend." They went into the back room. The man looked around and then he felt with his hand behind a large wooden clock.

"That's it," he said and a narrow opening of about 30 cm opened up from floor to ceiling in the wooden wall.

"It's important not to eat too much," he murmured as he squeezed through the opening. They came into a pitch-black room.

"Let me just turn on the light," the man said and William heard a click and the whole room bathed in light. The room was completely different from what William had imagined. At the far end was a red velvet sofa with associated armchairs. There was a pattern of medallions in the fabric that reminded him of what he had seen on the ground by the fountain.

"You have sharp eyes," the man says. "I see that you've seen the similarity in the patterns. Yes, indeed, he who seeks knowledge will find answers and sometimes answers you don't want to find," the old man said and sighed heavily, "but that may well be the case. I hoped and believed that you'd come and see me, but I wasn't sure. But I thought our meeting wouldn't come this soon as I did not know if the power in you was strong enough yet but it both pleases me and worries me that you're here now. You're welcome to sit down and I'll be right back with something to drink."

The man walked over to an adjacent kitchen.

William sat down on the sofa. He felt at ease. There was something about the old man and his shop that made William feel safe. He looked around the room and noted that the books were neatly arranged on the walnut bookshelves that stood along the four walls. A brass lamp hung from the ceiling and on the dark wooden floor was a brown and green silk carpet with hints of red. The room was neat and tidy. William got up and went over to the kitchen. He peered in and saw that the man was making coffee and thawed cookies in the microwave oven. The cabinet doors were made of thick wood and looked sturdy. The fridge was moss green and so was the microwave.

"Do you like chocolate cookies and syrup bread? It's my sister who baked them."

"It sounds delicious," William answered.

"I have juice made of lemons and elderberries. Would you like some?"

"It sounds good," William said.

The man picked up a plastic can from the fridge and pulled out a spoon and put several full spoons of frozen juice in a glass carafe. "Can you help me add water and mix," he said and handed William the glass carafe.

"Is it your sister that made the juice?" William asked.

"Mm," the man mumbled. "Now we're almost ready for some coffee," the man said as there was a pinging sound from the microwave. He pulled out a beautiful old porcelain platter painted with white and red roses and put the cookies on it.

"Can you bring the cookies and juice and I'll bring glasses, coffee cups, plates and coffee."

William took the platter with the cookies and the juice carafe and went to the sofa. The old man brought a tray and sat down in the left armchair.

"Welcome William, please help yourself. I don't think I've introduced myself. My name is Marcus," he said and offered his hand.

"I'm William," William said and smiled, "but you already knew that."

"Does it bother you that some people already know who you are?" Marcus asked.

"Yes, I think so."

"Then I can assure you that most people have no idea who you are. It is only among certain people that you are already well known, but for most people you are just another boy."

"That's good to hear," William said.

The man poured himself some coffee and leaned back in the armchair with his cup in hand.

"Excuse me," he said. "I usually drink my coffee in a certain way. Is it ok with you?"

"Sure," William replied, who was curious about what Marcus meant. The man took his cup, poured coffee onto the plate and then put a sugar cube in his mouth and drank the coffee from the plate.

"It's an old habit of mine but I do think the coffee tastes much better this way and it cools of quicker as well." William nodded.

"You see William," Marcus continued as he slurped his coffee. "You are a very important person to me and not only to me but to many other people as well."

William fidgeted a little nervously.

"It's probably going to take some time before you get used to the idea," Marcus said, "but I can assure you that you will. I've been in a similar situation myself. Of course, it was nothing like yours, but you could say that I've also had expectations on me and what I should do with my life. You could say that my destiny was already decided from the time I was born. I inherited it from my father, who in turn inherited it from his and so on, it has been that way for generations. All the time for the same purpose. To guide and transfer information between two people. Unfortunately, one person died before the meeting, which is why I'm glad the same thing didn't happen to you."

William shivered.

"You might be wondering a little about the mess in my store and I promise you that it's true when I said that I have the order inside my head. A lot of it, of course, is rubbish that I have stacked just to confuse any visitors. Not that I have many visitors, but those who find their way here often have some evil purpose and therefore it is important that I confuse them. I've been working really hard at pretending to be a confused, demented old man for surely 40 years now. Before that, I just pretended to be confused and absent minded. You know one that other people easily make fun of and speak ill of when they think you don't hear, but I do. This spectacle has been inherited in my family and the purpose has always been that those who come here should not take me or my ancestors seriously and not believe that we in any way pose a threat or that we possess any knowledge that may be dangerous for them. A lot of times I've had to bite my tongue when they've said mean comments to me though, but it's part of my role not to reveal who I really am.

Secretly, over several hundred years, my family has collected material, magazines, letters, books, objects that we found valuable in some way. We've also been eavesdropping on conversations that we've written down. You have no idea what people talk about when they don't care about a confused man that sits nearby. They don't even bother to whisper. Everything is recorded and carefully catalogued."

"Then there must be more rooms than this one," William said, who understood that not everything would fit in the room they were sitting in.

"You're right, it's all locked in a vault below us."

William nodded. "My grandfather is in an order, are you in one as well?" William wondered curiously.

"No, it's never been relevant to me. You see, I don't trust anyone. In an order, you often entrust your secrets to your brothers, and I dare not do that. Besides, my cover would be revealed to the order and I have nothing to gain from that. When there are several people sharing a secret, there are more opportunities for someone to leak the information to others. In addition, there's no order that is interested in a member who seems confused and thus cannot contribute to their work. No, enough about me. Now you have to tell me what you're looking for that made your inner compass find me?"

William fell silent. He didn't know how much to say. After all, he was carrying sensitive information. He felt on the map that was in his inner pocket. William took off his jacket and put it down beside him.

"I don't really know where to start," he said truthfully. "I think I need to think about it for a while."

"I understand," Marcus said. "You are already carrying secrets and you need time to decide what you can reveal to me and what you need help with. I'll just drink my coffee and if you want, I can pick up a book and read while you think." Marcus reached down under the table and picked up a book with black leather cover.

A pinging sound was heard.

"Oh, Marcus said, that's unusual, I already have a visitor. I usually don't have many at all. No more than one per month and sometimes it goes several months without anyone entering the shop." He stood up laboriously. "Stay here, I'll be right back." Marcus pushed apart the wooden planks and went through the hole and closed the opening behind him. William was left alone on the sofa. William felt a little restless. Suddenly it was hard for him to sit still. He started to walk back and forth. Strange that someone visits the old man right now. Just when I got here. At the same time William was busy thinking about what to tell Marcus. He also needed to think about Marcus' safety. He only needs to share information that did not pose a threat to Marcus. Information that he didn't risk being pressured to disclose. William decided to ask who William was but not to mention anything about his tomb or the unnamed tomb he had seen below the cathedral. William sat down, but he still couldn't get rid of the uneasy feeling. It can't hurt if I quietly sneak out just to see who the visitor is, he thought. I don't have to show myself. William got up and snuck out through the opening. He deliberately didn't close it in case he needed a quick retreat.

He quietly snuck through the rooms and stopped in the room that was just before the entrance. He saw a tall man that leaned over Marcus and hissed something that William could not perceive. Suddenly, the man grabbed Marcus by the throat and pushed him up against the wall. William saw the old man gasp for air. I can't stand here and watch him be killed, William thought feverishly. What should I do? I need to think of something quickly. William picked up his phone from his pocket. What if I had the phone number to the store? Then I could have called and maybe diverted the man that way. Think fast, William thought. I have to find another way to save Marcus. William came to think of that at one point he had downloaded a police siren as a ringtone. He put it on and hoped the man would be intimidated. Otherwise, there was no choice but to fight him. William prepared to attack. He picked up a heavy vase that he could hit the tall man in the back of the head with if the ringtone didn't work. Di do di do, the police siren started weakly and then increased in strength.

"What the h… is this!" The tall man exclaimed. The man dropped Marcus, who fell to the floor. The tall man stood over him and hissed high.

"Lucky for you, old man, if I somehow find out you weren't telling the truth, you can count on that I'll come back and then you might not be so lucky." With long strides he hastily left the store.

William ran up to Marcus, who was gasping for air.

"Are you alright? Do you want me to bring you a glass of water?" William asked. Marcus shook his head. He held out his hand and William realized he wanted help getting up. William felt Marcus whole old body shake.

"You want me to help you get back to the room?" Marcus nodded. William extended his arm and the old man took it gratefully and William supported him as they walked back to the room and the armchair. William helped him sit down and then he ran to the kitchen to get a glass of water. Marcus gratefully accepted the glass and drank a few sips of water. William saw the glass shaking in Marcus's hand.

"They are on to you," Marcus said silently, "the man who came in asked me if I'd seen a boy around fourteen or fifteen years old. I told him that I rarely get visitors in my shop and that I find it difficult to remember who has been here. That's when he pushed me up against the wall. I then said that I could not remember any boy and that it was mostly adults who found their way to my shop."

Marcus looked William in the eyes. "We need to find another way for you to get here. We'll talk more about it before you leave, but now I need to hear what you need help with." William saw that Marcus gathered himself and took a deep breath. He was quiet for a few minutes then he asked William. "What are you looking for?"

William needed a few seconds to recover. Not because he didn't know what he wanted to ask Marcus about, but to take in that someone was after him and that that person thought he was going to seek out Marcus. After a short moment William said with a low voice. "I'm looking for information about a boy named William. He lived…" William became silent and thought, I actually don't really know when he lived but I know he was seventeen years old when he was murdered.

Marcus froze. "I know very well who you're talking about. Remember that I told you that the purpose of collecting information in my family was to convey information between people. The William you mentioned was going to visit one of my ancestors but disappeared under mysterious circumstances just before the meeting was due to take place, later he was found dead. He died for, what was it now," Marcus thought for a moment, "I think he died almost five hundred years ago. A very tragic story. He accomplished so much for our country and was in the middle of something when he was murdered. How anyone even can imagine to murder a boy is

incomprehensible to me, but he probably posed a great threat to someone. I think it must be some kind of conspiracy against him that led to his death. You see, he was a very clever kid who possessed deep knowledge of magic. In my family we have always believed that it was someone close to William, someone who he trusted who led the conspiracy."
William shivered.

CHAPTER 9
THE VAULT

"If I remember correctly a package came to us from William a few days after his death. You know back then postal services was not the same as it is today. It was probably one of his servants or a friend who left it to us."

"Do you still have the package?" William asked.

"Of course, I have!" Marcus answered almost a little offended. William was relieved that he would at last get some information about William.

"Shall we go down to your vault?" Marcus asked.

"My vault?" William said wondering.

"Yes, you see, I'm just the trustee. It is you and the other William who are the rightful owners. My family are just the information collectors." Marcus put his hand in one of his pant pockets and picked up a yellow key and handed it to William. "Here you are!"

"Thank you," William said who felt how heavy the key was in his hand.

"It's made out of gold," Marcus said explanatorily. "And by the way, I'll give you one of the two keys to the entrance door as well so that you can enter the normal way if need be. Shall we go downstairs then?"

"Have you rested enough? William wondered.

"Yes, I have and we have no time to lose." He got up and went over to the kitchen. William followed after him.

"This is a bit clever, at least I think it is," the old man said while walking over to a tall wooden cabinet. "My pantry," Marcus said and opened the cabinet door. The shelves were full of various marmalades, pickled cucumbers and canned food. Marcus grabbed a dent in the wood and pushed the entire rear wall of the cabinet downwards. Behind the cabinet wall there was a door. Marcus opened the door and reached for a light switch. William saw how black and relatively short, forged lanterns lit up. I don't think they're more than a meter high, he guessed. At the end of a stone walkway that led downwards William glimpsed the vault. It looked like a large stone building with a thick steel door. On the steel door was a large brass wheel. They went quietly to the vault.

"Put the key in here," Marcus said and pointed at a keyhole that was just below the brass wheel. "Then turn the wheel." William did as he was told and the door opened up surprisingly easy. It didn't squeak or resist when he cranked the wheel.

William entered the vault and he saw that it looked like a very large library. The shelves went from floor to ceiling and they were packed with books. The shelves stood in long rows one after the other. When William looked at the ceiling, he saw that there were hanging signs that explained what themes the bookshelves contained.

"It's ok to come out. He's the owner of the vault," Marcus said and pointed at William. William saw something moving in the shadows at the back of the vault. He squinted and tried to see what it was.
"It's OK," Marcus repeated. William sensed a small figure amongst the bookshelves far back in the room.
"He's a little shy and wary. You see, he hasn't met anyone but me."
"I will come out now," William heard a weak voice whispering.
"Yes, please do so that I can introduce you to William," Marcus replied.
The cutest creature William had ever seen emerged. He was about a meter tall. He had two short legs, two arms and two hands. His hands were twice the size of those of a grown man and his ears were also big, kind of like two egg-shaped circles. Nose and mouth were small and his skin was covered with hair. He had a little fuzzy light brown hair on his head. He looked so cute that William wanted to pick him up and give him a big hug. He was wearing overalls, a T-shirt and black clogs which made every step he took noisy. The creature gently walked up to William and reached out his hand to greet him. William marveled at how smooth and soft the creature's hand was when he shook it and it felt a little strange that his own

hand almost disappeared into the big hand. It was a soft and gentle handshake.

"Uhm," the creature said and cleared his throat. "My name is Joey."

"My name is William," William said.

"So, you're the owner of the vault," Joey said and looked at William with his big, beautiful and expressive eyes.

"Yes, Marcus told me that I am but it is all new to me so I don't know what it really means," William answered truthfully.

Joey's face cracked into a faint smile. "Perhaps I can show you around?"

"That's an excellent idea," Marcus said, "as you're the librarian of the vault."

Joey seemed to stand a little taller and William understood that he took his task very seriously.

"Let's start from the entrance itself," Joey said and pointed. "The bookshelves at the beginning of the room contains the newest books and the further in you go, the older the books are. If you look up at the ceiling, there are signs hanging, on the first sign you can see that is says 21st century, then follows the 20th century and so on. The oldest books are several thousand years old, from the time when the art of writing came to in Thyrridea. Books and letters are placed in order of different themes on the bookshelves. For example, themes can be people or events that have taken place in our history. As you can see, there are some comfortable armchairs and tables placed a little here and there so that you do not have to carry the heavy books far and then easily put them back in the correct place. Most of the time I do like that and that saves me some walking. I'm the one who cleans, dusts and wipes the floor in the vault so it stays clean and fresh. The oldest books need care and I regularly lubricate their binders so that they do not crack."

They walked the different aisles while Joey was talking. "Here in the middle, there is a reading corner." William saw three armchairs facing each other with four side tables standing between the armchairs.

"So that we can be able to sit together all three of us and discuss important things," Marcus added.

They arrived at a tall cabinet with large doors.

"Here are various magical objects stored. They've been collected for centuries," Joey enlightened him.

"When you learn to master more advanced magic I will introduce you to them." Marcus said and opened the cupboard. "Some instruments are a bit old-fashioned and unwieldy, but most of them are actually useful."

William let his eyes wander over the objects. Some, as Marcus had said, were large and looked a bit clumsy to use while others were considerably smaller and looked handier.

"I have written small notes that is placed on the shelves to describe what kind of devices they are."

William had time to notice that there was a memory device that extended and found hidden memories, a truth machine, an invisibility device and so on.

"Many of the functions of the devices can be replaced with magic spells, but they can also amplify spells. For example, if you were to meet a person and you both threw the same spell, yours would be stronger if you used a magic device at the same time. You could say that the devices are an arsenal of magical weapons. You choose the weapon that you think will benefit you the most in the battle." William nodded. Marcus closed the cabinet. They continued further into the vault.

"What are the big glass balls that are stacked on the bookshelves?" William asked and pointed.

"It's event bubbles," Joey answered. "For centuries, Marcus's family has observed various events. They've recorded the events into these crystal balls. If you pick up a crystal ball and look into it, you will see and hear different events. It's like snapshots of events from the past. Events that might be of importance to you."

William picked up a crystal ball. It sparkled in all the colors of the rainbow. The ball was about 7x7 centimeters in size so he could hold it comfortably in one hand. When William looked closer at the ball, he saw two older men standing and talking. William heard how they discussed with each other.

"If you want to hear better what they're saying, hold the ball even closer to your head," Joey enlightened him.

"This is really cool!" William exclaimed. "How amazing it is to be able to see them and hear what they say."

Marcus smiled contently. "It takes a little time to make an event ball."

"If you want, I can show you where I live," Joey said.

"I think that'll have to wait until another time," Marcus said. "Now we're in a bit of a hurry and we need to find the package William sent us just before he died."

"All right," Joey said. "Wait here and I'll find it." He quickly ran away down an aisle.

"If anyone finds things quickly, it's Joey. He's lightning fast and finds his way around the vault like it is his own pocket," Marcus said, laughing.

William heard the clapping from Joeys clogs as he moved through the vault. Suddenly it went quiet for a short while and then the sound of the clogs could be heard again. It wasn't long before Joey was back with them again.

"Here," he said and handed over a brown package to William. William saw that the package was sealed with a red seal with a squiggly 'W' on it. He was about to open the package when Joey stopped him.

"Look at the seal, it says open privately," he said.

William looked closely at the seal and he saw it written in small, small letters.

"You better follow William's wish," Marcus said. "You can choose if you want to open the package here or if you rather want to take it home and open it there."

William thought for a moment. "Hmm, I think I'll sit in one of those armchairs and think about it,"

"You do that," Marcus said. "Joey and I will leave you alone. If you want us, pull the velvet-red tassel," he pointed at a tassel that hung from the ceiling down beside one of the armchairs. "Then we'll be here right away." Markus and Joey left the vault and William sat down in one of the armchairs.

He closed his eyes and thought. What a strange vault he was in. Everything that was collected and stored here, all the snapshots, books and conversations that had been written down. William could understand that there were probably many people who wished he had never met Marcus or found this vault. Then his thoughts began to wander to the other William. He must have been special with such a powerful and deep knowledge of magic. I can hardly believe he lived about 500 years ago. The idea was almost staggering. William felt incredibly closely connected to William so that it felt as if he had lived in this century at least. His thoughts were swirling. It's amazing that William left me a package 500 years ago. It's almost inconceivable. William turned the package around in his hands. It was wrapped with a brownish paper that was tied up with a thin but strong string. William looked at the red seal. A long time ago, it would probably have been bright red, but over time the color of the seal had faded and become a more brownish red. William slowly loosened the string below the seal and carefully unwrapped the paper. Under the paper was a metal box. William uttered the spell that Arild had taught him that allowed no one to locate him. When the spell was in place he opened the lid of the metal box. In the box there was a rolled-up letter and a clear transparent stone, which was flat-cut at the bottom. William started to read the letter.

"From William to William" it said on the top row. *"Hi William. I'm 16 years old when I write this to you. I will leave this message to my best friend Alexander who will leave this letter at Marcusson's vault in case something happens to me. I don't know if you know it yet, but you and I both bear the mark of the compass. Through my studies in magic, I have found out that there will be another that bears the mark of the Compass in some hundred years' time and that he, like me, will also be called William. But our backgrounds are a little different. When I was a baby, my mother left me to an orphanage here in Libra and after that I became a foster child in a family. What I've learned about you from my studies is that you're going to come from a stable family, a home that's not divided like mine, but I'm not going to complain. I've been very lucky and I go to a very good school. Enough about my private situation. It feels a bit strange to write this letter to you, but since we are both bearers of the compass, I think we will have a lot in common. I want to tell you that no one but my mentor knows that I am the bearer of the compass and I think it makes sense if you, like me, make sure that only a few people know that you are the bearer of the*

compass and even better if no one knows. I have a very good mentor at my school. His name is Mr. Argilini and is a teacher at the school. He constantly helps me develop my knowledge of magic, but we do it in secret so that no one knows how much I know. I think you, like me, are learning more about your inner compass and where it can lead you. I recommend that you also get a mentor to help you develop your magic and your abilities.

At this moment in time, there is a large-scale internal conflict in Thyrridea, King Valdemar is doing his best to resolve the conflict, but it is difficult. It's dark times and it feels like a lot of people are driven by their own unspoken agendas. You must constantly pay attention, protect the truth and keep your head cool but your heart warm and watch your tongue. I always wear a thick leather bracelet around my wrist so that no one will see the compass mark. I think it is also a good idea for you to hide your compass mark. I've put a spell in the glass stone. Take the glass stone and pull it over your mark and the mark will disappear for a while. Unfortunately, the formula doesn't work on me as I have placed a strong protective spell on me and these two spells cannot work together. I wish you all the best, my namesake, and I believe that our destinies, even though there is about five hundred years between us, will be connected in some way. Best regards, William."

William sat with the letter in his hand for a long time. It was like William's words had gone right through his heart. I can't believe he only became 17. Suddenly,

William was filled with an enormous rage. William would usually never swear, but now he stood up and screamed straight out into the vault. "Why on earth, why?" The words echoed briefly in the vault, but were quickly absorbed by all the books on the bookshelves. William sat down in the armchair again and instead of rage, a great sadness and resignation came upon him. Feelings that you may feel when you lose a very close friend or brother or sister. "Why?" he whispered silently as tears ran down his cheeks, "why?" William cried.

Eventually, there were no more tears to cry. The grief was just as great, but the tears had run out. William picked up the glass stone William had left him and looked at it. He decided to do as William had said. He looked closely at the stone that reflected the shadows in the vault and pulled the stone slowly over his wrist. William felt a tingle in his skin and then he saw how the compass mark gradually began to disappear until it was completely gone. William took out his lighter from his pocket, placed the letter on the ashtray that stood on the small round table between the three armchairs and then he set the letter on fire.

"Now no one will know what the letter said except you and me, William," he whispered quietly. Then he leaned back in the armchair. The whole time the questions repeated itself in his head. How am I supposed to help William? How am I supposed to find his killer? The questions repeated itself over and over in his head. At last, William got up.

"This is of no use," he said aloud to himself. Nothing will happen if I just sit here." He took the stone in his right hand and found his way in between the bookshelves. The whole time he thought that there must be something in the vault that can help me. The shelves were nicely organized with small dark green notes that said century, then there were subtitles that said magic, which in turn had subtitles with protection spells, etc. But William's gaze stuck to a subtitle that said graves and ornaments. He slowly went over there, below the note there were three lines of both older, thicker books with leather covers and thinner books and loose papers that were just spun together.

William took out the bundle of loose papers and sat down on the floor and began to skim through the pages. William was very careful because the paper was old and fragile. The papers told him what different burial ornaments stood for, for example, it said that there was often a brief description of the deceased on the grave. The more significant the person, the more lavish the grave was. It was common for very wealthy people to have richly ornate burial sites. Sometimes they had their own chapels and their own small family cemeteries. The grave was seen as a central and important place. One final place that showed your social status. Sometimes the person was very involved in what the decoration would look like, but in sudden and unexpected deaths it was family or friends who had to decide the decoration, largely depending on the money that the family had. William put the papers back together and put them back on the bookshelf.

William had a strong feeling that he was looking for something special but he didn't know what it was. He held the stone tightly and walked slowly further into the vault towards the time when William was alive. He held the stone in a hard almost convulsive grip as he walked. Somehow the stone felt very important to him. As if he had received a very important gift from William. A gift that was very special. He sat down on the floor between the bookshelves and put the stone in his two hands. He closed his eyes and mumbled quietly to himself "How am I supposed to help you?" William felt a faint burning sensation from where the compass mark had been. The sensation got stronger and stronger. "Ouch!" William screamed, frantically looking for something he could cool down his wrist with. As the heat in his wrist increased, the stone became colder and colder. "My wrist is on fire, he screamed!" At last he took the stone and put the flat side of it on his wrist. It fizzled and smoke rose from his wrist when hot met cold. The whole vault shook and it got completely dark as if a short circuit had cut the power.
Oh, William had time to think before he heard a scream that William was acutely aware of wasn't his own. William lifted his eyes off his wrist and looked straight

ahead. He saw a boy standing right above him. The boy was in some kind of stone room.

"Hurry up William!" he heard someone whisper with a strained voice. "They'll be here anytime now."

William realized that the boy in front of him was William. The boy turned to the one with the strained voice. "Soon, I just have to do one thing first," the boy said.

"Run into the tomb and I'll try to fend them of until you're ready," the injured man whispered. With great difficulty and with the help of his sword he raised himself a bit from the floor. "Forever together," the injured man whispered. William saw the boy quickly bend down to the injured man, who seemed to be around 35 years old. His armor was all red with blood that was seeping out from his chest. The boy gave him a quick pat on the cheek and took out a bottle and said, "When the time comes, drink this and you won't feel anything." William handed over a small glass bottle to the injured man. William could see that he was whispering something in the injured man's ear but he couldn't make out what he was saying. Then William quickly got up and ran into the other room. There was fire everywhere.

"Where is it?" he cried out while covering his mouth with a cloth so as not to inhale the black smoke. William saw him close his eyes and utter a spell and immediately a fireball appeared, hovering in the air in front of him, showing him the way towards a stonewall. William pushed on a stone and the wall opened up and he stepped through into a dark vault. Behind him he heard a roar and the sound of someone hitting the ground. It got all quiet when the stonewall closed behind him.

William stood completely still with the fireball in front of him. He looked straight at William. As the older boy looked at him William felt a strong stream of energy going all the way down to his stomach.

"There's so much I want to tell you, but I have very little time. I don't know how much time I have left in this life. I've been betrayed by someone close to me. I don't know who, but it has to be someone I trust a lot. I have several times considered to send you a personal message. You see, we're the same in many ways, you and me. I would have liked to pass on most of my knowledge of magic and the lessons I have learned to you, but unfortunately it does not seem to be possible. I sincerely would have liked to spend more time with you, to be able to tell you what I have been through and exactly how we are alike. You see, many times I've felt lonely, but when I found out through scrolls and prophecy that another one with the mark of the compass would be born, I was incredibly happy. It felt like my heart started to sing and a warm feeling spread inside of me, in many ways you're like a little brother to me. And as a big brother, it's my duty to try to save you from facing the same fate as I."

Tears slowly began to fall down Williams's cheek as he looked at the older boy. I can't believe I've had a big brother. William looked at the older boy. William thought he looked older than 17. He looked like he was about 20. There was something warm and safe in his eyes. William got the feeling that he almost wanted to crawl up into his arms, or at least sit next to him. William looked at the older boy and immediately found that he reminded him of himself in many ways. He had the same light brown hair and ice blue eyes. Even their facial features were a little similar.

"I wish we had a little more time together you and I," the older boy said, "but I want you to know that what we have between us will always be there, no matter what happens. If I die, I will watch over you and you will be able to feel my presence through the compass mark. That's what connects us. That connection is stronger than everything else. Even stronger than death," he said and became silent.

"There seems to be trouble outside," he said and turned his head, "so I'll have to try and speed things up."

William heard the screams. The older boy continued.

"No matter what happens to me and what you're going to see, I don't want you to be blinded by hate and anger. Such feelings only darken your heart and make you not see clearly. Instead, try to gather energy to move forward and fulfill my mission. Even your time is limited. When I've been dead for 500 years, my magic will end. The messages I have sent you will be destroyed. My enemies know that and they will do everything in their might to prevent you from receiving this message. Today it is the 1st of September, 1522."

William thought quickly, there's only three weeks left before it all goes away. He swallowed hard and felt a slight sense of panic.

"I don't want to put too much of a burden on you either," the elder William continued, looking him in the eye. "I don't really know how far you've come with your knowledge of magic, but I do know that you are of my flesh and blood and that we are therefore equal in many ways in how we solve problems and how we act. However, heed my words, trust only a few people and even if you trust someone fully, I don't want you to make the same mistake as I did and tell that person or persons everything. I understand now that even people close to you can play a sometimes very dirty game and keep their cover for years without revealing themselves. That was my mistake. That one of the two or three people that's been closest to me have betrayed me. Therefore, only tell someone what that person needs to know to help you. Don't ever tell anyone everything you know. Just tell them fragments so they don't get the whole picture. Never let another person ever know all your thoughts even if it's your closest friend. Always be careful and pay attention to nuances in people's communication. Look closely at nonverbal communication. How close are people to each other when they talk, what kind of glances do they give each other and so on. You have honesty and truth in your heart, but don't expect anyone else to be like you just because they claim to be your friend. The person who has betrayed me has only done friendly acts and proved several times that I could trust him. Through this, the person has gradually gained my trust for several years. He has thus lured me into his trap. I say him because my three closest friends are men. Maybe all three of them betrayed me, I don't know. If you find out who betrayed me before 500 years have gone past, I'd love to know. Otherwise, when the mission is complete, I want you to let it be known who betrayed me and how the whole plan was put into effect.

I'm also going to send you a few letters that I wrote when I was 16. My friend Alexander will leave the letters to the Marcusson family, who I was supposed to meet. I wish I could say that I trust him with all my heart, but right now I don't know. I never expected to be in a situation like I am now. If you received this message, he has done what I asked him to do, but does that mean he is not the traitor? Right now, I don't know. It could be part of the plan. The messages might be copied or distorted, I don't know." William reached out with his hand. "Take my hand in yours. Close your eyes when you do." William did as he was asked, he reached out and took his hand and to his surprise he felt as if he held a real hand in his and the Compass mark appeared clearly before his closed eyes. In the darkness, the whole mark burned like fire. William felt a warm stream of energy pass into his body. It felt like he was getting an electric shock. His whole body vibrated. The force flowed first to his heart and then it followed the blood out into one arm, down the leg and then through the next leg and up into the other arm and back to the heart. William also felt the force flowing through the passages in his brain. The feeling was so strong that it felt like something touched him deep inside his inner self. That the Compass Mark touched his darkest feelings of doubt and anxiety and filled him with strength and determination. At the same time, he heard a soft voice whisper from his inner self. "Now you're a part of me. We are connected through life and death forever, my beloved little brother. Part of me will live on in you. Now my opponents can't access my magic. Manage it well my beloved brother." The voice fell silent.

William opened his eyes and looked up at his older brother. He stood there big and tall in front of him. William looked at his hand and closed his eyes to remind himself of what it had felt like to hold his brother's hand. William saw a dark shadow coming over his brother's face.

"I must hurry up and tell you what I know," he said. "If my suspicions are true, a lot will change in Thyrridea, he said with a serious look on his face. Through the aid of magic and by talking to various people close to the former king, I have indications that it is likely that he was murdered by supporters of his brother and his order. According to several sources, the former king was slowly poisoned by small quantities of arsenic in in his food. Therefore, he has gradually become sicker. His son reportedly suspected that something was going on, but just as he returned from a long journey home to assist his father, the son died in what is said to have been a drowning accident. His body was found in one of the canals. It was claimed that he had had too much to drink and accidentally fell into the water, but when the body was autopsied, no water was found in the lungs. This was silenced and the doctor who examined the body was said to be mentally unstable and was confined to a hospital. A new examination of the body was carried out and it was established that the king's son had died of drowning and that at the time of drowning he had had large amounts of alcohol in his blood. King Valdemar contacted me because he feared that his son had been murdered and he himself worried about his own life."

William pulled a small roll of paper out of his metal armor. "Here's the letter he sent me. It's dated July 10. On July 11, the day I received the letter, the castle flew their flags at half-mast and the king was pronounced dead. I immediately went up to the castle to show my condolences while I wanted to catch a glimpse of the dead king. When a king dies, it is customary for his body to be placed in an open casket and for the people to have the opportunity to say goodbye to their king for a day. When I came up to say goodbye to the old king, there were guards standing along the entire aisle and you could not get closer to the old king than five meters. Everyone was kept at a distance. According to the guards, the king's brother had ordered increased protection because he feared someone would try to take the body. Who would do that? There is no reasonable explanation. I think the king's brother was worried that someone would get close enough to the dead king and, through magic, examine the body and find large amounts of arsenic. In order to cast such a spell, one must be near the body in order to find out the cause of death. Within just a week, both father and son were buried.

In one of my previous conversations with the king, he had told me that he wished to be buried in a coffin, but the king's brother claimed that it was expressly the king's wish that he should be burned and that the ashes should be scattered at sea. In this way, the brother cleverly avoided that someone would try to examine the remains of the old king. When the king's brother took over as the new ruler, he made some changes in the country. Subtle changes that the common man did not notice, but I noticed, for example, the school got a new governance where the principal needed to regularly inform the king and a board of council the king had appointed about events at the school. What we worked on and researched and so on. The king's knowledge of the school and its work thus increased. New positions were filled and new procedures were introduced. The king began to attend school ceremonies and made himself a symbolic part of the school."

William sighed and wiped sweat from his forehead. "I've tried to keep a low profile and not openly tell anyone but my three closest friends what I know. Soon they'll be in this room, so I'll have to end my message to you."

William saw the older boy gather himself.

There was a very loud noise and a large part of the stone wall cracked. Dust and rocks fell everywhere and in came a man dressed in a black velvet cape with a mask in front of his eyes. He raised his sword against William, who ducked and returned the blow. The fight began. William felt incredibly helpless just sitting there and not being able to do anything to help his big brother. It was the worst feeling he had ever experienced. To just watch as someone you care a lot for defends himself. The fight was very even. The other man cast magic spells as the battle went on and William defended himself with other spells. William saw how lions, tigers, huge scorpions and giant spiders were formed just to be dissolved by Williams protective spells. The battle was just between the two of them. The man with the cape saw his chance and threw himself forward at William and stabbed with all his might but William just managed to avoid being stabbed by the incoming sword. William quickly turned around and stabbed the black-clad man in the back. The man fell down in front of his feet. The younger William saw a dark figure sneak in through the opening in the wall. William screamed to warn his older brother but he couldn't hear him. William saw the dark figure mumble something. The pictures of William disappeared and he understood that this was the last time he would see of his brother alive.

"No, you can't die!" William screamed as large tears rolled down his cheek. "No, you can't. You can't." William felt something inside him burst and he screamed out in despair. William cried so that his whole body shook. Suddenly he saw a flashing light that dazzled him. On instinct, William raised his arms to protect his face. William felt something hit him in the chest and he fell backwards. There was a surge of heat from his compass mark and an enormous force went through his entire body. William fainted. When he woke up and opened his eyes, he didn't know where he was at first, but then memories quickly came back to him and he was filled with an enormous anger and hatred.

"I will find and kill him," he said grimly, "believe me, whoever did this to my brother is going to die," William screamed. William's words echoed through the vault. William was furious, his whole body shook. "I will seek revenge!" William roared.

To his surprise, he saw that a crystal star lay in front of him. It shimmered in all the colors of the rainbow. William picked it up in his hands and felt a warm feeling of love spread through his body. He was strongly reminded of what William had said, that he shouldn't let his heart be darkened by hatred and anger because it would make it harder for him to see clearly.

Um, William thought. I'll keep calm, I promise. William felt different in a way but he couldn't put his finger on what it was. Somehow, he felt both older and more mature. It must be the magic that William brought to me that I feel. William suddenly understood what his brother had meant by saying that he would be with him.

"Yes, truly, you really are with me," William said aloud, feeling the blood pounding in the compass mark in response.

"Let's see," William said and carefully studied the star. "It's really beautiful." William turned it over and over in his hand. It was transparent but in the core was a dark spot that William couldn't see through. There must be a meaning to why I got this. William studied the star carefully to see if it had any opening. "Where could it be?" he said out loud to himself. He felt with his hands to see if he could find anything, but he didn't. Looking towards the core of the crystal star, he saw that the dark center shifted in color depending on how he held the star. The color went from black to a lighter gray, much like a shadow, William mused. He concentrated and looked towards the core. Now he could see dark clouds passing by in the core and then it cleared up and a light grey mist spread inside the star. William blinked and sat completely still, almost afraid to move. William heard the sound of a soft wind. He put his ear to the star to hear better. The sound got louder and he could hear a full storm going on in there, then the sound faded and he heard something that sounded like a whisper.

"William, William." William could hardly believe it was true and rubbed his hand to his ear to make sure he heard it right. He put his ear to the star once more and once again he heard the whispering through the whistling sound. "William, William."

"I'm here," he murmured.

"Say the words 'through rain, water, light and darkness, the search goes through time'." William spoke the words and just as he had finished the whole crystal became transparent and a shimmer of light spread through the star. William had to close his eyes so as not to be dazzled.

William felt that something appeared in his left hand. He opened his eyes and the light was gone and the dark core was back in the star. William looked at his left hand. In it there was a gold ring with a green emerald and a letter. William immediately recognized the letter and shivered. It's the letter that William showed me, he thought. He looked at the letter. The letter had turned a bit yellow and it looked a bit worn but it hadn't aged much. William saw the royal seal. He carefully opened the envelope and unfolded the paper that felt thick yet fragile in some way. It must be because it's hundreds of years old, William thought and was a little worried it would break. He really had to make an effort to read the squiggly letters. The letter clearly stated that the king believed that his son had been murdered and that he himself was next. William put the paper back in the envelope. By chance, he happened to take a closer look at it. William saw that there was something very faintly written on the back. He took the envelope closer to his eyes to make it easier to see what it said. He went over to one of the armchairs and used the reading light to see the faint writing better. *"Go to my grave/W"* it said. 'W' must stand for William, he thought. Alright, I have no time to lose. He put the ring and letter with the map in his inner pocket. He was about to pull the red velvet tassel when he stopped. Where should I hide the star? he thought. William looked at it where it lay on the table next to him and he felt that he didn't want to leave it behind. I need help, he thought. What if Arild had been here. He began to quietly mumble to himself. "Arild, can you help me? Arild, where are you? Arild, I need your help. I want you to take care of William's star for me." William heard faint steps behind him and felt a hand on his shoulder.

"You came," William said relieved, looking up at Arild's familiar face.

"I see you've been sad," Arild said. William sniffled.

Arild gently stroked him over his hair and said "I'm here with you now."

William threw his arms around his neck and hugged him tightly.

"Now, now my child," Arild said with his soft dark voice. "I'm with you now."

William felt tears once again running down his face and he buried it against Arild's shoulder. William felt incredibly relieved to see Arild again. Arild hugged William and when he noticed William was calmer, he said, "I understand that you want me to take the star for safe keeping."

William looked up surprised, then he remembered that Arild had the ability to read his mind.

William nodded. "Then you also know what happened to William."

"Yes," Arild answered. "You were thinking about him and what had happened when I held you in my arms." Again, William felt relieved. It felt good not to have to explain what he had been through. It was as if there was a wordless understanding between him and Arild.

"I think you need to hurry to his grave. Do you want me to help you and transport you there?"

William thought for a moment. "Yes," he said, then he came to think of Marcus and Joey. "Actually no, I think I need to tell them I'm leaving first, else they'll probably be worried and wonder where I've gone. Besides, I want to say goodbye to them."

"I can wait while you say goodbye."

"That would be kind of you," William replied.

Arild picked up the star and held it in one hand. "It's really beautiful," he said thoughtfully. "I'll try to find some more information about William that hopefully might be of use to you."

William shone up. Arild mumbled something and William realized it was an invisibility spell because after three seconds he couldn't see him anymore. William was left alone. He walked up to the velvet tassel and pulled it. William had been expecting some kind of sound when he pulled it. Maybe I didn't pull hard enough, he thought, and reached out with his hand to pull again. But right then, the door to the vault opened and Marcus entered, closely followed by Joey. Marcus noticed that William looked a bit stressed.

"I need to find a quick way out of the vault," William said. Marcus nodded.

"But first I want to thank you Marcus, and your entire family, for all the sacrifices you've had to make over the centuries to gather information that might be useful to me and..." William was about to say my big brother but quickly changed his mind and said, "...and William the Elder. I understand that there have been sacrifices that have been very difficult and costly to make. Where you haven't been able to live the lives you might otherwise have done. Lives where you wouldn't have had to face mocking and condescending words from other people. If people had known about your intelligence and knowledge, your status in the society would have been completely different. I just want to thank you from the bottom of my heart."

Marcus had trouble holding his tears back so he blinked frantically. "Your gratitude brings tears to my eyes, Marcus said with a shaky voice.

William walked up to the old man and gave him a hug.

"I really wish there would be some way that I could compensate you," William said.

"That you care about me is gratitude enough for me," Marcus replied. "To me you're the most important person there is and I'm proud to be your informant."

William saw the sincerity in Marcus's eyes and then he turned to Joey and held out his hand.

"I would also like to thank you for all the work you have put into getting the material in the vault in order and for being here for Marcus. The fact that you're a true friend of his means a lot to me."

Joey took the outstretched hand and hugged it tightly.

"Now you need to get out of here quickly," Marcus said. "Follow me and I'll show you a way out."

"I already know how to get out of here quickly." William interrupted him. Marcus looked questioning at first.

"I'll manage," William said, kindly patting the old man on the shoulder.

"If you ever have to get to the vault without using the front door of the store, just climb into the well that you saw in the small square outside. There is a ladder inside that goes down to the aisle that leads here."

"I'll remember that," William said smiling.

"We do not say goodbye," Marcus said, "instead we say we'll meet again."

"We will," William replied.

"We'll leave you now, good luck with the mission and I hope we'll see each other again soon."

"I hope so too," William said.

Marcus and Joey left the vault. The moment the door closed, Arild appeared.

"Are you ready, William?" He asked.

William went next to Arild and said, "Yes, I'm ready." Arild mumbled something and they disappeared in a whirlwind, first out of the vault and then the journey continued in the dark.

"We are in the burial paths," Arild said.

William barely had time to grasp how they were travelling because they moved very quickly. William closed his eyes and thought of the elder William. After a while, Arild said, "We're almost there."

William opened his eyes and noticed that he stood by the stairs down to the unknown tomb he had previously visited below the cathedral. Arild looked at him. "I'll leave you now. Take care of yourself and I'll see what I can find out about William. I'll get back to you as soon as I find anything worthwhile." William nodded and Arild disappeared swirling through the air.

CHAPTER 10
WILLIAM AND FRITZ

William walked down the oak staircase. He walked with careful steps to avoid any creaky noises from the old wood. He slowly went downstairs in the dark. He came to the room with the stone columns. He quietly approached the tomb but stopped before entering. He thought he heard something move in there. William's heart started to pound harder. Who could it be? He silently crept forward and peeked through the opening. His heart pounded so hard that he could hear the heartbeat in his ears. He immediately thought there was something familiar about the dark silhouette he saw sitting down by the grave. William saw that the male figure seemed to be reading a book. William drew back into hiding again. Strange, his fear was now completely gone. It must be someone I know, he thought. William decided to peek once again through the opening. The person just turned up his face and the light from the glass mosaic in the ceiling made it possible for William to clearly see who it was. What? it's Grandpa? William was completely taken aback.

"Grandpa, what are you doing here?" he whispered.

"But William, is that you?" Fritz said and rushed over and hugged William tightly. William was still astonished. He could barely believe his eyes.

"How did you get here?" William asked. "Did you use the hidden path from my room?"

"No, my boy," his grandfather said, looking at William. William could barely think.

"You haven't told anyone at your order about William, have you?"

"No, Fritz said and shook his head, "of course not." William calmed down when he heard it.

"You know," William said, "it's very important that we keep this to ourselves." Fritz nodded.

"But how did you find William's tomb?" William wondered.

"I got help," Fritz answered calmly.

"Help from whom? You just said you didn't tell anyone." William felt confused. Goblet that had been hiding behind Fritz looked up.

"Psst," Goblet said, "I helped him."

Amazed, William looked around.

"Here I am," Goblet said, who could no longer hold still and went forward at a tremendous speed and stopped right in front of William. "I did, I did, I helped him, but I wouldn't have done it if William hadn't wanted me to."

"So, you knew William?"

"Yes, of course," Goblet babbled on. "He was my best friend and now I finally get to see him again, or rather, I get to see his final resting place," Goblet said quietly. Then he pulled himself together and carried on. "You know, William and I shared many adventures together and I've been sleeping for hundreds of years and now I'm extremely ready for new adventures. By the way, I haven't really introduced myself yet. My name is goblet," Goblet said, leaning forward and then backwards as if he bowed. "And my name is William, William said and did the same thing.

"I already know who you are. William talked a lot about you. You two carry the mark of the compass," Goblet giggled happily. "I just want you to know that I'm at your service. Of course, at your service as well," Goblet continued giggling while turning to Fritz, "but mainly to William. It's lovely to finally meet you. How I've longed for it." Goblet made a valiant attempt to compose himself and said, "I mean, it's a pleasure to meet you," then he couldn't keep it together any longer and he excitedly went around and around the tomb. "Yoho! I can't believe the three of us are going on an adventure. It's so exciting. I can't wait, I can't wait," he kept shouting.
William looked at Goblet and then at his grandfather and they both burst into laughter.
"Yes, he's really positive and cheerful, you might say," Fritz said, then he added a little more seriously, "but if it

hadn't been for Goblet, I would never have found my way to the tomb. I think we'd better update each other on what's happened."

"You're absolutely right, Grandpa," William said earnestly.

William sat down with his grandfather, who described what had happened at his order, that the priest was missing and about the secret items left to him by the former Grand master.

William shivered. "Are you saying they've taken Father Ormund?"

"I'm afraid it seems that way," Fritz said and hugged his shoulders.

"It's terrible," William said, trembling.

Goblet, that had listened to the conversation while he had flown around the room dizzy with joy, now flew down and sat down in front of William and Fritz. Goblet told William what he had already told Fritz.

"I can't believe you knew my big brother," William said.

"Yes," Goblet said, "you are brothers and both bearers of the compass mark. But how did you get here?"

William told them about his contact with William but he didn't mention anything about the vault, Marcus, Joey and Arild. He kept them to himself. Fritz gave William the book and quickly explained that it had belonged to Alexander. William browsed through the book quickly.

"Then we can rule out Alexander and probably Father Orfius because he kept the secret that Alexander was alive and that after his so-called death, he was not subjected to anymore assassination attempts."

"Yes probably," Fritz said, rubbing his beard. "So, who do we have left?"

"Let's see, we have Grand master Glowney, magic teacher Master Agerlini and the high nobleman Mr. Bergial," William noted.

"We also have to verify that King Valdemar and his son really were murdered and, if so, how it was done and who was behind the deeds," Fritz filled in.

"What do you mean?" William said irritated. "We know they were murdered. We have the letter from the king stating that he suspects that his son was murdered and that he feared for his own life!" William felt how upset he became.

"You're absolutely right, William, and I totally agree with you," Fritz said calmly. "But if we're going to get to the bottom of this, we need more evidence that they really were murdered. If we can prove that the king and his son indeed were murdered and who did it, there will certainly be consequences, even today. That's why we need solid evidence that no one can question." Fritz concluded

"Mm," William nodded, "of course you're right. We need clear evidence to clarify what really happened to the king and his son about 500 years ago."

"Exactly," Fritz replied. "I think this is the right mystery to start with. After we solve this one, we're going to find out who killed William and why he was murdered."

"Then we have no time to lose, if I understood you correctly, the clues that's connected to magic will disappear very soon. That means we have to act quickly."

"Yes exactly," William said quickly. It felt good to have grandpa with him on the mission, he thought. William ran into the other vault and looked up at the ceiling, at the sun and the sea. "It's very high!"

"Yes," Fritz said, "it certainly is. I do not really know how we can get up there."

"I think I know a way," Goblet giggled, "but you can't be afraid to have long legs."

"What, long legs?" Fritz wondered.

"Well, I'm just saying that you can't be afraid to have long legs. They will disappear after a while."

"Ah," William smiled. "I think I understand."

"Well, I guess I better do it," Fritz said, "as the letter was addressed to me."

"I think so, too," William smiled.

"But I don't want to hear any laughs," Fritz said.

"We promise," Goblet and William said in chorus.

Goblet walked up to Fritz, cast a spell, and Fritz's legs quickly began to grow. "Oh my!" Fritz exclaimed.

And the thing was, it looked so funny. Only the legs grew on Fritz but the rest of his body stayed exactly the same size as before.

"You haven't thought about taking up Triple jump?" William joked.

"Very funny," Fritz said a bit strained. It was a somewhat exhausting to go through a growing leg spell. It really felt like someone was pulling and tearing your legs. Not that it hurt exactly, but it felt. It did.

"Finally, I can reach it!" Fritz shouted from the ceiling as he stretched out his palm and placed it on the sun. William and Goblet had turned their backs to Fritz as they shook with laughter, but as soon as they heard Fritz shout they turned around. And what they saw was amazing! After Fritz's hand had touched the sun, they heard a clicking sound followed by a sound like that of a large old iron wheel spinning around. It creaked something terrible. William and Goblet covered their ears and Fritz was so relieved that the spell had ended and his legs quickly shrunk back to normal length that he did not even hear the creaking sound. Behind William's grave, the large stone wall opened up.

"It must have been on an iron rail, so ingenious of Alexander and Father Orfius," Goblet shouted, who had already arrived at the opening. Goblet stopped and said humbly. "I think I'll let you go first, William."

"It's dark in there. I can't see anything," William said, straining his eyes to see anything in the dark. He walked slowly and felt with one foot in front of him so as not to stumble upon anything. Fritz followed behind him and

Goblet hovered next to him. William tried to walk straight ahead.

"Oh, what's going on!" William cried out. The stone he stood on sank into the ground. When William looked down, he saw how the stones were laid in different patterns around him. They sparkled like stars in the night and lit up the whole room. He looked down at the stone he stood on and saw that it was glowing. William felt heat radiating from the stone touch his body. It was not unpleasant but more like a warm pleasant heat aimed at him. William relaxed throughout his body and felt pleasantly calm.

"In about 500 years or when the stars are in this position, Williams' magic linked to the clues will be destroyed. Use it well and find out who killed him."

"It's Alexander's voice," Goblet said out loud. William nodded and looked down and saw that he was standing on a dark night sky, which was to some extent covered by a thin layer of dust. William looked around the room. He quickly realized that Alexander must have lived in the room. At the far end of the room was a bed with a dark blue canopy. William had a strange gut feeling. It didn't feel right in any way that Alexander had to live underground just to not get murdered. He would have needed to see the light and the sky at night, William thought. William took a few steps into the room. Even if William had not known that Alexander had come from a high-ranking noble family, it would have been hard to miss. As he looked around, he saw a white marble table and a sofa dressed in a slightly clumsy baroque style. In one corner was an ornate desk with associated wooden chair. William noticed as he walked around that there was warmth coming from the floor and its starry sky. It felt kind of like the underfloor heating in the bathroom at home. It felt comfortable. William thought it created a little homier feeling and the air didn't feel cold and raw like it did in William's tomb. Next to the desk there was a dark bookshelf with seven or eight thick books. William realized that it must be magic books that had belonged to William. I wonder where Alexander kept William's secret items. William looked around but couldn't see any in the confined space.

"Achoo," Goblet sneezed. "It's the dust," he said. "I have a mild dust mite allergy." William started giggling.

"So, you can't stand dust?"

"That's right," Goblet answered before being interrupted by another sneeze. "We'll have to hurry out of here," he said "before I start to sneeze again."

Fritz reached for a packet of paper napkins that he had in one pocket. He pulled out a clean napkin and put it on top of Goblet. "Here you go," he said.

"Thank you very much," Goblet replied and blew his nose loudly so the napkin flew up and fluttered in the wind.

"There's something I'm not seeing," William said. "I wonder where Alexander kept the magical items."

"That's a good question," Goblet said, and began to roam the room.

"Not here," he said while looking under the bed. "And not here either," he said, looking under the desk.

"Could it be here?" Fritz wondered and pointed at the big stone that William stood on earlier."

William immediately got down on one knee to examine it more closely. He had to squint because the stone shone so brightly. He looked closely and felt the smooth surface. Gently, he pushed the stone down. Then he heard a click and the stone rose up again. William removed the stone and beneath it was a silver chest. William picked up the chest and put it on the floor.

"Open it!" Goblet shouted excitedly.

William opened the lid and in the chest there was a handful of objects. The chest was lined with a dark blue velvet fabric. William couldn't take his eyes off the magical items. There was a transparent glass ball, shimmering in light blue. Next to it was a crystal rod and a white candle in a silver candlestick. Underneath these items was a thick black book. William picked it up and opened it. He knew immediately that it was William's magic spell book. It looked a bit like the book Longtail had given William but it felt well used and the spells were lined up one after the other and were divided into distinct categories. William saw that his older brother often had written something next to the spells to explain in more detail how they were to be used. William shivered. I can't believe I'm sitting here with his magic book, after almost 500 years. It's almost inconceivable. William looked at the front page. It said with squiggly black ink *"William 1510"*. William put the book in his lap and it felt good somehow that he now had it. Kind of like a family heirloom that is passed on from generation to generation.

"Have you considered that this is part of your legacy?" Fritz asked.

"Yes," William said, "and it feels so good that I get the opportunity to take care of these objects."

"And use them," Goblet filled in and then he got a little more serious in his voice, "but after 500 years the objects will lose their magical abilities."

"Does that apply to you, too?" William wondered, looking at Goblet. Goblet nodded and couldn't stop a sob.

"Yes, unfortunately, I think it also applies to me. But let's not think about it," he said in a cheery tone. "I'm sure we'll figure it out."

William stroked Goblet gently with his hand.

"Come on now, you have to look at the other items in the chest," Goblet said encouraging.

William looked in the chest again and saw that there was a gold medallion with a thick gold chain and an hourglass that was made of black wood but the sand was gold-colored. William picked up the hourglass.

"Do you see how strange the sand counts down?"

"You're right, William, we don't have much time," Fritz said thoughtfully. William hung the gold medallion around his neck and carefully went through the rest of the items. There was also a map of the stars in the sky. William rolled out the map and saw that there was a small cross at one of the stars. Beside the cross it said *"William is born."* It almost felt a little scary that by reading the stars you could find out who was going to be born. Fritz saw how William reacted. He put his hand on Williams's shoulder and said calmly. "There is a lot of magic, you have time to learn more about all the elements William."

At the bottom of the chest was an ink pen, a graying photo of a man and a lock of hair. It's probably a lock of hair from William when he was little, William thought while he neatly put all the items back in the chest. Well, almost all anyway. The crystal rod and the magic book he put into his jacket. He then took the chest under his arm and sat down on the bed. As he sat down, a large cloud of dust came from the bedspread.

"Was that really necessary?" Goblet exclaimed upset as he tried to smother a series of sneezes.

"I'm sorry," William said, "but why don't you go out to the tomb room? I'll come along in a little while."

"Of course I can," Goblet said a bit offended as he floated out while his sneeze attacks continued. Fritz followed Goblet out because he understood that William needed to be alone for a while.

CHAPTER 11
A VOYAGE

William sat on the bed. Slowly, he let his eyes rest on the sofa, the desk and the bookshelf. There was something lovely about this place. It almost felt like being at sea for some strange reason. The sea roared in his ears. William closed his eyes and listened to the roar of the waves, but then he shrugged. Am I going crazy? He lightly pinched his arm. No, I do really hear the sea. Slowly, he opened his eyes and looked around. The whole room bathed in a lovely blue glow and by the stone walls it was as if waves were slowly hitting the walls and there was no sign of the opening to the tomb. William was astonished. Amazing, he thought. The stones shone like stars and almost black water run amongst the stones. William wasn't afraid instead he was filled with a very pleasing feeling.

"Oh, I'm sailing," he exclaimed spontaneously. And indeed, the bed with its dark blue canopy now looked like a boat where the dark blue canopy had formed a dark blue sail. Out of a loudspeaker came Alexander's voice. "Hi William! Welcome to my quarters! I've spent many fun hours here and now the place is yours. First, I want to explain a few things to you. 1. You do not have to worry about Fritz and Goblet. If you wish they can participate in your journey whenever you want. 2. If you look at the stones over there, you will see that they have changed color and that dark water now surrounds them. The water symbolizes the night sky and the stones stars 3. You're perfectly safe in here. No one can ever hurt you while you're here. With the help of William's books, I have put a very strong magic over the room and the boat and it is actually not possible to break the spell. 4. If you do not already have, please put on William's gold medallion immediately. It was a medallion that William always wore and that you should always wear when traveling with the help of this room. 5. I want you to put all of William's things back in the chest, except for the gold medallion, the magic wand and Williams magic book. You should then carefully close the chest and place it at the bottom of the boat below the steering wheel. With this ship and this room, you can sail anywhere you wish, just use the magic wand and navigate with the help of the stars in the sky." William could feel the boat heel.

"And don't worry if the boat heels, it's just like life sometimes. It's twists here and there, but there's nothing to worry about. I wish you the best of luck on your journey and with your mission. Or like your big brother said. 'There is only one who can take my place and who will wear my medallion and that is my little brother.'

Good luck to you, William. I believe in you and I know William always did too." The voice faded away and then completely disappeared.

William was in shock. This must be the strangest thing ever. William had been through a lot of strange things, but he never would have thought that a room could transform itself with the help of magic.

"Oh my god! The chest with William's possessions floats over there. I have to save them before they float away." William placed the magic wand and the magic book on one side of the ship and began to laboriously crawl over the railing. I really hope I don't have to swim, he thought as he jumped off the boat. But swimming was actually exactly what William had to do. Big waves rolled in and William swallowed at least two mouthfuls of seawater before he could get to the chest. He grabbed the chest and pushed it in front of him back to the boat.

But what do I do now? How am I going to get the chest into the boat and Fritz or Goblet wasn't there to help him.

"Hey, guys!" William cried. "Can anyone help me? Grandpa, Goblet, hello!"

The moment William called out to his grandfather and Goblet they appeared on the boat.

"But William!" Fritz called out, horrified. "What are you doing there?"

Goblet was a little faster. He saw the chest in the water and quickly floated down to it and made two quick movements with his body and a white powder poured out over the chest which immediately began to soar. Fritz quickly got hold of the chest and put it down on the floor of the boat.

"William, wait!" he shouted as he saw a large strong rope lying in the fore of the boat. Fritz threw down one end to William who quickly grabbed hold of it and pulled himself up. Tired and out of breath, he finally landed in the boat.

"But what on earth has actually happened here?" Fritz asked. "Where did all the water come from?"

William told grandpa and Goblet what had happened. Goblet became completely excited and shouted, "That's cool. That's so cool! So, we can go anywhere we want. I can't believe the bed became a boat, it's really amazing," Goblet shouted while he flew up to the top of the mast. "Ship ahoy!" he shouted down to the others, then he floated down to William.

"Where do you want us to go?"

"I don't know for sure." William still felt a little dizzy from the sudden change of the room.

"I can't believe it," he said, and turned to his grandfather. It's unbelievable, but at the same time he also felt relieved. He no longer had to feel the same sadness for Alexander because it turned out that he was not trapped underground and he could freely transport himself wherever he wanted. It made his life considerably more fun and interesting. Of course, it must have been very difficult for him to not have any contact with his parents and relatives. But having his own boat and a lot of magical items that he could use must have made his life really exciting.

"Such adventures Alexander must have been on to find out who murdered William," Goblet said dreamily. "What if I could have been on one of them, but of course, now I am and what an adventure this seems to be," he said, laughing. "Thank you, my friends," Goblet said and floated up and touched William's cheek while he made a kissing sound.

"What are you doing?" William asked and immediately wiped his cheek. Goblet, who realized that William didn't like it, quickly flew to Fritz and hid behind him.

"Peekaboo," he said. "You're always nice to those who are smaller than yourself," Goblet cried out. "Remember that I helped you with the chest."

"Ok then," William said somewhat irritated, "just don't do it again."

"I won't," Goblet said, swirled away laughing, not particularly disheartened that William didn't like his kiss.

William sat down as far forward in the boat he could and looked at the high waves that now had increased in strength. The wind also started to blow stronger and stronger and the boat really tore into the anchor that held it in place. Large clouds towered up above them and William looked down at the stars shining in the dark water. William looked at the off-white sail that hit the wind. I wonder where we should start our search. He instinctively felt that they needed to find out more about what had happened to the old king and his son. Their fate seemed somehow connected to Williams, but in what way he didn't know.

"Grandpa, do you have Alexander's book?" William shouted through the fierce wind. Fritz nodded and held on to the railing as he walked towards where William sat in the bow. He looked up the first page of the book. William had to help him hold the pages down so they didn't flutter in the hard wind.

"We'll see," Fritz said as he read through the first page.

"This is about what happened after William's death," Fritz murmured. "What do you want me to look for?"

"Something about the old king."

Fritz and William quickly searched the first few pages but it was difficult in the strong wind.

"It's a bit cold on the hands," Fritz said, and William nodded.

"Here," William exclaimed and held his finger to a sentence in the middle of page 8, which said *the castle Kalvador flew its flags at half-mast to mark the king's death.*

"That's where we're going," William said and pointed at the word Kalvador. "I just wonder what we need to do to make the boat take us there?" William said.

Goblet, who had been waiting a bit further away heard William shout and came flying to them.

"I think you should take the magic wand, point it at the word, read the word out aloud and then point it at the stars in the water."

William lifted the crystal rod and did as Goblet said. At once, the boat weighed anchor and steered off into the fierce wind.

"Hold on!" Fritz shouted. The boat headed straight for the open water. The bow went straight into a wave and then turned upwards again. Water splashed over all three of them and the wooden deck became soaking wet.

"It's a good thing there are holes at the sides so that the water can run out!" William screamed in the wind.

Fritz turned and saw that there were holes near the wooden floor at regular intervals.

"The sail," Goblet cried out. William looked up and saw that the sail was loose at the top of the mast.

"We need to secure it," William shouted, "I'll climb up." William got up and he had to hold on tight to the railing as he walked so as not to fall over. Once he got to the mast, he started to climb. William, who had a good physique and was a seasoned athlete, smoothly climbed the mast. When he was up, he lashed the sail tightly.

"That's it," he said out loud. The mast moved a little back and forth in the wind. William looked around and noted that it was very dark on the horizon. We're probably going to have a thunderstorm soon, he thought. I'd better hurry down. William saw that the ship was in the middle of the open sea and because the fog was dense, it was difficult to

196

see towards land. William felt that it started to rain. It was a cold rain that whipped his cheeks. William hurried down. When he put his feet on the deck it felt a little safer. There must be a galley, William mused. William looked around over the deck. He saw that Fritz and Goblet were still in the bow. I'll try to go to the back of the boat to see if I can find anything. William walked across the wet wooden deck. As he approached the stern, he saw a round black iron ring. He bent down and saw that the ring was attached to a wooden hatch, cut out in the deck. He pulled the ring gently and opened the hatch and looked down. On the wall was a gas lamp that spread a pleasant glow over the wooden staircase leading down. William quickly closed the hatch and began shouting and gesticulating to the others.

"Grandpa, Goblet, Come here! I've found the cabin." His grandfather and Goblet didn't seem to hear him. I'll shout one more time else I'll have to go over to them, he decided. "Grandpa! Goblet!" William saw how Goblet started to move and then Fritz also got up. William waved with one hand and screamed, "Come!" Goblet was quickly at William's side but it took a little longer for Fritz as he had to hold on so he didn't fall in the hard wind. As his grandfather got closer, William lifted the hatch. First Goblet floated down the ladder and then Fritz and William brought up the rear. The hatch closed after them with a bang.

"It's cozy down here," Goblet exclaimed as he flew around in the room.

"Well done my boy," Fritz said. The whole of Fritz's hair was soaked and water run down his face. "We all look like half-drowned cats," he said, laughing. "It's been a long time since I've been this wet."

William nodded. He felt that he was drenched to the skin. "We'll probably be dry soon," Fritz said and pointed at the lit fireplace in one corner of the room. William looked around. There were two beds in the room. William sat down in one of the beds and sank into the soft mattress.

"I can't really understand," William said. "It doesn't smell old and musty in here, it smells homely. Kind of like when you get home and there are freshly baked buns in the oven."

In the middle of the room was a brown Chesterfield leather sofa with two armchairs. On the square dark wooden table there was fresh fruit and sandwiches. There were also two porcelain jugs and three cups with associated plates. One cup was significantly smaller than the other two. There were also white linen napkins. A little further into the room stood a bar cabinet with different types of whiskey and crystal glasses.

"I'm a bit hungry," Fritz said, "but first I want something to warm up with." He went over to the bar cabinet and poured some whiskey into a low round crystal glass and sat down in one of the armchairs.

"Now I'm starting to gain some heat back into my body," he said with a sigh.

William joined his grandfather and sat down on the couch. It crackled pleasantly from the fireplace.

"It feels good to be indoors, William said. William noted that it felt like the boat was rocking less when they were indoors than it had felt on deck.

"I wonder how long we're going to be here," he said half aloud to himself.

"I don't think you can ever really know that," Goblet said, "but I'd guess we'll find out when we get there one way or another. I think I'm a bit hungry as well," Goblet continued and then he whispered something and one of the jugs hovered up towards the small cup and poured smoking hot coffee into it.

"Oh, how lovely," Goblet exclaimed. "I think I'd like some milk in my coffee as well." Goblet looked around.

"There," William said and pointed at a smaller jug that had been hidden behind one of the large jugs.

Goblet flew up and peered into the small jug. "Yes, will you look at that, of course it's milk," he said cheerfully. He sat down and mumbled something quietly to himself and the little jug started to soar and poured milk into his cup.

"That's it," Goblet said contently. "You have to excuse me. I've become so used to being alone that I've started saying spells out loud. I can think them out quietly instead."

"No, it's all right," William said.

"Do you want something to drink? Goblet asked. "I can pour it up to you if you want?" William looked at the sandwiches, they looked really tasty. William looked into one of the jugs and saw that there was hot chocolate milk in it. That's what I want. He reached for a sandwich and was about to grab the jug when it started hovering. The smoking hot chocolate milk was poured into his cup. "Please, go ahead," Goblet said contently.

"Thank you very much," William answered and immediately took a sip of the hot chocolate.

"Do you think there's some whipped cream as well?" William asked.

"Of course, I'll arrange it!" Goblet replied and, in an instant, a small silver bowl that been standing on the round mahogany table came hovering up to William who helped himself to three spoonsful of cream that he put in the chocolate milk and leaned back.

"Ho ho ho," Goblet chuckled, "think that we are here, all three together. It's amazing! And if I understood you correctly," he continued and turned to William, "we don't have to worry about anything when we're here?"

"Yep, that's right," William answered contently.

"Think, what a place, absolutely amazing," Fritz sighed who had found a pipe that he was now sucking on, while slowly letting the smoke curl out into the room. William yawned really wide.

"Oh," he said, a little apologetic, "you don't notice how tired you are until you relax. I think I'll see if there's a pajamas under the pillow."

"Pajamas," Goblet mumbled and indeed under the pillow was a lovely cotton pajamas in dark blue. William quickly jumped into the pajamas and crawled into bed. William felt safe. He heard from a distance that Fritz and Goblet were chatting, then he fell asleep.

William dreamed of large beautiful ships with fine gold sails with large dark blue royal crowns on them. The ships sailed majestically on the sea and sometimes there were three ships sailing next to each other and sometimes there were two ships. He dreamed that he laughed happily while navigating one of the great ships. It'd been a long time since William had one of those really lovely dreams. As you know, it's not often that you dream such wonderful dreams, but once you do, the feeling is usually with you all day once you wake up. And waking up, that's exactly what William did. He opened his eyes and noted that the fire in the fireplace had burned out, and that Goblet and grandpa were still sleeping soundly. They probably stayed up for a long time chatting yesterday, William thought as he slowly got out of bed. I'm glad the clothes have dried, he murmured, pulling his shirt over his head. He walked as quietly as he could towards the back wall where he discovered a small door.

No wonder I didn't see the door yesterday when it was dark. He gently turned the dark wooden handle and the door gently slid up. William bent down to go through the door, but once through he could stand upright again.

"A kitchen," he exclaimed, "that's great!"

The kitchen consisted of an iron sink and oak benches and cabinets. In the middle of the floor was a round kitchen table, also in oak with four oak chairs around it. What is that? William wondered and pulled away a dark brown curtain that hung down the wall. Behind the curtain there was a huge glass window. You could see the water wash over the window and in the next moment you looked out over the water as the ship moved with the water.

"Cool," William exclaimed. "I can sit in here and still see where we're going." Suddenly, a muted sound was heard. Kind of like clock chimes. William looked around to see where the sound came from. But just as he started to move in the direction of the sound, it stopped. That's weird, he said. But then the sound came back, "ding-dong." William listened carefully and heard that the sound came from the larger room. William went out to the large room and there on one wall was a big wooden clock mounted. "Ding-dong" it chimed again and William could see the rattle from the two brass weights that hung in chains down from the clock before the clock chimed. Let's see what time it is, he thought, and went closer to the clock. To his surprise, there were not the usual numbers on the clock face. Instead, the name 'Kalvador' was at the top of the dial where the number twelve usually would be. The big hand was pointing down where number six should have been. Hmm, William thought. Could it be that there are six hours left before we arrive at Kalvador Castle? William looked at the clock face again to make sure he had seen it right. He now saw that it said another lap around the dial. Then it must be 18 hours left, 12 + 6 hours. "Ding-dong" the muted sound was heard again from the clock. I'll probably have to wake Goblet and Grandpa, William thought and looked at the two of them who were sleeping and snoring soundly. William went over to Fritz's bed and sat down on the edge of the bed.

"Wake up Grandpa, I think we'll be in Kalvador in 18 hours," William whispered.

"What, did you say we're almost there?" grandpa asked and sat up dizzy in bed.

"Are we there!" Goblet exclaimed and immediately flew out of bed and came over to William and Fritz.

"Well, not quite yet, but in 18 hours if I understand it correctly", William said and pointed at the clock. "According to the clock on the wall, it is about six hours and a whole lap until we're there."

"Wow! Then we need to hurry," Goblet said energetically. "I thought it would take at least a week to get there. I'll make you breakfast if you want? I just need to wash off a little first, it'll just take a moment." Goblet sailed into the kitchen and William heard him rattling around in there.

"What do you want to eat? Goblet shouted from the kitchen. "You can choose from rice pudding, milk, two kinds of bread, cheese, coffee, tea and hot chocolate."

"I'd love to have some rice pudding," William said.

"The same to me as well Fritz called.

"Breakfast will be ready in about 10 minutes." Goblet turned on the tap and washed himself quickly and dried himself with a napkin. Dried himself might not be the right word, it was rather the napkin that went around him, wiping him dry after he quietly had uttered a spell. "Where do you think the bathroom is?" William wondered, who was used to modern facilities, even on boats.

"I'm not so sure there is a bathroom on this boat," Fritz answered. "We might have to get some water with a bucket and rinse off up on deck and brush our teeth there. At least we have some soap and two toothbrushes and toothpaste," he continued and pointed at a small table next to his bed.

"Do you have a bucket with a rope in it?" Fritz called out to Goblet.

"Sure," Goblet replied, "I can arrange that." He quickly came out of the kitchen with a dark blue bucket with a long rope attached to it.

"Thank you very much," Fritz said.

"Don't forget the towels," Goblet said, nodding towards the beds. William saw that there were two white terry towels neatly folded on the chairs. William took the towels, soap, toothbrushes and toothpaste while Fritz took the bucket.

Fritz went up the small stairs first and opened the hatch. It was a lovely morning and the sun was shining.

"What a lovely weather we have," Fritz exclaimed.

"Yes indeed," William replied happily. "There's no sign of the storm we had yesterday."

"No, it has been blown away," Fritz said, laughing. "Let's see if there's a ladder down to the water, in that case, it would be nice to have a morning swim." They both went and looked over the ships railing.

"Here!" William shouted and pointed to a wooden ladder.

"Perfect," Grandpa said. They undressed their pajamas and climbed into the water. Grandpa brought the soap and put it on one of the wide wooden steps.

"How refreshing it is with a morning swim," Grandpa said contently as he sprayed some water out of his mouth. William felt that it was really nice to swim in the calm water. They scrubbed themselves with the soap and rinsed off the soap with a swim. Fritz got out of the water first and wrapped himself in the towel. He handed William a towel that William wrapped himself in before getting up on the wooden deck. The wooden deck was a little warm from the sun. Then Grandpa took and hoisted down the bucket and gathered some water to brush his teeth in. William put some toothpaste on his toothbrush and dipped it in the bucket. He brushed his teeth thoroughly and spat out the biodegradable toothpaste foam into the water. It feels like a scene from a commercial, William noted cheerfully.

"What a lovely day it is today and what a great view! The tranquil water! Yes, just like a scene from a commercial," Fritz said.

"Just what I thought," William replied.

"Breakfast is served," Goblet said solemnly, "and by the way, I found both toilet and shower in a room next to the kitchen."

"That's excellent!" William answered, "and it'll surely taste good with breakfast now."

They went down to the cabin and quickly into the galley, that is the kitchen on a boat. On the round table Goblet had served chocolate milk, pudding and cheese sandwiches with cucumber.

"Wow, it looks great! You're a splendid cook, Goblet!" William exclaimed as he sat down at the table.

"Yes, certainly," Fritz agreed as he swallowed his first spoonful of pudding. After they were halfway through their breakfast, Fritz put down his spoon and said thoughtfully.

"What do you really think we will face in Kalvador?"

"Hard to say," William replied. "But I think we should prepare for the worst."

"What do you mean, the worst?" Goblet wondered.

"I mean it feels like anything can happen there. Our task is to look for evidence that the king and his son were murdered, but also to find out who did it." William kept talking. "I believe that Alexander has probably been there several times to seek evidence, but something must have stopped him from succeeding. I don't know why, but there's something about that place," he ended the sentence quietly. There was a moment of silence around the table.

"Yes, I think you're absolutely right," Fritz finally said. "I think all three of us needs to prepare mentally. We have no idea what secrets Kalvador hides.

"Ugh," Goblet said with a sigh. "Now I don't feel like eating anymore."

"It's important that you eat," William cautioned him. "I think we will need all the strength we can get."

They continued to eat their breakfast in silence and then washed up the dishes.

William felt the need to be on his own for a while. He slowly got up on the deck and sat down with his back to the fore of the boat. He grabbed the medallion with his right hand. If only you'd been with William, he whispered quietly. I wonder what sorcery that surrounds Kalvador? From a distance, William heard the bell chime once more. Now there's only seventeen hours left, he thought. He hugged the medallion harder. Finally, he picked it up and examined it more carefully. There was a round green stone in the medallion. The green stone captured a ray of sunshine and it flashed in a green-blue shimmer over the boat.

"Oh, what is this?" William wondered. William took off the medallion and examined it carefully. It was a very beautiful piece of jewelry. I wonder where William got it? William pondered as he turned the medallion around. William had always liked things of gold. It was something that he had inherited from his mother and grandmother who were also very fond of things of gold, such as gold frames and gold mirrors. The back of the jewelry was perfectly smooth. William touched the surface gently. I really wonder what will happen in Kalvador. William felt his stomach clench a little bit with nervousness. William hugged the jewelry tightly. A few moments later when he was about to hang the medallion back around his neck he was surprised because he noticed there was something written on the back of it. *"You don't have to be afraid. Just follow the medallion //W"*

William felt joy bubbling up from his stomach.

"Grandpa, Goblet!" he shouted and ran below deck. "William left me a message!" William quickly recounted what he just had experienced, how nervous he had felt and about the message from William.

"Indeed," Fritz said, "maybe that's why you should wear the medallion around your neck. I'm sure William has put a strong spell on it, so it can sense your feelings. Yes, William, your predecessor cared very much about you! It's absolutely amazing!"

"And I care about him," William answered quietly.

"Let's be happy now shall we," Goblet said. "William wouldn't have liked it if we were sitting here feeling sorry for him. Or as William always used to say. 'Done is done and the only thing we can change is the future.' And the future, gentlemen, it is in our hands," Goblet concluded.

"You're absolutely right," Fritz said. "I am so happy and proud that I have gotten to know both Alexander and William. I'm also very proud of you," Fritz said and hugged William.

A discreet coughing was heard. "Yes, yes, of course, I'm also proud of you, Goblet."

"I thought so," Goblet said while he pursed his lips theatrically before smiling.

"I think it is time for us to search the boat Alexander created thoroughly. Maybe he has hidden more things for us to find," William said.

"Of course, where should we start?" Goblet wondered enthusiastically.

"I think each of us can start wherever they want. It'll be like a treasure hunt for us, you might say," William said.

"Ho, ho, ho," Goblet chuckled, "and I who have always liked treasure hunts!"

Fritz, Goblet and William counted to 50 before they started the treasure hunt.

Hm, where to start searching, William thought. It was still very cozy in the kitchen. And it was a good idea because

Fritz had gone up to the upper deck to look there and Goblet looked in the cabin where they slept. What could be hidden in here? There was something about the window. To put a glass window into the hull of the boat. It must be for something other than just looking through it? Admittedly, it was extremely good that you didn't have to get up on deck to see out when it rained and blew, but even so, William reasoned to himself. He pulled the curtain from the window and looked out. Because the sea was completely calm out there, William saw the sky shining bright blue. No, I have to focus on the window, he added, somewhat irritated with himself. The window was divided into squares with metal rails around each square. It has to be to make the window as strong as possible. William looked closely at the window and its leaded glass. William began to think about how the boat was actually controlled. The boat steered towards Kalvador when I used the magic wand and then we have the clock where it also says Kalvador. In addition, the clock tells us how many hours it takes for the boat to reach Kalvador. William tried to think rationally. It can therefore be said that the boat is somehow controlled by the wand and by the clock. But somehow the window must also be involved. William pondered on his assumptions long and well. Could it be that the only purpose of the clock is to show how long it is until we reach our destination or does the clock also have any other purpose? William felt his thoughts go around and he didn't find any solution to the problem with the boat, its steering and the window. It has to be connected in some way, he thought frantically to himself.

William examined the window thoroughly. But he couldn't find any button or anything else strange about the window. Oh well, William thought resignedly. I'll get the magic wand. Surely there must be a spell that tells me what the window is there for. William walked quickly to his bed and took out the wand. It was under his pillow, just where he had put it. He hurried back to the window again. He swished with the magic wand in the air, but he couldn't think of anything sensible to say.
"Oh, I'm so stupid!" he exclaimed. I'll get Alexander's book. I'm sure there's something in it that can help me find out how it all works. He remembered that grandpa had read the book yesterday before William had fallen asleep and indeed, the book was on the shelf below the small coffee table. William took the book and the wand and sat down at the round table in the kitchen. He noticed that the book felt heavier than before, almost as if it had been filled with more pages since grandpa had found it in William's vault. And indeed, when William opened the last page of the book, he saw that an invisible ink pen was in the process of writing in blue squiggly letters everything that had happened to William yesterday and today on the boat.

"What on earth!" he exclaimed. *"William became very confused"* the pen wrote. William became very annoyed and closed the book with a loud bang.

"What kind of book is this?" he exclaimed outragedly. It felt both frustrating and annoying that the book recorded everything about William since William had boarded the boat. William clenched his teeth hard. Eventually, he calmed down.

"William," he said out to himself as it sometimes feels good to talk loudly to yourself. "You picked up the book so that you could come up with some kind of clue to how the boat is controlled and what the clock and the window does. Just calm down, will you." William took a few deep breaths and tried to focus.

William opened the book again and pointed the wand at an empty page in the book and said, "if there is any secret to how the boat is controlled reveal it to me." Out of the wand came a lightning bolt and a wind. The wind caused Alexander's book to scroll a few pages forward. On the blank page, the pen began to write *"and William walked up to the clock, tapped with the magic wand three times against the clock, and the whole secret appeared."*

"Aren't you going to write anything more?" William wondered. He really thought the pen would reveal everything, but the pen remained in the same place. William waited for a while, drumming impatiently with his fingers on the book. But nothing happened. Finally, the pen began to write, only this time with a pencil. *"Come on, William, I haven't got all day."* William was amazed. A book that communicates with me. William really didn't know what to think.

"All right, let's go!" he said and closed the book and went over to the clock.

William hit three times with the wand on the clockwork. The clock started buzzing, at first a low buzz then the buzz got louder and louder. Just as William thought that the sound would have to stop, the buzzing subsided slightly and something like a red pathway formed from the clock to the window in the galley. William rushed to the window and discovered that the window's leaded glass panes had become a large map. William looked at the map and quickly realized that the red flashing dot that was slowly moving on the map was the ship. The round table had disappeared and, in its place stood a large round steering helm. The steering helm looked like it was moving by itself. It first spun a little to the left and then spun to the right, but that's not what surprised William the most, no it was the fact that there was a boy in his late teens steering the ship.

"Oh, hello!" William said surprised. "Are you in charge of the ship?"

"Yes, I am!" The boy replied. "Alexander created me when he made the ship so he and I have made a lot of trips together." William somehow felt relieved. He had wondered what Alexander's life would have been like and whether he had spent much of it all alone.

"What a relief! Then Alexander always had company on his travels!"

"Yes, yes, he did," the boy answered.

"Excuse me for asking, but what's your name?" William wondered a little curiously.

"No excuse needed," the boy replied. "My name is Axel. And you're William, of course?" he added a somewhat cautiously.

"Yes, I am, but how did you know my name?" William wondered.

"Alexander and I spent many hours and journeys together and he told me that in a few hundred years there would be a boy named William who would sail this ship."

"I understand," William replied. Now William felt his curiosity overwhelm him and he had at least a hundred questions for Axel.

"It's all right, just ask your questions," Axel said before William had time to ask any questions.

"Yes," William began tentatively. "How long did you know Alexander?"

"Let's see," Axel said and thought for a while. "I think Alexander was around my age when he created me, yes," he said while he was thinking," about 14 to 15 years old I imagine."

William cleared his throat. "When, um, did you stop knowing him?"

"Oh, you mean when Alexander died?"

"Yes, that's what I mean," William said quietly.

"Oh, Alexander grew old but he was always very vital. He became 83 years old and just before he died, he and I had been on a long voyage with Old Maran."

"Old Maran? Is that the name of the ship?"

"Yes, yes, it is. She's very ingeniously built and can handle most things. Alexander and I had such a fun life together. One of the last things he said to me before he died was that I would have to wait a while and then I would have to sail with someone named William, who was the younger brother of the William Alexander knew. And now I'm here and once again on my way to Kalvador."

"Did you and Alexander go to Kalvador many times?" William wondered curiously.

"Maybe not that many, but probably at least 10 times," Axel answered. "The last time I was very worried because Alexander was gone a very long time and when he finally got back to the ship, he was very injured. It took him a long time to recover."

"Did Alexander ever say anything about why he went to Kalvador?"

"Yes, of course, to find out who had murdered William, but he never talked to me about what he experienced in Kalvador. He didn't, and I didn't want to ask. You know, some experiences you just want to keep to yourself."

"I know exactly what you mean," William said.

"You know, Alexander and I sailed to a lot of different places and I think, of course, I can't be sure, but I think most of the places Alexander visited were somehow connected to William. But sometimes we just took and randomly picked a destination on the map and set off. Then we had a real vacation! And everyone needs a real vacation from time to time."

"Yes, you're absolutely right about that," William said while feeling that he also needed a vacation.

"When we're done with this adventure, you and I can go on vacation," Axel said shining up.

William felt a tingling sense of joy! "Yes, we'll do, it will be great fun!"

"But now we're on our way to Kalvador Castle and I understand we do it for William."

"Yes, among other things," William answered. Then it hit William. He must, of course, tell Axel that he is not alone on the ship, but that he has his grandfather and Goblet with him.

"Well, you see, I'm not alone on the ship."

"Of course you're not, you have me," Axel replied.

"It's not that. I also brought my grandfather Fritz and Goblet."

"How exciting, you have to introduce me!" Axel said cheerfully.

"Introduce to whom?" Fritz said who had just entered the galley. William turned around.

"Yes," he said, "I want to introduce you to our helmsman, Axel, this is Fritz, my grandfather, and Fritz, this is Axel who is running our ship."

"Nice to meet you, really nice," Fritz said and shook Axel's outstretched hand. "So, you're the one who controls our ship! Actually, I thought about it a little bit. Have you made many trips?"

Axel told him about all his travels with Alexander and how much fun they had had.

"Have you been to Kalvador before?"

"Yes, several times," Axel replied, "but I've never been ashore. Alexander has programmed me to take care of and steer the ship, but I don't know if I'm able to go ashore."

"I understand," Fritz said. "What a wonderful assignment you have."

"I know," Axel said smiling.

"What are you guys talking about?" It was Goblet who came floating in.

"Axel is my name and I'm the helmsman of the Old Maran."

"Pleasant, Goblet is my name. I'm one of William's creations."

"How funny, and I'm one of Alexander's creations," Axel replied!

It was obvious that Goblet and Axel had much in common as both were created by humans.

Goblet and Axel started chatting. They talked about Alexander and about William and how similar the two had been. They told of their respective hardships with their creators and all the adventures they had experienced. William sat and listened. It was wonderful to hear two happy people sitting and having a chitchat with each other. It was almost like school. When he and his friends hung out, sometimes they just sat at someone's house and chitchatted just about everything. William laughed out loud when he heard about funny situations that Goblet and Axel had been through. The evening quickly passed by and it began to darken outside.

"It's probably best that we have some supper," Goblet said and quickly arranged a meal for them. They ate and laughed. William felt happy. Slowly he felt the fatigue wash over him so he went to bed while Fritz, Goblet and Axel remained in the galley laughing and talking.

I have to remember, William thought before he fell asleep, that I have to check with them tomorrow if they found anything special on the ship. But Axel might know something as well. William fell asleep happily.

He woke up early, but stayed in bed for a long time before getting up. When he silently went out to the galley, he was surprised to see that Axel already was up and stood by the helm of the ship. "Didn't you sleep last night?"

"Alexander created me so that I don't need any sleep. I am constantly alert and can make sure that the ship operates correctly."

"That feel's good, then I know someone is always awake when I sleep." William loved that feeling, it gave such a sense of peace.

"If you can't sleep you can come and talk to me," Axel said.

"I forgot to ask yesterday, but did Goblet and Grandpa find any other exciting surprises with the ship?" William asked.

"We talked a little last night about what surprises there are on the ship and I told them about the kitchen cabinet to your left." Axel pointed to a cabinet door, "if you turn the knob and spell out what you want to eat and drink, and magically, it will be in the fridge or if the food or drink is hot it will be in the cabinet."

"Excellent!" William exclaimed. He went to the kitchen cabinet. He turned the knob and spelled out cheese sandwiches and chocolate milk. Seconds later there was a ping from the cabinet.

"Just open the door," Axel said. William opened the cabinet door and, indeed, there were two cheese sandwiches on a platter and a cup of steaming hot chocolate.

"It's perfect. No need to cook, and no need to go shopping either. I think a lot of adults would have wanted it like this. To not have to cook and shop, it can hardly get any better."

William ate his sandwiches in silence. In general, William liked to have peace and quiet around him in the mornings. His whole family used to eat in silence. It was a time for recovery before the day started. Axel understood what William wanted so he kept quiet while William ate. When William had finished eating, he sat in silence for a while longer. Then he came to think of Kalvador.

"When do you think we'll reach Kalvador?" William asked.

Axel looked at his watch and said, "in about 3 hours."

Oh my, William thought. In three hours. That's not much time. "Time goes by really fast," he said.

"Yes, it really does," Axel replied. "But do promise me, William, that you'll be careful."

"I promise I will be," William said. Then he hurried and put on his clothes. Now let's see, the magic wand I'll put in my jacket's inner pocket and the medallion I'll have around my neck. I might as well take Alexander's book with me as well. William carefully sneaked up the stairs and onto the upper deck. It was still early morning. The morning haze was still there, but it was pleasantly warm outside. I'm sure it'll be a hot day, William thought. He sat down in the bow with the closed book on his lap. He let his thoughts wander. I wonder what Kalvador will look like and what we will be up against there? William thought of Alexander, who had been there a few times, and wondered if he would be able to get closer to the truth than Alexander had. He sat there by himself and thought for a long time. How long he sat there immersed in his own thoughts he didn't know. It's always hard to have a sense of time when you're thinking. At last, he put the book on the floor and stood up and through the haze he saw Kalvador castle emerge majestically on a cliff.

CHAPTER 12
KALVADOR CASTLE

William looked up at the castle where it was located high up on a mountain. It had four tall towers and at the top of each tower a flag flew with the royal emblem. The flags moved gently in the wind. The castle was built with light brown sandstone and looked really grand from afar. It was robustly built and there were not many ornaments. The rock wall went straight down to the water. William estimated that the castle lay about 100 meters up from the surface. William picked up his binoculars and zoomed in on the guards patrolling from the towers and along the castle walls. Strange, William thought, the castle is so well-guarded, there is no war or other threat now. William aimed his binoculars at one of the guards. He looks really cruel, William noted. What's he wearing? William thought puzzled. It looked like some kind of metal armor though it wasn't clumsy and heavy like the armor knights usually wore. It must be a modern variant, he concluded. The armor appeared to be of a thin sheet metal that bent and followed the movement of the guard smoothly, almost like a metal suit. On his head was a helmet that covered a large portion of his face. There were only holes for the eyes and the mouth. William zoomed in on the guard's eyes, two cold blank eyes staring watchfully. Ugh, William shivered, he hardly looks human. The sword he had on his right side flashed when hit by the sun's rays. The guard appeared to stare out at the water to see if there were any intruders.

It's fortunate that Alexander put an invisibility spell on the ship, William thought. I wonder if the guard can see the waves that the ship creates? William looked anxiously at the water. As the ship slowed down, there was not much movement in the water from the ship as it went forward. Phew, that was lucky. Somehow it felt like he was being watched. William felt tense all over his body. Strange, they can't know we're coming. He tried to shake off the feeling. Of course, if they are to keep a secret, they are surely ordered to be constantly alert and ready for battle. William picked up his monocular again and saw that there were about 30 guards patrolling at the top of the towers. To William it was a strange feeling to not really know what he was looking for. He instinctively touched his medallion to make sure it was still there.
"We're going to get through this," he whispered quietly. "It's time for the truth to come out."
All at once William felt calm in his body. It must be William's magic that affects me. William went down to the cabin to gather some strength before arriving at the castle.

He lay down in bed and looked at the clock and found that there was half an hour left before they arrived. Fritz and Goblet sat in the galley and talked. With five minutes to go, the clock started to chime several times. "Ding dong, ding dong." To William the chimes felt almost fateful. The uneasy feeling came back immediately. I wonder what I will actually find? Fritz and Goblet immediately came out of the galley.

"It's time," Fritz said.

"Not like that," Goblet said. "I think it sounds better if we say let's go instead."

"Alright," Fritz said, "let's go!" William left the chest behind but brought the medallion, magic wand and ring. They all went up to the deck.

The ship was only 20 meters from shore. A little further ahead was a harbor where there already was a number of large sailing ships. In the harbor there were guards patrolling that controlled the ships and visitors. William thought at first that they were going to dock there but the ship continued past. Instead, they approached a small peninsula about 100 meters away from the harbor.

"Maybe that's where we're going," William said, pointing. Fritz nodded. The boat slowly approached the small peninsula.

"I wonder how we are to anchor the ship?" Fritz said, but he didn't have to think about it for long. When the ship was a bit from shore, it stopped and they heard a splash when the anchor went into the water.

"Now we just need a small rowing boat to get to shore," William said.

Goblet immediately went off to check the sides of the ship. "There is a small boat here," he whispered and pointed. William and Fritz came over.

"Let's see," Fritz said. "we need to lower the boat into the water with the help of the ropes." Fritz took one rope and William the other and they lowered the little rowing boat into the water.

"Wait," William said. "We need to check if we too are invisible and not just the ship." William leaned over the railing to see if he could see his reflection on the water's surface.

"I'm invisible," he concluded. Fritz and Goblet did the same and all three of them where pleased to note that they were invisible to the ordinary eye. They got into the little boat and Fritz rowed them to shore. Once they had pulled the boat up on the small sandy beach, Goblet said:

"Perhaps it's best if we hide the boat in a bush in case someone who doesn't see it stumbles upon it." William and Fritz agreed. Together they hid the boat among the trees and just to make sure they put some branches over it. "That's it, now it's out of the way," Goblet said happily. They found a narrow path and began their trek up towards the castle. William and Fritz had to be careful where they put their feet so that they didn't stumble on any root or branch lying on the ground.

It was a hot day but it was cooler in the forest as the trees shaded the heat from the sun. William felt the medallion against his chest as he walked.
Suddenly he heard a soft, somewhat squeaky voice say. "Not so fast. Slow down a bit."
"What?" William said and turned around. "Did you say anything Goblet?"
"Nope," Goblet answered.
"Then who could it be?" William asked puzzled and looked around.
"It's me," he heard the soft voice say, "down here." William looked down at the ground but saw nothing.
"Come out so that I can see you," William said.
"I can't be more visible than I am. I'm hanging right here." William picked up the medallion and looked at it.
"Are you the one talking?" William asked.
"That's right." William saw a mouth move on the medallion as it spoke. "Wait a second, I'm just going to open my eyes so I can see you. I've been sleeping for a long time," the medallion said and yawned, "but I woke up from bumping around so much when you jogged."
"Excuse me," William said politely. "If I had known you were asleep, I would have taken it easier."
"It doesn't matter," the medallion said. "It was time for me to wake up as soon as we got closer to the castle anyway."

The medallion opened up her little flirty green eyes and looked at William. "I'll have to introduce myself. My name is Iris."

"And my name is William."

"Mm, I know that. William told me. I mean the older William," Iris said and stifled a yawn. "Brr," the medallion said and shook back and forth. "I just need a little while to wake up. Do you have some water? I feel dry in my mouth."

"Of course I have," William replied, and brought out a bottle that he had in his backpack.

"One drop is enough," Iris said.

"Mm," William said while trying to pour as carefully as he could.

"That was refreshing. Thank you very much, my young gentleman. Now I feel much better. Let's see now, what could it be?" Iris said and thought for a while, "about 200 meters from Kalvador. What are you looking for?"

"Any evidence of what happened to the old king and his son." William said.

"You mean proof they were murdered?" Iris said, "Oh, that'll be a challenge," she mumbled. "But not entirely impossible, sure, the odds might be 100:1, but certainly not impossible no."

"You mean we only have a hundredth of a chance to succeed?" Goblet said, swallowing.

"That's right," Iris replied, who didn't seem too worried and yawned again. "No, I need to compose myself," she said curtly. "It's no good that I hang around here yawning. I'll just have to do my morning gymnastics."

William felt the medallion lift from his neck and jump down to the ground. "A little stretching might help." William looked in amazement at the ground where the medallion did various stretch exercises. First, Iris bent backwards a number of times then forward, to the left and finally a few times to the right.

"Now I'm awake," Iris said, and her soft squeaky voice was gone. William thought that her voice now sounded like the voice of a female teacher he had in school. Iris once again settled around Williams' neck.

"Now I'm ready, she said and turned to Goblet. "To answer you correctly, about a thousandth of a chance, but then I took your accumulated experience into account and ended up with about a hundredth chance or to be correct 0.009998."

"It doesn't sound very encouraging," Goblet said dishearteningly.

"But at the same time, there's a small chance that we can do it," William filled in. "What do you think? Are we all ready to continue our mission?"

"Of course, and you know you can count on me," Fritz said.

"Count me in," Goblet replied quickly. Iris was silent.

"Iris, what do you think?" William asked.

"Do you ask me?" Iris said and seemed uncomprehending? "I can't say no, without me you hardly have a chance at all."

"I understand that," William said, "but you too have a choice."

"Not really, I was created by William solely to help you in this mission. This is what I am designed for and it is as natural for me to be helpful in this mission as it is for you, for example, to breathe."

William didn't really understand what she meant other than that the mission seemed to be important to her and thus he said. "So, can we count on you?"

"Definitely," Iris answered, "otherwise my entire existence is wasted."

"We should continue forward on this path for about 20 meters then we turn off on a path to the right. From there we will be able to see the entrance to the castle and figure out a way to get in."

"Let's go," William said. They walked in the thick and dense terrain. They had to constantly watch out and fend off for branches that tended to scratch them in the face if they didn't.

"Here we should turn right," Iris enlightened them. William looked to the right but didn't see a path.

"I'll guide you," Iris said. "The path is overgrown."

They headed slightly upwards. After a while, William heard an engine noise. "Is that a car?"

"Yes, we are approaching the road leading up to the castle," Iris said. "We need to go a little closer to get a better overview of the entrance."

As they approached the busy road, they began to slow down. "Over there you see Kalvador," the medallion said. "Look up through the trees." William looked up and there in the distance he saw the castle, bathing in sunshine. We need to get a little closer. They continued forward and when William looked down, he saw a road far below winding upwards towards the castle. Kalvador was on a cliff. The castle looked majestic. Around Kalvador was a deep moat filled with water. Across the moat was a paved bridge leading to a stone-paved large roundabout. William saw a black car similar to the one he was picked up in when he arrived in Thyrridea drive across the bridge and stop outside the large brass door. The driver opened the rear door and a man and a woman stepped out of the car.

"Do you think I can borrow your binoculars?" Fritz asked. "Of course," William replied. "It's in my backpack, in the middle compartment." William turned his back to his grandfather so he could open the backpack. "There it is." Fritz closed the backpack and aimed the monocular at the two guests. "What do you know, that is Brother Sauluson. I had no idea that he had a visit scheduled with the king. How about that."

"Who is Brother Sauluson?" Goblet asked curiously.

"He's part of the same order as I am," Fritz answered. "We'll see if he tells us about this meeting at our next meeting or if he keeps that information to himself. It's going to be exciting to see."

Two guards stood outside the door and before the man and woman were let in, they were carefully searched by the guards with some kind of detector. Then the guards opened the door and let them in.

"Is it the only entrance to the castle?" William asked.

"I think so," Iris said. "There used to be secret passage under the moat into the castle but it was destroyed at the time that William was murdered."

"Then we'll have to figure out how we're going to get in," Fritz said.

"You are invisible," Iris said, "but at the same time they can hear you and if you happen to touch someone, they will feel it."

"I suggest that we camp a little further into the forest and rest until it gets dark. We will find a way in if we consider our options."

"Ok," William replied. They went back into the forest and found a clearing where they sat down.

"Do we have a map of the castle?" William wondered.

"Wait a minute," Iris said. "There's a little note in the medallion. Open me up and we'll see." William opened the jewelry and indeed, instead of a photograph there was a small, folded piece of paper. The text was very small and William had difficult to see what it said.

"I can enlarge the text," Goblet said who saw that William squinted and could not read what the note said. Goblet mumbled something quietly and suddenly the whole paper grew. From being about a square centimeter in size it grew to letter size.

"We're lucky to have you," Fritz said to Goblet.

"Thank you, I am happy to help." All four of them began to study the text.

"No, it's not a map," Iris said a little disappointed, "but wait a minute. I'm a bit out of practice," she said apologetically. "I'm just going to close my eyes for a while and see if I can find the information stored in me."

"You mean that you are to search for information stored in your long-term memory?" Goblet asked Iris.

"Quite right," Mr. Goblet, Iris said in a polite tone. She closed her eyes and hummed. "Not there. Could it be in this folder? No, not there either. I'll search the next folder. What happens if I enter this file?" She asked herself. "Wait a minute, here's something. Wow, this file was really big, several mega bites."

"It's like you have a computer in there," William said.

"I don't really know what a computer is," Iris replied, "but I have a lot of information stored in different files."

"You could say that a computer can be used to store large amounts of information, from images to large documents." William clarified.

"Then I think my memory works like a computer," Iris said.

"Ok, how can I show it for you." Iris thought for a moment. "Yes, now I've figured out how to do it," she said happily. Iris opened one eye and out of it came a green ray of light. In front of them a hologram appeared, a multidimensional sketch of the castle and its various rooms.

"Awesome," Goblet exclaimed. "This is much better than a map."

Iris chuckled contentedly. "I can enlarge all the different rooms if you wish."

"Perfect, that's exactly what we need," Goblet continued excitedly.

William looked at the castle and quickly noticed that the castle was large and that it was a five-story building, one of which was a basement that ran throughout the castle. William also noted that stairs and doors were visible in the hologram. In the middle of the castle was a large hall.

"That's where they hold all banquets," Iris said, who saw that William was looking at the large room.

"Hmm," William began, "we have to figure out how to get in." He looked closely at the hologram for any secret passages into the castle. William saw that, as Iris had previously said, there was a secret passageway from the moat up through the basement but that it was blocked.

"It's going to be hard to get in without being noticed," William murmured. All four of them where deep in thought.

"Yes, we don't want to risk being discovered," Fritz thought aloud. They looked closely at the hologram to see if there was any other way in.

"It's going to be difficult," Goblet said.

"Yes, William said, "it would be easier if we could fly in."

"Of course, that's it. I'll fly in and scout the place out, after that I can guide you in. But we still have to have a rough plan," Goblet said thoughtfully. "It's probably best if we get in at night when most people are sleeping, then it would be good if you could put some kind of transmitter on me so that you can see where I am in the castle."

"How are you going to find your way in the castle?" Fritz asked. Goblet thought for a moment, then he said,

"I just have to take Iris with me or I'll have to memorize the hologram."

"But if you take me with you, William and Fritz can't see the map."

"That's right," Goblet said. "I just have to memorize it." William looked closely at the hologram.

"I wonder where to hide secrets in a castle?"

"Good question," Fritz said. "Sometimes there is hidden compartments behind paintings, behind bookshelves or under a stone in the floor. It will be hard to find out where it's hidden."

"The room is probably well guarded," Iris said, "with both guards and magic spells."

"Can you find out if there are magic spells in one of the rooms?" William asked.

"Wait, I'll check. Not there and not there," Iris said out loud as she went through the files. "Wait, here's something." Iris opened both eyes. From one eye came a green ray of light that showed the castle and from the other eye came a black ray of light that clearly highlighted two of the rooms in the castle.

"Hmm," Goblet said, "that's black magic."

"Ugh," Fritz shivered. "At least we know what we're facing."

"Yes," Goblet said seriously. "I think I need to refresh my old magic skills."

"Me too," Iris agreed.

"Then we know what to do until it gets dark," William said.

They all settled down in the clearing. They sat close enough to see each other but still with enough distance for each of them to have their own space. William sat down in the thick grass and leaned his back against a rock. He looked around and saw that the others looked very busy. Almost like they meditated. I wonder how to prepare? William thought. He opened his blue backpack and picked up the letter from old King Valdemar as well as the ring he got from William. He slowly read the letter and clearly understood the cry for help. William tried to understand the powerlessness the king must have felt. To suspect that his own son had been murdered and that he himself was next. William read the letter over and over again to see if there was anything he had missed. If there was any hidden message or meaning somewhere. He checked every single letter but couldn't find anything. It's a bit strange, William thought, it still feels like the letter is crucial in some way and that it will help us. I got the letter and the ring from William. There must be a meaning behind it. William put the ring on his ring finger and to his surprise it fit perfectly. William had learned that if you were thinking about something you could not solve, it was good to take a break from it for a while. He let go of his thoughts on the letter and the ring and looked at the others who seemed deep in thought. I really hope that the mission goes well, he thought, with the realization that it would be a difficult mission. He looked at all three and felt how much they meant to him. It would be terrible if we didn't make it, but as Longtail had said, it was better to face what you had to do in battle and William felt that the mission really was inevitable. I can't disappoint either the old king or my brother William. This is something I have to do, no matter the cost. William closed both eyes and felt the smell of moss and forest fill his lungs. He felt relaxed and at the same time determined. William fell asleep. In the dream, he met his older brother who were all dressed in white. He really shone and his presence felt very real.

"Little brother," he said, "don't forget to bring the letter and the ring to the castle. You need both of them to find what you're looking for."

"I promise," William replied, then he felt his big brother touch his arm and look into his eyes as he said,

"There are many of us watching over you."

Then he was gone. William woke and stood up. The others were still sitting down and doing their own preparing for the mission. Then it was true what I felt, I had to bring the letter and the ring with me.

William started to look for wood to start a cooking fire with. He knew they needed something to eat and something to keep them warm when the evening came. Soon he had collected enough dry twigs. He put them in a pile and made sure that there was no grass near to keep the fire from spreading when he lit it. He looked at the canned food they brought and decided to cook spaghetti Bolognese.

"Do you think it's time to eat?" Fritz asked.

"Yes, we need to have something to eat before we go into the castle."

"Good idea my boy," grandpa said. It had already started to get a little cooler and they could feel the evening air approaching. "I have matches to try to get the fire going," Fritz continued.

"Maybe we need some more dry grass." William said and went to gather some. When he returned, Fritz had not yet managed to get the twigs to catch fire.

"Here," William said and handed over an armful of dry grass and dry moss that he had found.

"Perfect," Fritz said and smiled, "now it'll be easier." Within a few minutes the fire burned brightly. He took out a saucepan and a can opener from his backpack.

"Yes," he said happily. "There will be food soon." He handed over the can opener to William, who opened the two cans and poured the food into the saucepan, which he then put directly into the fire. William regularly stirred the food in the saucepan. Meanwhile, Grandpa took out plates, mugs and spoons.

"It's good that everything is made of paper so we don't have to do the dishes, instead we just put it on the fire when we've finished eating," grandpa stated out loud.

"Dinner is ready!" William called out.

Goblet immediately came flying over.

"Can someone pick me up?" Iris said.

"I can help you," Goblet said, "I've just memorized a spell on how to create a couple of legs that lasts for 24 hours."

"That would be nice," Iris said, who was already happy to not have to be carried everywhere. Goblet mumbled a few words and after two seconds Iris had two legs that were about a decimeter long.

"This feels strange," she said. "I think I'll try a little jumping. Yippee, that was really funny." Iris bent and stretched her legs. "What amazing little creatures, she said cheerfully. Let's run. Ready, Steady, Go." Iris ran as fast as she could to the fire. When she arrived, she was really out of breath.

"I'm not in the best of shape, but give me a little while and it'll be better. Thank you very much Goblet, it was really kind of you."

"My pleasure," Goblet replied chivalrously. "I'm happy to be able to assist."

They all ate with a good appetite.

At the end of the meal, everyone was a little tense.

"It will be completely dark soon," Goblet said. "It's time I went down to the castle."

William looked at his watch and saw that it was half past ten.

"We need some kind of transmitter on me and a microphone so I can communicate with you."

"I've already arranged it," Iris said and ran over to get what looked like a little black button. It serves as both a transmitter and receiver. "I have another button that I thought we'd put in William's ear so you can communicate directly with each other."

"That's cool," Goblet said. "Come on, we have to try it."

Iris put one button in Goblet's cup and William put one in his ear. Goblet flew away. "Can you hear me?"

"Yes, I hear you," William answered.

After five minutes, William heard a little whisper. "I'm now outside the castle. See if you can see me on the hologram."

William asked Iris to start the hologram and indeed, a small red dot shone above the castle.

"It works well," William said. "We can see you."

"That's good," Goblet replied. "Let's see where it's easiest to get in."

William saw the red dot go around and examine the castle. I wonder if there may be a side entrance that is not guarded in the same way as the main entrance? How strange, I don't see any other door. There must be some kind of side entrance. Goblet went around and examined the towers.

"At the bottom of each tower there is a door leading in from the courtyard. I think I'll check one of the four towers."

The hologram showed how he entered one of the towers and flew upwards. They heard how out of breath Goblet became. "I almost feel a little dizzy," he whispered. "There is a narrow spiral staircase leading up to the top. Wait, here's a door that seems to lead into the castle." They heard the handle being pressed down and the door squeaked a little when it opened. "I'll close it behind me in case anyone comes. Wow, it's dark in here. I can hardly see anything." They saw Goblet go straight ahead.

"You will soon reach another door," William said.

"I'm glad you warned me." Goblet slowed down his pace. "Here it is," he said and peeked carefully through the keyhole. They heard the sound of footsteps approaching.

"I'll hide," Goblet said and went up to the ceiling.

Two soldiers came in. They closed the door behind them and turned the light on. In the ceiling, a large brass lamp lit up. Goblet saw that the corridor he had been floating in was practically empty except for a worn tapestry that hung on the wooden wall.

"I don't understand why the King suddenly wants to double the security of the castle?" One soldier said to the other.

"Yes, the whole thing is very strange. He acts as if he were in grave danger. Our country is not threatened in any way. No, the whole thing is strange. Suddenly, we're to act as if everyone we meet is a potential enemy. Even little children."

"Yes, it's weird. Suddenly we get a picture of a boy." One of the soldiers took a picture out of his pocket and unfolded it. "If he shows up at the castle, we are to immediately take him to the king, who will then decide his fate. I think the king must have gone a bit crazy. I think he's getting delusional."

"Yes, truly," the other soldier laughed. They opened the other door, turned off the light and disappeared into the tower.

"The picture was of you William," Goblet whispered.

"Then the king suspects what is going on," Fritz said. "We have to be extremely careful." William nodded,

"But it also means that he is aware that he has something to hide, and that is even worse," William said thoughtfully. "If he acted without knowing and did not know about the background, it would have been a different matter. Then maybe he could have helped us, but that's not the case. It's frightening to have someone like that as ruler of the country."

"Yes, unfortunately he can do a lot of damage," Iris said, sighing.

"But now we know which side he is on and it is to our advantage to know it already so that we do not have to discover it at a later stage," Goblet whispered. "Let's see. Do you think I should try to get to the two rooms that were marked with black on the hologram?"

William thought for a moment. "Yes, but be careful."

"You never know what danger you'll face," Iris filled in. William looked at the hologram. "To get to the two rooms, that appear to be next to each other, you should first pass through, let's see, one, two, three rooms and then you should take the door to the left in the other tower and continue straight ahead until you get to the center of the building."

"So, I will continue straight ahead and when I arrive at the tower, I will take the door to the left and continue in the other castle wing."

"Correct," William replied. "When you're about half way through the wing, take the third staircase and go down two floors. Then you will be right outside one of the two rooms. Once you pass through the first room, the second room is right behind it."

"Ok, now I think I have a pretty good idea of where they are in the castle. I'll move on then."

William began to feel a little nervous and had a feeling of anxiety in his body. Goblet opened the next door and it was dark in that room as well.

Strange, it feels a bit deserted in this part of the castle, as if there's no one here. Goblet looked into the shady room. He noted that this room as well was sparsely furnished. The floor was a beautiful rough wooden floor and the ceiling had large wooden beams. He quickly passed through the other two rooms and arrived at the tower room where he took the door to the left. When he opened the door, he felt a creeping discomfort. The rooms in the wing he just had passed through had given him a warm feeling in his body. Even though the rooms themselves were fairly empty, there was still some kind of pleasant atmosphere when he passed through them. Here the feeling was the opposite. There was a compact, almost threatening silence when he entered the first room. Goblet tried to shake off the unpleasant feeling, but couldn't do it. It felt like he was going to his own execution.

"Ugh," he whispered.

"Do you see anything?" William asked worriedly.

"No, not exactly, but it's a very strange, almost a threatening atmosphere in here. I feel like I'm on edge." There were no windows in the room and Goblet did not dare to look for a light switch and he was also not sure that there was any. Goblet stood on the floor to rest for a while before making his way through the room. At that moment, he heard and felt how he was hit by what he thought was a sword. He heard the blade meet his metal body and pain went through him. Goblet was caught off guard so he fell and the blow sent him smashing into the wall. Everywhere in the room, long steel spears came down from the ceiling and up from the floor and drilled through every little part of the room. William heard the noise from the spears and how Goblet rolled on the floor and crashed into the wall.

"Are you alright? Are you hurt?" William cried with panic in his voice. He calmed down when he heard Goblets voice. "I'm all right, only got a dent, but no living creature would have been able to get through this room," Goblet said. "The entire room is pierced by metal spears."

Goblet stood up and flew carefully between the steel spears up to the next door. I don't know if I dare to open it, he thought, closing his eyes, but I have to. He felt the dent. It could have been worse. What if William or Fritz had been with him? When the initial shock had settled, he gathered courage and pushed down the handle.

CHAPTER 13
THE WALLACE MIRROR

He was surprised by what he saw. The first thing he saw was his own reflection. It must be a magic mirror, Goblet thought, looking at the black frame that was lined with gold around the mirror.

"Who dares to enter my room?" a dark voice boomed through the silence.

"It's me, oh enchanted mirror," Goblet replied.

"It was of no use for you to put on an invisibility spell, I can see you clearly anyway."

"It's not because of you that I have the spell," Goblet answered. Goblet quickly became aware that he needed to gain the trust of the mirror in order to pass into the other room and therefore said out loud. "It's for people and objects that don't have a deep knowledge of magic. These are the ones I want to avoid."

"I see," the mirror replied with a slightly softer tone, but then quickly changed its mind again. "But don't think you'll be able to get past me, you have no chance."

"I know," Goblet answered truthfully. "I've read about mirrors like you. No one can get past you if you don't want to and all the spells that I throw at you are just mirrored back on me."

"Reflected on you," the mirror corrected him with his dark voice. "Tell me, why should I spare you?"

Goblet noticed that the mirror was looking for his name and therefore filled in, "My name is Goblet."

"Why should I do that, Mr. Goblet?" the mirror said. When Goblet looked into the mirror, he saw huge flames being thrown up, then he saw a storming sea, followed by a dry desert.

"You have to choose which way to get past me. Either you enter a sea of flame, or you choose the hot desert or you are thrown into the sea. The choice is yours Mr. Goblet. I would like to point out that no one has ever made it through any of these earth elements."

"Hmm," Goblet said. "You give me a difficult choice, but they all lead to the same point in the end."

"Exactly," the mirror replied. "I'll wait, the choice is yours."

"Why isn't anyone allowed to get past you and into the next room?" Goblet asked challenging.

There was a flash and a couple of eyes in the mirror shot out a beam of fire that hit right in front of Goblet. The floor in front Goblet was incinerated and a small pile of ash remained.

"You ask too many questions, Mr. Goblet, why all these questions? I'm guarding the gate to the room that no one's allowed to enter."

"But you can't do that," Goblet said. "I need to pass another room and then at least two flights of stairs before I'm in front of that room."

"It's not possible," thundered the dark voice that now was really angry. Who are you who comes here and questions my assignment? Don't you know who you're talking to? I can destroy you before you even have time to blink and maybe that's what I'm going to do when you anger me in this way."

"Forgive me, I didn't mean to upset you," Goblet said. "It may be that I have received the wrong information and not you. My information is from a hologram I've seen of the castle."

"I want to see that hologram," the mirror thundered.

Oh no, Goblet thought, now I've really messed up.

"That'll be difficult because I don't have it with me."

The mirror began to shake with anger. "Then where is it?"

Goblet didn't really know how to answer the question. If I don't answer the question honestly, he's going to destroy me, so really, I have no choice.

"Her name is Iris," Goblet answered.

"Tell me where she is and I'll get her," the mirror said with a grim voice. Goblet hesitated.

"Tell him," William whispered in Goblet's ear. "Tell him to bring us all. Then we all get into the castle without attracting any attention."

"If you're to pick up Iris, you have to have to pick up the others, too," Goblet said.

"So, there's more of you?" The mirror said curiously. "A small group?" Goblet nodded.

"All right," the mirror said with his stern voice. "Where are they?"

Goblet explained where William, Fritz and Iris were. Goblet saw in the mirror how pictures of the forest came up.

"You said they're in a grove of trees by a small fire?"

"Yes," Goblet replied.

"Then I'll do a heat search," the mirror said. Goblet saw in the mirror how he searched large parts of the forest where they had been. Soon a zoomed in picture of William, Fritz and Iris came up where they were sitting by the campfire.

"Are those the ones you're talking about?" The mirror asked.

"Yes, that's my friends," Goblet said.

"They'll be with us soon," the mirror informed him and began to utter a spell.

Goblet saw how the image in the mirror became all smoky and after a few seconds the image cleared up and first William, then Iris and finally Fritz jumped out of the mirror.

"Good, now we're all here," William mimed to Goblet, but Goblet didn't have time to answer before the mirror began to speak.

"You must be Iris," the mirror said and focused his eyes on Iris. "I've been informed that you have a hologram of the castle."

"That's right," Iris answered.

"I have been tasked for centuries to guard the entrance to the most sacred room in the castle," the mirror continued.

"A room that is fragile and contains something very valuable."

"Who gave you the assignment?" Fritz asked.

"My master, the magician Kanarra and former King Valdemar's brother."

"Do you know exactly what you're guarding?" William wondered.

"No, it's a well-kept secret. I asked my master when I got the assignment but he said it was so incredibly secret that it was best for me that I didn't know what it was. He said it was out of concern for me that I was not told what it was. However, now I am very confused as to whether it really was as he said or if there was another hidden purpose."

"Wait," Iris said, "I'll show you the hologram." The room was illuminated by the green hologram.

"There are two black-marked rooms," the mirror said grimly. "This suggests that black magic has been used."

"You were right," he said while looking at Goblet. "I don't

guard anything valuable and sacred. Behind me there is no such thing at all. Just an ordinary room. I've been deceived and made a fool of."

"I understand you're upset," William said, "but now you know the truth."

"I'll make them regret it. I have tried to see what was behind the door many times, but I have not been able to see anything. I thought it was such a powerful magic that I couldn't see what it was but now I understand. There's nothing at all behind the door. I wonder why they put me here at all? There must be some purpose to it, or was it solely that I would prevent any intruders? I've decided to help you. I oppose black magic and I understand now that I have been used for its purpose which I truly regret, but when you as a magical object become connected to a person, you do not have the right to question your master. When we talked about black magic, he said he was against it as much as I am. No, something is not right. He may have been deceived, too, but I don't believe that. It's like there's a missing piece of the puzzle somewhere. I wonder what's really going on here? The whole thing needs to be clarified, once and for all. Let me introduce myself, my real name is Wallace and I belong to the Montbarbessa family."

"My name is William Silvercrona"

"And my name is Fritz and I am William's grandfather."

"Now that we're all introduced," the mirror said, "let's discuss how we proceed. Actually, there's not much of a choice. We need to get to the black-marked rooms on the hologram."

Everyone nodded in agreement.

"I feel there's something special about you, William," Wallace said. "Are you the leader of the group?"

"Well," William said, "leader might be too much to say…" William was interrupted by Goblet.

"Yes, he is leading us, he's just a little modest."

"What do you think, William, do you want us to move on to the magical rooms?" Wallace asked.

"Yes, that's where we need to go," William replied.

"You need to take me down first," Wallace said.

Together, William and Fritz lifted down the heavy mirror and leaned it against a wall so he could look directly at the door.

"Let's see what's hiding behind the door," Wallace said as William turned the key and pushed the handle down.

"Wait!" Wallace exclaimed. "I have to check the room first." The mirror closed its eyes and the room appeared in the mirror image. It was all white and looked empty. "There seems to be nothing in there," the mirror said, "but wait a little while I check it more carefully. What kind of smell is that? It's familiar in a way. Wait, there's a very faint smell of lavender."

William felt how he was getting tired.

"Close the door immediately," Wallace urged.

William looked at his grandfather and could see that he was tired as well because he tried to hide a yawn with his hand. William did what the mirror said and closed the door.

"The whole room is covered by a sleeping spell. Those who enter the room fall asleep and cannot be woken up again," the mirror said.

"Do they never wake up?" Iris asked in dismay.

"No," Wallace replied. "If not, wait…, there is a strong herb that grows at the top of Mount Dountley."

"Do you think you could find the herb and bring it here?" Goblet asked and turned to Wallace.

"I don't know," the mirror answered truthfully. "I think it's out of my reach, but I can try."

The mirror closed its eyes again, in the mirror an image of the land of Thyrridea appeared with its clear waters and steep cliffs. It was dark, which made it difficult to see exactly where the mirror was. After a while the night sky became visible and William realized that the mirror was now traveling high up in the clouds.

"The mountain is in front of us now," Wallace said. William and the others saw a dark silhouette sticking up among the clouds.

"I'll be there soon. I just hope I have strength enough," Wallace said strained. "I have to land now."

They saw in the mirror image that Wallace had landed in a mountain crevice. "I didn't make it all the way," Wallace said disappointedly.

"Do you think I can pass through you and help you find the herb?" William asked.

"Of course," Wallace answered. "But I want you to know that the herb is very hard to find. It's very rare and it's not season for it right now. There has likely only been a few and I fear most of them have withered."

"But is it wise that you go by yourself?" Fritz said. "Wouldn't it be better if one of us comes with you?"

"I think I can do it myself, but if I need help I'll come back."

William took his magic wand and climbed through the mirror. The ground was slippery and wet. William didn't see much in the dark. I think I'll have to try with the magic wand. William made a quick gesture with the wand and said "Give me light." To his surprise, the whole wand lit up and spread a bright light. William climbed out of the crevice. He shivered in the cold night. It's probably freezing here, he thought quietly to himself. He stepped on something that cracked. When he looked down, he saw that it was snow that had frozen so that a hard crust had formed on top of it. William did not sink into the snow, but walked on the hard crust. He held the magic wand in front of him where he went or rather, climbed forward.

"Where can the herb be?" He mumbled quietly. "What is the name of the herb," he called back to the mirror frame that remained in the mountain crevice. Wallace heard him. "It's called Gibraltar Campion Silene tomentosa. It's not big, about a few decimeters high," Wallace answered. William climbed on and now it started to get steep. It was difficult to climb with one hand so William had to put the wand in his mouth and climbed with his cheek against the rock wall. He was about to reach for a new grip when he slipped. "Ouch," William shouted. He quickly got a new grip with his hand but felt his hand pounding. I'll have to look at it later, he thought, and kept climbing. When he had climbed about 5 meters, he came to a new ledge where he could stand freely and gather strength. It will be almost impossible to find the flower in the dark. William thought for a while and then he took the magic wand and said aloud "Find Gibraltar Campion Silene tomentosa." William saw a beam of light shoot out of the wand and land about 20 meters away on a small whitish flower.

"Fantastic, there it is!" William exclaimed. He put the wand back in his mouth and continued his climb. As he got closer, he saw that there was only one small flower left. The other two had already withered. How lucky I am, he thought. He reached for the flower and carefully picked it while he held tight with the other hand and his feet. Please let me not fall, he thought. He was just about to put the flower in his pocket as he lost his balance and fell.

"No!" William cried out. As he fell, he feverishly tried to figure out what to do. He took the magic wand and said out loud, "Take me to the mirror." To his surprise he stopped falling and a shimmering light spread around him, carrying him through the air to the mirror where he was gently put down.

"Wow," William exclaimed breathlessly. "That was a close call." William sighed with relief.

"I'm glad you found Gibraltar Campion," Mr. Wallace said. "Then I think we'll better take it and get back." William crawled into the mirror, or rather, Mr. Wallace as he preferred to be called. They travelled through the darkness and soon they were back in the room.

"Oh," Goblet said, "the scent of Gibraltar Campion. You found it! It's absolutely amazing."

The scent of the flower was very strong. It smelled like ten lilies and you all know how strong the scent of a lily can be.

"What should I do with the flower?" William asked.

"You should take the flower petals and spread them in the room. It should break the sleeping spell," Wallace answered.

William took the flower out of his pocket. It looked small and fragile, but the scent was very strong. William picked the white petals and carefully put them in his hand, then he entered the room and at once he felt the petals come alive in his hand. The flower petals moved around and when William opened his hand, he saw that the flower petals gave off a white shimmering light. The flower petals were still for a second and then they flew out in the room and then they dissolved and the whole room shimmered. It was as if a white glitter fell from the ceiling to the floor. Before it reached the floor, it reacted with some substance and the white glitter turned yellow and then completely dissolved.

"Beautiful!" William exclaimed.

"Yes indeed," Fritz agreed, who stood just behind him.

"Now the spell is broken," Wallace shouted.

"Shall we continue to the next room?" Iris asked.

"Can you check if you see anything before we go in?" William asked Wallace.

"Yes, a moment please." They turned around and looked at the mirror. The image of a large waterfall emerged.

"Oh my," Goblet murmured. "That wasn't quite what I expected. A waterfall instead of a staircase. Here it'll be easy to get drenched."

It was a large waterfall that fell straight down.

"Ugh," Iris said, "I don't like to get wet."

The image of the waterfall disappeared and Wallace cleared his throat and said, "My help unfortunately ends here. You see, I haven't enough magical power to see what's in the two rooms with black magic. My guess is that once you have passed the waterfall, you will stand in front of the rooms with black magic."

"That is what the hologram shows as well, William said.

"However, I can make sure that no other people pass through the room that I guard. I can promise you that, but unfortunately that's where my help ends," Wallace said.

"We are incredibly grateful for the help you have already given us," Fritz said.

"But what happens to you now?" Goblet asked. "You can't stand here and watch the room for hundreds of more years."

"No, I really have no intention to do that. When you have finished your mission and found what you're looking for, my spell will be broken and I will be free. I'll not be in anyone's service anymore."

"That's great," Iris exclaimed.

"Indeed," Wallace said with a sigh. "I want to go home to my family for a while, then I would love to be at your service again if you ever need me."

Fritz scratched his beard. "If you want, I could use some help. I'm in need of a magic mirror that tells me the truth and keeps an eye on the members of my order. I'm not sure everyone there does what they say they do. I think there are some things that needs to be sorted out and people who aren't what they claim to be."

The mirror's eyes shone up. "Of course, I'll be happy to help you with that."

"It's voluntary, of course," Fritz clarified, "and you can end it at any time you like."

"It suits me perfectly. I need something to do. I just can't go home and relax. I'd be bored to death. When you're done with the mission, all you have to do is pick me up here."

"We'll do," William said. "Now we have to figure out how to get past the waterfall. Does anyone have a suggestion?"

"Uhm, I've been thinking and I remember a spell that makes me bigger so that you all could fit inside me." Goblet said.

"You mean inside the cup itself?" Iris asked.

"Yes," Goblet replied. "What do you think of my suggestion, William?"

William thought briefly before answering. "I think it's worth trying."

"Keep in mind that we need to close the door behind us so that Wallace doesn't get soaked," Fritz said. "There is a chance that the water will flood in here when we open the door."

"I'll do it," Goblet said.

Everyone turned to the mirror in the other room.

"Thank you so much for all your help," William said.

"I'll see you all again soon," Wallace replied.

All four of them waved to Wallace and shouted good bye.

CHAPTER 14
THE WATERFALL

"Good luck!" Wallace called to them. Goblet closed the door and then he started to mumble a few sentences. William could barely make out what he was saying because he spoke very quietly. Goblet grew and grew and Fritz, Iris and William had to back off to give him space. In the end, he was huge and occupied almost half the room. "Now I'm done," Goblet informed them. William looked up.

"Now you can climb into me."

William quickly realized that he could not reach the edge. "I think I'll have to help you." Fritz said. "If you take Iris and put her in your backpack, then you can climb onto my shoulders."

William reached the edge as he stood on his grandfather's shoulders. "Yes, I can reach it now," he said contentedly. He first took his right leg over the edge, then the left. When he was in Goblet's bowl with both legs, he leaned over the edge and reached out his hand to his grandfather. "I think I can just reach your hands," Fritz said and made

himself as tall as he could. Fritz took a good hold with both hands while William pulled him up. When he reached the edge with his hands he said, "could you help me and catch my leg so I can get it over the edge."
He kicked up with his right leg. William caught it in the air and pulled it over the edge.
"Just my left leg to go. Ah, finally I'm up."
Fritz and William held onto the edge and looked down.
"I'd better let go first and go down the middle as I'm much heavier than you are." Fritz said
"Good idea," William agreed. Fritz let go and slid at high speed down to the bottom of the bowl.
"Watch out, here I go," William shouted. He let go and felt a tickle in his stomach as he slid down as it was quite steep and deep down to the bottom. With a thud, he bumped into his grandfather.

"Are you ready?" Goblet asked.
"Yes, we are."
Goblet mumbled two words and the door opened. William felt a wave of water hit Goblet and he went with great force into the door that broke.
"Hold on as hard as you can," Goblet shouted. A huge bang was heard when Goblet went through the doorway and knocked down part of the wall on both sides.
"Watch out, here comes the waterfall," Goblet shouted. It was difficult for William and Fritz to hear what Goblet

was shouting because the roar from the waterfall was deafening.

"Hold on to me," Fritz shouted.

"If we sit with our backs against each other and hold on with our feet against the wall, I think we have a better chance." William shouted back.

As William shouted what to do, he showed with his body how they should sit. Fritz quickly understood and within a few seconds they sat with their backs against each other and their arms intertwined with each other. They both took hold with their feet against the wall.

"Let's go!" William shouted and they went straight into the roaring waterfall. William pressed with his legs as hard as he could. Goblet went down at a tremendous speed.

"Ouch," William cried out when Goblet hit a hard rock that was sticking up through the water. A metallic bang was heard and Goblet was thrown to the left. William wasn't the only one screaming.

"Ouch..." Goblet screamed. On Goblet's right side there was a large dent in the metal. Goblet swirled around in the water. William closed his eyes to try to focus and said quietly to himself. "We'll be down soon. We'll be down soon."

It feels like an eternity, William thought, will the waterfall never end? Water splashed in where they were sitting and Fritz got it straight into his mouth and started coughing.

"We're nearly at the bottom," Goblet shouted. William held on tighter to his grandfather and they both prepared for the impact.

Bang! Goblet hit the ground with such force that both William and his grandfather went straight out of the cup. William felt their grip slip and he was thrown high into the air and landed with a thud. William gasped for breath. He had trouble breathing. After a while, he could breathe more easily again and he got up and looked around. He saw his grandpa lying on his stomach a few meters from him and Goblet had landed upside down a little further away. William looked at the waterfall which was about 20 meters from them. It was like the water was gushing right through the floorboards.

"Grandpa," William cried, but he got no answer. William looked at the lifeless body and a cold shiver went through his body. He must have survived the fall, William thought desperately.

"Grandpa, grandpa" he cried again, but this time he shouted even louder and with a clear desperation in his voice but still no answer.

"Grandpa, answer me, Grandpa!" William had almost given up hope when he saw Fritz moving.

"Ow, Oh my old body hurts."

"You're alive," William shouted with relief.

"Yes, barely," Fritz answered. William got up and slowly limped over to his grandfather. William felt badly bruised and his whole body was aching.

"Do you want me to help you up?" William asked.

"Well," William's grandfather answered, "I'll try to sit up by myself. I feel completely bruised."

Fritz tried to stand up but couldn't so he grabbed William's outstretched hand.

"Uh-oh," they heard from Goblet, "big body, great damage," he moaned. He mumbled something and William and Fritz could see how he shrunk back to his normal size.

"Now I feel a little better," Goblet said and began to inspect the dent. "Yes, it's not that bad. I just need a blacksmith, I'm sure a blacksmith can remove the dent. I can't believe we made it," he said in a cheerful tone.

"Yes, but it was a close call," Fritz replied, who was now leaning against a wall.

"You're right," Goblet said, "I wasn't sure it would work at all. It was a wild guess from my side, but we are alive all three of us. Shall we rest for a while before we enter the room with black magic?"

"Yes, I think so," Fritz said.

"Hello, let me out!" William heard a soft, tender voice shouting from inside his backpack.

"Oh, it must be Iris." William opened is backpack and Iris jumped out.

"That went really well," she said cheerfully, but as she looked at Fritz and Goblet, she fell silent.

"You two are injured and need medical attention."

"Well, not really," Goblet said. "It's just a little dent. I thought I'd fix it a little later."

She turned to Fritz and asked, "Can you move?"

"Just barely. I have terrible pain in my whole body."

Iris opened the medallion and looked at her dial.

"I'm afraid we have to hurry. We haven't got much time to enter the magic room."

"What do you mean?" William wondered puzzled.

"I don't know, maybe I should have told you a little earlier, but I was afraid to stress you out. We actually need to enter the room in exactly 4 minutes. If we don't, the door closes forever and no one can ever enter. I'm afraid it's better if you Fritz stays here. Black magic is able to use weaknesses and make them worse and I'm worried that you will not survive if you enter the room."

"Then I don't have much choice," Fritz said dishearteningly.

"No, you'd better stay here," William agreed.

"But it also means that I can't help you if you need it," Fritz said somewhat distraught.

"I know it's hard, but I think it's better if William and I go in by ourselves." Iris said.

"You can't mean that," Goblet cried out annoyed. "I only have a small dent."

"But imagine that dent growing and taking over your whole body. In fact, there is a risk that you too will die. Besides, it's better if you stay here taking care of Fritz in case something should happen."

Goblet turned to William. "Do you feel the same way?"

"Yes, I actually think so. It's better for all of us if you're here and takes care of grandpa."

"All right, I'll do it," Goblet said, "but when we're to find out who killed William, I want to be there."

"Of course," William said. Iris and William went to the door. William wasn't quite sure what to expect and he felt his heart beating hard in his chest.

"But," Goblet cried out. "William is injured, too. Why is he allowed to go into the room and not us?"

"William hasn't really got a choice. If anyone is to do this, it's William. There's no one else. I know he is bruised as well after the fall, but unfortunately that is a risk we have to take. We have to keep our fingers crossed that it all goes well." Iris said and looked at her dial. "Unfortunately, we haven't got time to talk about it anymore."

CHAPTER 15
ENTRANCE TO THE BLACK MAZE

William's heart was pounding hard as he looked at the big black door. Suddenly he felt scared. Afraid of failure, afraid of what would happen if he failed, afraid that his grandfather would not make it and afraid of how it would turn out for himself.

William had been taught early on by his parents that life comes with no guarantees, that you have to take responsibility for your own life and the choices you make. But taking responsibility was easier when you went to school and had friends, where the biggest problem was how to relate to different groups of friends. This was something completely different. The only time William had been subject to black magic was when he had been captured by Lord Theodorus. William shuddered. All these thoughts passed through William's brain in seconds and in a strange way it was what the mirror sensed and seemed to understand what William was going through.

William heard the voice from the mirror whispering in his ear. It felt like the mirror was next to him.

"William, remember that you haven't wasted your life the way I did. I can't believe I've been played as a fool and deceived all these years. Fight for me. Your pure heart will guide you. And, the mirror lowered his voice even more, if you really need me William, just shout my name. Then I promise I'll help you even if it's the last thing I do."

William swallowed hard. "Thank you from the bottom of my heart."

Iris felt stressed. "There's only 10 seconds left, William. We have to go in before it's too late."

William held Iris in his left hand and with his right hand he turned the key that was in the lock and slowly pushed down the handle. Before entering the room, he turned around.

"Don't worry about me. I'll be fine," he said but inside he felt uncertain. The big heavy iron door slid closed behind him.

"I can't see a thing," William whispered to Iris. It was really dark. It was a compact darkness that surrounded them. Iris blinked with her eyes to see if she could discern any contours but it was pitch black all around them.

"I'll see what I can do," she whispered. She searched her memory and found a folder with the title *'Lighting'*.

"Let's see," Iris said focused. *'To light up dark magic'* the title of a document said. "I'll try," she said quietly. As soon as she had double-clicked on the document, a whitish glow spread across the room.

Iris and William both gasped for breath. No wonder there was so much black around them. About half a meter in front of them, a huge black wall towered.

"Oh, what could this be?" Iris mumbled.

"I'm not sure," William said, "but I think it could be a maze."

"But there is no entrance. All mazes have entrances," Iris protested.

"This is not an ordinary maze," William replied grimly. "It is built of black magic. We have to try to get into the maze. Iris, can you search your memory if you find anything about black mazes and openings?"

Iris searched and searched in her memory but eventually she had to give up. "I can't find anything about mazes," she answered weakly.

Suddenly, a large red and gold mark appeared, burning on the wall. It looked like two rings that went a little into each other. William could feel the heat from the flames.

"You managed to get here," a cold, dark voice said. William felt how he became stiff all over his body. The warmth he had previously felt was gone.

"You know, William, you still have a chance to go home. Nothing has to happen to you. William saw two doors open in the dark wall. Behind one door, William saw his two parents sitting down and drinking tea with William's grandmother.

"If you go through this door, you don't have to worry that something will happen to you. You can continue to live your life here in Libra."

Door number two opened.

"You can also choose to return home to Sweden." William saw his former house. "You can return to your old school and your old friends. Of course, your parents and even your grandparents will follow you there. Then you can forget everything you've been through here. All of this will be erased from your memories. Why should you risk your life for something that happened a long time ago and doesn't concern you? It's a huge risk you're taking. To face the magic of darkness has its risks. Are you really ready to make such a sacrifice? How do you think your parents will feel if something happens to you? Are you really prepared to put them through such grief? Think carefully. It's your choice and the consequences are yours."

William felt his blood flowing through his veins.

"I will never let my big brother down. I promised to help him." William felt the strength come back to his body. "I've made my choice."

"I've noticed," the dark voice said, "but remember that I warned you. Now there's no going back for you."

The dark wall moved backwards and between it and William came a thick mist that covered the floor. Out of the mist stones of different sizes appeared.

"If you make one faulty step or if you stand on the wrong stone, you will fall straight through the mist and through a black hole until you reach the ground. No one survives such a fall."

William took a deep breath and closed his eyes. He opened his eyes and looked at the stones. Some of them was just barely visible in the mist. He closed his eyes and memorized the stone pattern. The stones all had different shapes, some were oblong, others were round. They seemed scattered randomly.

"Are you ready, William?" The voice shouted.

"Yes, I am," William answered.

"All right, but remember that I warned you. You have one last chance to withdraw."

William swallowed and concentrated on the first stones. Which one should he choose? William focused. There was something special with the stone to the left. William jumped. He just made it and landed with his right foot on the stone. A rumble was heard and William saw the stones beside him come loose and fall with a big bang through the mist.

"Well done, William," the voice said. "However, I forgot to tell you." he chuckled hollowly.

"You forgot what?" William wondered.

"I forgot to tell you that it's timed. If you haven't made it to the other side in four minutes, all the stones will come loose."

"But that's impossible," William looked at all the stones and swallowed.

"Don't tell me that I didn't warn you, William."

William felt his head spinning. He closed his eyes again, and as he listened carefully, he heard his older brother's voice. "The ring, William. Put on your ring."

William felt in his jacket pocket and there it was. He quickly put it on his right ring finger. The moment he did, a green beam of light came from the ring. The beam pointed to a rock far to the right. William readied himself and jumped. The stone held his weight and again a deafening roar was heard as the other stones behind William plunged through the mist. When William had made it about halfway through the maze, the mist began to thicken. William saw that some of the stones disappeared in the mist and were no longer visible. The green light from the ring showed that he had to jump to a stone straight ahead, but as William jumped, the stone disappeared into the mist.

"No!" William screamed and stumbled and lost his balance as he landed, but at the last moment he managed to regain his balance. I have to hurry before all the stones disappear into the mist, he thought. He quickly continued to jump from stone to stone and focused hard to land just right on each stone. Finally, there was only one stone left between William and the maze on the other side. The green beam pointed to the stone, but just as William was getting ready to jump, the stone disappeared completely into the mist. William made a quick decision. It was too risky to jump to that stone, but if he prepared the jump correctly, he might reach the other side. William took a deep breath and focused on the ground where he needed to land. He gathered every muscle in his body and jumped. Never in his life had William made such a jump. Not even when practicing long jump in school. William flew through the air and felt the damp mist against his cheeks and landed with a thud on the ground on the other side. Tears of relief ran down his cheeks.

"I made it! I made it!" he shouted out to the mist, but the voice that had spoken to him previously was now silent. William heard how all the remaining stones came loose and fell towards the ground far below. He lay down for a few minutes and caught his breath.

CHAPTER 16
THE BLACK MAZE

"Well done," Iris shouted from inside the backpack. William picked her up and put Iris on the ground.

"Now we need to find the entrance," she said. "I wonder where it could be?"

"We have to systematically examine the wall," William filled in.

"Umm ok," Iris said. William stood up and put both hands on the wall. He was surprised. William had expected it to feel like a normal hard wall, but it didn't. Instead, his hands sunk into the wall a few inches. It wasn't sticky, but rather soft and cold.

"Strange," William said out loud.

"Yes indeed, it feels strange," Iris replied. "My hands got really cold." She blew on them to get some heat back in her fingers. William and Iris began to search the wall.

After a while William said, "I can't feel any entrance." They both looked up.

"Do you think the entrance can be so high up that we can't reach it?" Iris asked.

"I don't really know," William answered, "but something feels a bit strange. We must have missed something, something we haven't found."

William rubbed his hands to regain some warmth in them while he continued to talk. "What is typical of black magic? It is the opposite of good magic. The wall feels cold. The opposite of cold is heat. Hmm, Iris, do you think you can feel if there is a spot on the wall that's warmer than the rest? If there is, then maybe it's the opening. Perhaps there is a small gap that the black magic has not been able to cover and that this gap is the entrance to the maze?"

"Well thought William," Iris said. "I'll use my infrared detector to see if there's any warmer spot on the wall."

A reddish glow spread from Iris and illuminated the wall. William noted that the red light was transformed into purple when it hit the cold wall.

"It makes sense," he said to himself. "When red meets blue, that is cold, it turns purple."

At first glance, William thought that the whole wall seemed to be purple. But when he looked closer, he saw that about a meter up and several meters to the left of him there was spot of reddish color on the wall, formed as a round circle.

"There! that must be the entrance," William called out pointing.

"I see it," Iris said laughing. "I can't believe we found the entrance. Do you want to go first?"

"Yes, I do." William stepped into the red circle and then turned around and picked up Iris who stood on the ground behind him. He then turned around and walked several steps until he reached a large oak door with the sign of dark magic imprinted in red and gold. A round black handle hung on the door. William pulled the handle and the door opened. William was surprised by what he saw. In front of him it was all pitch black.

"Iris, can you give us some light?

"Of course I can," she answered.

William saw that a dark corridor appeared. On each side of the corridor there were black walls. William felt on one of them. "It feels exactly as the big black wall."

"You mean just as cold?" Iris wondered.

"Mm, exactly and then just as soft until you get to the hard part."

"What do you think we'll have to do?" Iris asked.

"I think we'll have to start walking and see what happens."

"Black mazes can be really tough to get through. No one has made it through alive in the ones I've heard of."

"It actually feels a bit scary," William said.

They started to walk down the corridor. The cold from the walls made William feel frozen.

"I think I'll put on my jacket," he said, shivering. He put his backpack down and took out his jacket from the big compartment. He pulled up the zipper and pulled the collar close around his neck. "If I had known it would be

this cold, I would have brought gloves, hat and scarf."
They continued to walk forward.

"Look," Iris said. "Do you see that there is an opening in
the wall up front on the right?"
William looked and there was indeed an opening. As they
got closer, William saw that it was another corridor.
"Ugh, it's a maze," Iris stated. "What shall we do? Shall
we take the corridor to the right or shall we keep going
down the corridor straight ahead?"
"I don't know," William said truthfully.
"I think we should try the one to the right," Iris said.
"Ok, let's do so," William answered. They went further
and further into the corridor until William halted.
"Did you hear that?"
"Heard what?" Iris asked.
"That sliding sound," William said. "Listen."
They stood still and listened. It was completely silent. Iris
was just about to say that she didn't hear anything when
she heard a very faint sliding sound.
"Now I heard it, too."
William turned around. "Iris, we have to run. Look behind
us."
Iris quickly turned around. She saw how the two walls
behind them began to move towards each other. William
didn't wait for her to reply but just picked her up and
began to run as fast as he could back to where they came
from.

"Help!" Iris shouted, "we must hurry before the corridor completely disappears."

"Yes," William puffed, as he ran for his life. William felt how both walls touched slightly against his arms as he ran.

"Uh-oh," Iris screamed.

Towards the end William had to run sideways as the corridor was too narrow.

"I think we might make it," Iris said. "Just ten meters left to the other corridor."

"I hope so," William said with a strained voice. It was almost like the walls could hear what they were saying as they started to close faster. When William arrived at the opening to the other corridor, the gap was only about twenty centimeters wide. He squeezed his body through and he was just able to make it. When he turned around, he saw that the opening was completely gone.

"That was a close call," Iris said.

"Yes, it really was," William answered as he bent his head down towards his legs to catch his breath. "We'll probably have to be more careful about which corridors we choose, but I'm afraid most of them will contain unpleasant surprises. We need to be alert at all times."

"I don't dare to think about what would have happened if you hadn't heard that sound," Iris said.

William was too tired to answer so he nodded instead. Within a few minutes, he had recovered.

"We'll move on," he said. This time they walked much slower and carefully searched their surroundings. They walked in silence and listened intently for any sound. After they had walked for a while, Iris pointed towards two corridors a little ahead of them, one to the right and one to the left. William saw them but didn't really know if they should choose either one of them or if they should continue straight ahead.

"Iris," he whispered quietly. "Are you sure you don't have any information about black mazes? Can you do a new search?"

"I'll try," she whispered. Iris searched her memory and went through several folders that were full of various documents that could be valuable to William. William had almost given up hope when Iris looked up at him and said, "I found a file that oddly enough is black and it's like I can't open it, like I need a password or something. I've tried different ways but I just get that the file isn't available. But I think it has something to do with black magic because I can open all the other files but not this one. Maybe it's protected or something so that it can only be opened with the proper authorization."

"You mean that if you'd been captured and pressed for information, you wouldn't have been able to give them the information that's in the black file?"

"Exactly," Iris replied sadly, "but I don't understand. I would never give my information to anyone. I would rather have destroyed myself."

"I understand that," William said, "but maybe someone could have somehow obtained the information even though you had not given it to them. You never really know. It seems that black magic is powerful and that it can act in ways that we don't know anything about."

"Yes, of course it is like that," Iris said, sighing, "but if the prophecy is true, they will have a tough time against you. You will learn a lot about both white and black magic," Iris replied.

"I understand that," William said, "but right now I don't really feel like I have that much left to offer, but at least I will fight with the power that I have."

"Let's focus on finding a password. Can I pick you up?" he asked, looking at Iris. "I have a feeling that the password may have something to do with me."

"Of course," Iris answered. William picked up Iris.

"I'm going to examine you to see if I can find any clue." Iris nodded. William began by examining the front and back but saw nothing strange. Then he opened the medallion and looked at the clockwork. It glimmered like stars at night. He could see many different kinds of hands moving at different speeds. There were different lines of numbers in a circle. Some were written with common numbers and some were written in Roman characters. When a hand pointed to a place in the dial, you did not know what number it actually pointed at, because there was a long line of numbers behind each other. When he looked closely, he saw that there were symbols among the line of numbers. Symbols like he'd never seen before. The numbers and symbols shone in different colors, in red, blue, yellow, violet, white and black. The strange thing was that they constantly changed color depending on which hand that was pointing to the line at the moment. At certain times, two hands pointed at the same line of numbers and symbols, and then some symbols and numbers shone brighter than others. William thought it looked magical and beautiful, as if the clockwork was alive and breathing. Wait, William thought, did I breathe? He took the medallion to his ear and listened. Faintly, he heard very soft breaths and a ticking that sounded like small heartbeats.

"Do you have your heart in the clockwork?"

"Yes," Iris answered. "If something were to happen to the clockwork, I would die."

William looked at the clockwork again. Umm, a password for the black file. He closed his eyes and this time he saw the clockwork in front of him. What is the password? It must somehow be connected to me. What do I know that no one else knows? He repeated the question quietly to himself. What do I know that no one else knows? What could it be? William thought carefully. It can't be the king's name. A lot of people know that. It can't be my name either. It's too simple. It can't be Arild's name because my big brother didn't know him. What do we both know that no one else knows? It can't be the word compass because several knew that William was carrying its mark. William shone up. It could be Marcus. Only he and William knew there was something special about this man. One of the last things William did was send his greeting to him through the Marcusson family.

"Iris I think I've come up with a password that I'd like to try. How can I try it without you knowing what I entered?"

"Why can't I know the password?" Iris said a little disappointed.

"No, we have to consider why the password was protected from the start. If you were supposed to know it, you'd already have access to it. It is to protect you so that you cannot be forced by evil to reveal it."

Iris sighed. "William, of course, you are right. I was too eager that I didn't think clearly. But I actually don't really know how to enter the password. All I have to do is think it and the password will be entered. Maybe you can do something similar?"

"I can try," William said. He held Iris close to his eyes and looked intently at the clockwork. In front of him he saw the clockwork with its brilliant numbers and symbols. He thought intensely about the dark file. After a while, it was as if his eyes were drawn towards a symbol representing an eye. The symbol began to shine brighter than the others. He blinked to make sure he wasn't imagining it. A moment later, it was as if he could see through the symbol of the eye and into the clockwork. He saw a variety of folders and files neatly categorized in alphabetical order. He then noticed a folder that had no name. When he tried to take a closer look at the folder, he saw that he could not read the contents. Instead, it was all black, after a few seconds the word password came up in squiggly white letters against the black background. William thought of the name Marcus, but nothing happened. Shortly thereafter, all the letters of the alphabet were displayed. William immediately understood that he had to press the letters to enter the password. William pressed in the air with his index finger, marking all the letters of the name Marcusson. When he was finished, the folder opened. William immediately saw that one of the files was about black mazes. He pressed the file and a text came up. William turned to Iris.

"Can you read what's in the file?"

"Huh, No, you entered the password."

William nodded. "Then I'll tell you what it says. Wait a minute and I'll just read it first."

William was surprised when he started reading.

"Hi William, I have gathered some of my knowledge of dark magic and black mazes in this text. I hope you will benefit from it. Good luck little brother. /W"

"Oh," William said. "My older brother wrote the file." William continued to quietly read the text. Iris waited and waited and thought it took a very long time. She began to feel restless and walked back and forth in the corridor. To keep herself occupied, she counted how many times she walked back and forth. William began to read the first line where it said *"Mazes of black magic is very unpredictable. They can adapt and adjust according to the visitor. That means that you as a visitor will have to use all of your powers to get through the maze."*

William immediately thought of the stones that had sunk or disappeared in the mist. The document continued *"Once you have entered a black maze, you can count on being watched. The black magic both hears and sees you. Therefore, be careful of what you say. The first obstacle in a black maze is which way to choose."*

William looked around, everywhere he saw the towering black walls.

"Every black maze usually starts with a crossroad. You can choose to go to the right, left or straight ahead. It is crucial which path you choose to take. The path to the right leads to certain death. At the other crossroads, each choice means that you will face different difficult tasks. If you fail the task, you'll be eliminated."

William continued to read through the document.

When Iris was on her 14th turn, William said. "Now I've finished reading."

"Good!" Iris said and stopped walking. "What do the text say?"

"It made clear that black mazes contain a lot of dark magic. The person who creates the maze determines what it should look like and what trials it contains. This maze was created by the murdered king's brother and the kingdom's foremost and most powerful black magician. According to William, this magician often began his mazes with a side corridor that, like a trap, often closes in and crushes its victim."

"Well, what do you know," Iris said, "that's exactly what happened to us."

"William wrote that it was important to walk slowly and observe everything. That we look at the walls and the floor but also the air above us and that we listen carefully."

"We?" Iris asked, "did he mention me?"

"Yes, he did," William answered, "but he also wrote that we should walk in silence so that we do not get distracted by our own talking. In stressful situations it is important that we remain calm and that we do not act hastily and intuitively. Much of what happens in the maze is supposed to scare us and make fear control our actions. The nasty will be even worse and increase its strength. It's like the dark magic is nourished by our fears."

"Ugh," Iris said. "Then I have to stay calm."

William nodded "But that can probably be difficult at times," he added. "There is supposed to be a very soft, simple melody that we have to listen for and follow as best we can. At first it will be incredibly soft and barely audible, but gradually it'll get louder and louder. The melody will lead us to the center of the maze."

"Did it say what kind of melody it was?" Iris asked.

"No, just that we need to listen for the voice of the heart. Then it said that I should hold you in my hand and at regular intervals have a good look at your clockwork."

"That's good," Iris said, pleased, "then I'll be useful. I don't feel like I've contributed with anything special so far."

"You can't say that. You've been very helpful," William corrected her. "Don't forget, you knew about the time limit. Without you, we would never have been able to enter the black maze. The time would have run out and we'd been stuck outside the door."

"Yes, you're right," Iris said and felt warm in her heart.

"Then you must not forget that you showed us the hologram of the castle and helped me find the warm area on the black wall."

"When you tell me, I actually feel I've done some good."

"Mm, and I'm very grateful that you accompany me through this maze."

Iris became so happy that she jumped up and down.

"If I could, I would have jumped up and kissed you on the mouth," she said cheerfully.

William started laughing, "That's something I'm glad you can't do." If you've read about William before, you know he's not particularly fond of kisses. They both laughed.

"No, it's time for us to take on this maze." William lifted up Iris and looked at the clockwork, but no symbol shone more than anyone else. Then we'll start our adventure in the labyrinth. William walked slowly and held Iris in a firm grip. He tried to listen, but he didn't hear any melody at all. It was completely quiet all around and the cold started to go through his jacket and he started to feel frozen. He looked closely at the black walls to be prepared in case they changed their mind. He continued straight ahead and as he approached a crossroad he stopped. William didn't feel that any of the corridors appealed to him. To make sure he made the right decision, he looked at the clockwork before proceeding straight ahead. There was no indication that he should choose another path. William continued straight ahead.

He walked straight ahead for a long time and William almost began to believe that it would only be one long straight corridor. He felt like he was starting to lose focus. He blinked a few times and blew on his hands to get them a little warmer. A pair of gloves would have been wonderful right now, he thought quietly. Wait, what is that?

CHAPTER 17
MUD

William looked at the wall and it looked like something was running from it. What is that? He thought and soon he realized it was black mud that ran from the walls and that the floor began to fill with black mud. William tried to keep his composure as the mud flowed faster and faster. He moved forward as fast as he could but he had soon mud up to his waist. William looked methodically around to see if there was anything he could climb up on, but the mud lay like a black lake all around him. William struggled to stay calm, but it was difficult. He understood that soon he would not be able to reach the bottom anymore. I need the light from Iris and if I need to swim, I can't hold her in my hand as she would be completely drenched in mud.

"Iris," he said in a calm voice. "Do you think you could hold on to my hair while I swim?"

"Of course," Iris replied, who understood the gravity of the situation. William glanced at the clock but it showed nothing special. William put Iris on his head and started swimming. The mud was thick and sticky and it was difficult to swim properly. I'll try crawl, he thought. William slowly made his way through the mud. Instead of focusing on the fact that it seemed hopeless, he rather focused on the progress he had made. The calmer William felt, the slower the mud rose. William noticed that and tried not to think that he was getting tired. He stopped and treaded mud so as not to sink below the surface. He noted that he was not far from a wall. There must be an exit, he thought. I'll get to the wall and then we'll see what happens there. He continued to swim and until he was almost there.

When he stopped and turned around, he saw a movement in the mud. At first, he thought he was imagining it, but then he saw the movement again. His heart began to pound harder and William saw how the mud began to flow at high speed down the walls. I have to stay calm. I have to stay calm, he quietly repeated to himself, almost like a mantra. He swam as fast as he could towards the wall. He realized that Iris also had noticed the movements in the mud. She whispered while she tried to keep her composure. "It's a giant snake."
William looked around and saw the middle part of the snake. It was about 40 centimeter in diameter. The snake was light brown and appeared to be several meters long. The snake moved with wave-like motions through the

mud. William's heart was pounding hard. He thought feverishly about what to do.

"Iris, can you pick up the knife I have in my backpack?" Iris jumped down from his hair and opened the backpack. She quickly found the knife and handed it to William. The snake was now about 3 meters away from them.

"William," Iris said, "my clockwork shows that there should be an exit in the wall, but I think you need to dive down to find it."

"Hold on," William said. He took a deep breath and dived down. As he could not see anything in the mud he felt with his hands along the wall. William felt the movements of the snake in the mud. It will be here soon, he thought. I need to find the opening. He was quickly running out of air. There, could it be the opening? William felt feverishly with his hands and indeed there was an opening in the wall.

William was halfway through the opening when he felt the snake wrap itself around his left leg and squeeze tightly. William felt how he started to lose feeling in his leg as the grip tightened. It can't be my destiny to die fighting with a snake here in the mud? It felt somehow surreal. William felt how his lungs was about to explode from lack of oxygen.

"I got you now!" the snake hissed, "I got you know, little William Silvercrona. No one leaves my swamp. I've killed far more important people than you and they taste sooo good," he hissed as he started to pull William towards him.

William tried to twist his leg quickly to the right but the snake was too quick and stopped him. William tried to resist and held on to the wall by the opening with a firm grip with his hands but the snake was stronger. I need to get some air! he thought in panic. He already started to feel dizzy from lack of oxygen. William felt that he was running out of strength.

"Don't fight me William," the snake hissed. "It's your destiny to end your life here in the swamp with me." William shivered and panicked. I must stay calm, he thought. I fight against it, that could be what I do wrong. He thought about what he had read in a newspaper a long time ago, about what to do if you're attacked. If someone has a knife, run, but if they have a gun you need to attack. The snake is overpowering me, just like a gun. I need to attack. He quickly let go with his hands and turned lightning fast around and stabbed with his knife into the part of the snake that was holding onto his leg. Blood sprayed out and turn the mud red. The snake screamed and loosened his grip around William's leg. William took the opportunity and dived through the opening as fast as he could. He felt how the snake tried to get hold of his foot again but he kicked hard and then he was through. As William came through the opening, he expected the snake to follow him, but luckily, the opening closed as soon as he was through it.

William lay exhausted on the floor. He gasped with effort. It took a long time before he could talk.

"That was a close call," he said between breaths and shivered.

"Too close," Iris whispered.

Both Iris and William felt completely exhausted. When William felt that his strength began to return, he stood up on shaky legs and hung Iris around his neck.

"What do we have here?" he wondered out loud.

It certainly looked a bit different. The walls were still there, but they weren't as high as before. It was brighter, but still a little shady. William removed some mud from his face. It was like they had arrived on a plateau of some kind.

"I don't know? Do you think we should climb the wall and see if we can find the best way out of the maze?" Iris asked. William thought for a moment.

"It sounds like a good idea," he said slowly. "Of course, it might be what the black magic expects us to do and we'll go straight into some kind of trap."

William fell silent for a few minutes as he thought. Eventually he said, "Oh, so difficult, but I think we'll try and we'll see what happens."

Said and done, William tried to find a foothold on the wall while he pulled himself up with his arms. Iris was still on the ground.

"Do you see anything?" She wondered worriedly. William didn't answer. He had some way to go before he was at the top of the wall. When he reached the top, he was baffled. Each path of the maze ended with a wall or a deep gorge. There was no way to get through the maze. It wasn't just a maze built of black magic. It was also the maze of death. In places, he could see skeletons. He exhaled. He tried to take a few deep breaths before he slowly made his way down the wall.

"Well," Iris said urgingly. "What did you see?"

"I have to think a little bit," William answered evasively.

"Do you have to think about what you saw?"

"Exactly," William answered.

William thought quietly. Could it be an illusion I saw, just to make me give up? Or was it real what I saw? Have I just been lured into this maze? William thought back and forth and then he decided. No, it must be an illusion. They must want me to give up. If there wasn't to be a black maze, why would William have programmed a file into Iris about black mazes?

CHAPTER 18
THE BLACK BIRDS

William thought for a moment. He took a deep breath and said, "Iris, we'll continue. I didn't get any clue from what I saw when I climbed up."

"Typical," Iris sighed. They continued to walk down the corridor and soon they noticed that it sloped downwards, which in turn meant that the walls became higher again. The walls continued to get higher and the path they walked on was constantly getting narrower.

"I wonder how this is going to end?" William whispered.

Soon they were walking on a very narrow path with very high walls. Iris turned on her light.

"I don't think there will be any ambient light at all soon." Iris was right. The walls merged into a vault above them. Just as William started to feel uneasy, a room opened up in front of them. At the far end there stood a podium carved out of stone and in the wall above the podium the stone wall was hollowed out and, in the cavity, lay glowing firewood.

"What a strange room," William whispered and a shiver ran down his spine.

"Yes, truly," Iris whispered. "I think we should turn back." They quickly walked back the way they had come from and soon they were back in the black maze. Iris shone with her light around them. It was the same cold and dark walls. At first, William thought it felt good with the cold as opposed to the heat he had just experienced. Both William and Iris felt too tired to say anything so they quietly continued forward in the maze. They walked on and on.

William looked around and felt that it was alarmingly still and quiet. When they had walked for, what William thought to be 15 minutes, he sensed a silhouette ahead of them in the dark. He stopped Iris and pointed at it. Iris shone her light at the dark figure. William could hardly believe his eyes. A large black bird leaned against the wall. The bird looked like a huge raven. The bird made no sound.

"What should we do?" Iris asked. "The bird doesn't move. It looks like it's dead."

William looked at it and indeed it looked lifeless. William searched for some signs of life, but he couldn't see if it breathed. "I don't know," William answered truthfully. "Let's get a little closer and see if it wakes up."

William and Iris slowly moved closer and closer but the bird didn't move. William sensed that there was something unpleasant about the bird.

"We can't just leave it if it's dead, can we?" Iris asked.

"No," William agreed, "but I'm not quite sure what to do. We have to be ready, but ready for what? It's impossible to know," William whispered back.

He stood still and considered his options, but concluded that they really didn't have much choice. If it was a test, they still couldn't get away from it. William looked around, looking for a place to retreat to if they had to but he only saw the dark corridor that seemed to lead straight ahead.

He instinctively felt that he needed something to protect himself with. He took off his backpack and brought out his magic wand. He took the wand in his right hand and put on the backpack again. The magic wand spread a slightly dull, almost gray, glow. William was pleased to see that no mud had gone into the backpack.

"I think we should take a closer look at the bird," William whispered. Iris nodded and both of them slowly and carefully walked towards the bird, as if they were afraid to wake it up. The bird was completely still and now they were only two meters from it.

"You can stay here," William said, turning to Iris. "I'll go closer and examine the bird." William felt tense but at the same time calm. I'm ready, he thought quietly in his mind.

Now he stood right in front of the bird. He lifted the wand to take a closer look at the bird's eyes to see if it was dead. He saw that the eyelids were closed. The bird's chest was not moving and he could not make out that it was breathing. William stood face to face with the huge bird. William was about to turn around and say something to Iris when the bird's eyes suddenly opened and William stared into a pair of blood-red eyes.

"Caw caw," the bird shouted with a tremendous force and stood up. William fell backwards.
"Caw caw," the bird shouted. "You thought I was dead, but I can assure you that I am very much alive."
William felt the angry red eyes stare right at him. William felt how evil radiated from the bird's eyes. William backed away to get some distance between himself and the bird but the bird came threateningly towards him.
"We're alive," the bird croaked, "and there are many of us." The bird opened its large beak and croaked loudly. Out of the bird's mouth came black ravens. It was like a black whirlwind came out of the bird's beak.
"We will soon take over. The black magic will regain its rightful role," the birds croaked.
The croaking was deafening. William held his hands to his ears to muffle the sound. The ravens swarmed above him before they as one dived straight towards him. William brought up his magic wand and held it above him.

"Don't touch me," he hissed. The magic wand flashed and fired a lightning bolt that hit one of the ravens.

"Ouch," the raven croaked.

"Take his backpack," several of them croaked.

The birds came towards William. There were so many ravens that it looked like a big black cloud.

William lifted the wand again and this time he screamed, "Leave me alone!" A big lightning bolt fired from the wand and instead of hitting one of the birds, the bolt flew around him. William looked around and saw that the bolt had made a field of shining light all around him. The birds attacked and William didn't dare to look. "This is it," he thought and sent a thought to his parents and grandparents. "Soon they're here," he thought, trying to keep his composure.

"No, what's this?" the birds croaked. William opened his eyes and saw that the birds could not penetrate the shining light around him.

"Let's try again," the birds croaked, looking at William with their angry red eyes. They took off from several meters away and flew at high speed towards William. This time, William didn't close his eyes. He met several of the birds' hateful gazes. They folded their wings and looked like projectiles with their sharp beaks. They came at him from all directions. This time the birds spread out because they thought that it would be easier to penetrate the light that way. William fell over because the force against the protective light was great. It was like a pressure wave that hit him when the birds hit the protective light. William looked around. He saw that three or four birds had made it a little further into the protective light but that most of them lay beaten outside the shield. William stood up and took a few steps closer to the birds that had managed to get through the protective shield to a certain extent.

"They've been burned," he said out loud. He walked closer to one of the birds that lay dead on the ground. The feathers were almost completely burned off. The smell of burnt meat spread around him.

"Cow Cow," the remaining birds croaked, too bad we couldn't get hold of your backpack with the magic items. The birds gathered in a large cloud. William heard the birds croaking but he couldn't quite make out what they were saying. Suddenly they fell silent. William saw that they were looking at Iris that stood a short distance away.

"No," William screamed. The birds flew in a line formation towards Iris.

"No!" Iris screamed as one of the birds lifted her up with the beak. Iris frantically tried to get free. She kicked and punched with her legs and hands on the beak.

"Do you have her?" One of the birds croaked.

"He's got her," the others croaked in response. "Cow cow, we did well."

"William, help me!" Iris cried out.

William picked up his magic wand. He didn't really know what to do. I need to learn more about magic and how to use it, he thought desperately. I'll have to try anyway.

"Let her go," William shouted, pointing his wand at the bird, but to his surprise nothing happened. There was no flash coming from his wand.

"Cow, he doesn't know how to use his wand," the birds croaked. "That's good," they kept croaking. "He can only protect himself with the wand, he can't save anyone else, caw caw caw. You don't know much about magic, that's good, caw."

William was boiling with anger. Once again, he pointed the wand at the bird holding Iris and screamed to let her go but nothing happened. William knew the birds were right. I have to find another way to save her.

He opened his backpack and saw that there was a rope in it. I didn't put that in my backpack, it must've been grandpa. Hurriedly he tied a loop at one end of the rope. I hope it works, I only have one chance or it'll be too late, he thought. William aimed and threw the rope. He saw it flying through the air and land right around the bird's neck. William grabbed the other end of the rope and pulled with a little jolt which was all that was needed. The surprised bird let go of Iris. Iris fell through the air and William just managed to reached out with his hand and catch her. The other birds saw what was happening and immediately they attacked William. William took out his magic wand and shouted "No!" The birds halted midair. They knew they had no chance against William so they flew away.

"You got away this time, but we'll get another chance," they croaked in chorus. "Believe it, we'll get another chance, we'll get another chance." They flew further into the labyrinth until William no longer could see them. When they were no longer in sight William took down the wand and exhaled.

"That was a close call," Iris said.

"Yes, really," William answered.

"I thought I was finished," Iris said, and William felt how she was shaking in his hand. "There, there," William said comforting while he patted her gently on one side. "You know you shouldn't count me out so easily."

"Where did you learn to throw lasso?" Iris asked,

"Well," William said. "It was actually the first time I tried it. It must've been beginner's luck."

"No way, you must have an innate talent for it." Iris said.

"You know," William said, "I didn't have much choice. I couldn't use the magic wand as it only protects me."

"Mm, that's right," Iris said.

"But we sorted it out."

"You," Iris corrected him, "you took care of it. It takes a lot to be that quick-witted. I'm really proud of you, but now we need to continue."

CHAPTER 19
MEETING WITH THE NEUTRAL MAGICAL TREE

"When I was in the bird's mouth, it must have pushed some small button of some kind because suddenly I heard another ticking sound and a dark voice saying that we have to hurry as time is running out. With each passing minute, the dark magic grows stronger in the maze and if we are to survive, we need to be quick."

"Then we'd better get going," William said. William picked up Iris in his hand and began to run. He ran forward in the dark corridor until he reached a corner.

William stopped. "Oh," William exclaimed as he looked around the corner, it looked like part of the floor was gone. Because it was dark and hard to see, he reached out with one foot.

"There is still floor here," he said half-high to himself. He took another step forward. Still solid ground, he moved his foot slowly forward. "Oh, the floor ends here." William took a step back.

"Iris, can you shine with your light here?"

"Sure, one moment, I'll turn on the light."

"The hole is pretty big," Iris said. "I'll walk up to the edge and shine the light down into it.

"Just be careful. I don't want you to fall down."

Iris nodded. William could see that the hole was only about a meter wide but enough for him to fall helplessly down. He lay down on the ground and stretched his head over the edge. Iris shone with her light straight down, but all they could see was darkness.

"Can you hear that?" William wondered.

Far down in the hole he could hear a faint sound of wind blowing and a soft cool breeze touched his cheek.

"It seems like there's an opening down there," Iris said.

"Yes indeed, but we can't be sure," William replied. "Shine a bit more on the sides."

Iris first directed the light beam to the left, then to the right side and then towards the back wall. As she finally pointed the light beam to the side in front of them, they both cried out. "Look, an old rope ladder!"

"I wonder if we're supposed to climb down?" William wondered.

"I have no idea," Iris answered.

"Do you think that the new ticking sound you hear can guide us?"

"Let's try," Iris said. William lifted her up and stretched his arm down as far as he could into the hole.

"Is there any difference to the ticking sound?"

"I'm not sure, lift me up again and try again."
William lifted Iris out of the hole and put her on the ground.
"I think I should have a sound meter that measures barely audible sounds." She said and searched amongst her files.
"Here! I found it. Now you can see it," Iris said, who had put the symbol on the clockface. William took a closer look at Iris.
"Yes, I can see it," William said. William looked at the little oblong symbol. He saw five black but rather weak vertical lines.
"Do you see the five black lines?" Iris wondered.
William nodded.
"Take me down into the hole again and I'll see if the sound gets louder."
William picked up Iris again and took her as far down the hole he could. He held her tightly because he was worried that he would drop her.
"You can take me up now," Iris shouted. "The ticking sound was a little louder down there. I had to disregard the sound of the soft wind first but after that I noticed a slight increase in the ticking. It reached 6 lines on the meter."

"We have to go down there then," William said.
"You think the ticking sound is going to lead us through the maze?" Iris asked.

"Yes, I think so," William answered, scratching his hair. "It makes the most sense. Since time is limited, I think if we move towards the ticking sound, we are approaching the most central part of the maze."

"You decide," Iris said. "I trust your gut feeling."

William took a deep breath and then he said,

"It's probably best if we hurry up and climb down."

"You can put me in your jacket pocket and I can light the way from there. I believe we'll need all the light we can get."

"Good thinking," William said. He picked up Iris and put her in the chest pocket of his jacket.

"I'll try to shine as brightly as I can."

William put his feet on the first step of the rope ladder.

"I hope it doesn't break," he said and jumped a little on the small wooden plank that formed the first step. He quickly climbed down. When he had climbed for a while, he looked up. Far up he saw the opening.

"It's really dark down here," he said, looking up at the faint light from the opening. I can't believe I found it pitch black up there and down here it's even darker. William continued to climb down. William thought he had been climbing for a long time when Iris lifted herself a bit out of the pocket so she could shine with her sharp beam straight down.

"Not much left now," she said. "About twelve meters, I think." William climbed on.

"What?" William exclaimed. He felt with his foot and he couldn't find any more steps. "The rope ladder ends here." Iris shone downwards. "You're right about that. What do we do now?"

"I'll try to get as close to the ground as possible," William answered. He took a good hold with both hands on the final step and gently took his feet off the step and lowered himself down until he hung fully stretched.

"I can't reach the ground anyway," he said. "Hold on, Iris, I'll let go."

William didn't really know what to prepare for, if he were to fall a long way or if it would just be a little jump.

"One, two, three, now I'll let go!"

Thud, William landed softly on the ground.

"I wonder where we are?" William mumbled. He felt with his hand around him. "Here's a bunch of leaves. Here's something hard. It seems to be a branch. Wait there are several branches," William mumbled. "Did we fall straight into a trap?"

"Wait, I'll light it up around us." Iris crawled out of the jacket pocket. She shone the light around them.

"No, it doesn't seem to be a trap," she said. "It's not a pit we've fallen into, quite the opposite."

William changed position a little.

"Oh, it's moving."

"Hold on," Iris said. "I wonder if it could be..."

She pointed the light beam straight down. "Yes, of course it is."

"What is it?" William wondered. Iris directed the light so that William could see.

"Are we in a treetop?"

"Yes," Iris said, "but it's not a regular tree. This tree belongs to neither light nor dark magic, you could say it is a neutral tree. A tree that relies solely on facts, skills and knowledge."

"What does such a tree do in the maze?" William asked in amazement. "It should be part of the dark magic."

"You might think so," Iris said, "but the fact is that when you build a black maze, there must be neutral elements in it. It can't be only elements from the dark side, if so, the maze would collapse."

"Like dark matter in black holes," William filled in.

"You could say that, much like black holes in space," Iris said. "There must be some kind of counterweight to the dark magic. Mazes that are not dark contains as much dark as light magic, but dark mazes do not have light magic as their counterweight, but use neutral elements to build up the structure. It also means that black or dark mazes are significantly more sensitive and can easily collapse because the balance between light and dark magic is not 50-50. Rather, they contain about 70% dark magic and about 30% neutral elements. It's difficult to balance it properly," Iris said thoughtfully.

"What do we do now?" William wondered.

"We'll have to wait and see what kind of test the tree will give us. I believe that it's considering what to do with us at the moment," Iris replied.

"Ok," William said. "Then I'll sit down a little more comfortably while we wait."

He crawled closer to the trunk and leaned his back against it. This is really comfortable, he thought. William felt relaxed for the first time since entering the black maze. There was something peaceful about sitting high up in a tree. It was a little warmer and he didn't feel frozen anymore.

"I hope we come across more neutral elements," William said.

"You can always hope but chances are slim. I know what you mean, we don't have to be on our guard the same way as before."

William and Iris sat quietly for a while and listened to the sound of the soft wind.

"You are welcome to come down," a dark voice said.

"What?" William said puzzled, then he quickly realized that it was the tree talking. It wasn't the first time William had encountered a talking tree. William rose up a little.

"How do we get down?"

"I'll show you," the voice replied. "Ask your little friend to shine a light on the trunk behind you."

Iris did what the tree said. William could now see a door in the tree trunk.

"Press the door and it'll open. When you look inside, you'll see a wooden slide down. Slide down and I'll be back when you're there."

"Ok," William said and turned to Iris. "All we have to do is open the door." Iris nodded. William pressed with one hand on the door and it slid open with a creaking sound. When he looked down, he saw a wooden slide in light-colored wood. William reached out with his hand to feel it. The wood was smooth and shone in the glow from a black lantern that burned on the right side of the wall. William looked around and noted that it was a very large tree because the inside was about 10 meters in diameter. As he leaned forward, he saw a light shining far down below.

"You don't have to be afraid," the tree said. "Nothing strange is going to happen to you in here. Dark magic has no power over neutral elements. You will be put to a test, but that's something different. Being tested is nothing out of the ordinary. I just need a measure of your skills."

"Come Iris," William said and lifted her up into his arms. He sat down in the slide with his legs first and let go. William felt a tingling in his stomach, it wasn't a nasty feeling but a good one. He laughed. William saw that the wooden slide was tilted in a way that it would not go too fast.

"This is really fun," Iris laughed. William saw that they were getting closer to the bottom and he felt it was a little warmer in the air. The slide ended just above a red plush sofa.

"Oops," William said as he fell to the couch. "At least it was a soft landing," he laughed.

William realized now what was shining and giving warmth. In front of him stood a black stove that burned and crackled homely.

"Welcome to my home," the deep voice said.

William looked around. It felt comfortable even though there wasn't much furniture. The only thing in the room was the plush sofa and a brown carpet. There were no paintings or tapestry on the walls.

"I've been waiting for you," the tree said. "I had given up and thought you'd never come to visit but it seems I was wrong. I started to think that they had hidden me too well in the maze so you wouldn't find me."

"Well," William said, "they had made a hole in the ground that I probably was supposed to fall into."

"My Goodness," the tree exclaimed, "you wouldn't have survived a fall like that. And that's for sure. Tell me, was there a rope ladder?" The tree asked curiously.

"Mm," William answered.

"That's good then. You see, our agreement was that there would be at least one safe way for you to get down to me," the tree said.

"Are there any more neutral elements in the maze?" William wondered

"No," the tree replied. "Since I'm quite big, my presence was enough to stabilize the maze."

"Otherwise it would have collapsed," William filled in.

"Correct," the tree said. "What do you know about neutral elements?"

"Not very much," William answered truthfully, "please tell me."

"All right I will," the tree said. "This maze is very special. It was created with one single purpose." The tree fell silent a moment before he continued. "The purpose was to prevent you from learning the truth about William and the old king's death. The two events are related."

"I suspected as much," William said in a low voice.

"The maze was created by the most famous black magician of the time, Mr. Kanarra, and the murdered king's brother. They placed the maze in the castle and made sure it would be well guarded so that it would be difficult for you to get in. No one but these two knew that the black maze existed, others would have been terrified if they know about it.

A black maze, as I said, is not stable and very complicated to create. Sometimes it is difficult to predict how time will affect the maze and therefore it's very risky to be near a black maze. If anything goes even the slightest wrong in its creation or if the balance is just slightly off, the maze will collapse by itself and devour everything in its vicinity."

"Kind of like a big black sinkhole," William mumbled.

The tree nodded. "The whole castle and the people in it could have been devoured. They would have been trapped in the black hole forever. There is no time, no light. They would have been floating around in the dark forever."

"How come that you were placed in this maze?" William asked.

"I didn't choose to," the tree said, muttering. "But my master, who owned me, thought that something was going on, and before he died he sent me a message that I should go to the new king and offer my services. You see there are very few neutral elements and we are very rare and thus incredibly sought after. They were very skeptical of me at first and didn't really want to use me. They searched for two months for some other neutral element but they couldn't find anyone and their time was limited so they had to use my powers. Otherwise, they would not have been able to create the black maze. But I helped fate a little," the tree chuckled, "and sent out a message to my relatives, the few who remained that they should stay away from the new king and his magician."

"You mean there's only you and a few of your relatives left?" William asked.

"Correct, here in Thyrridea there are only me, my uncle, my great-grandmother and one of my cousins left but in other countries I know that there are a few more but there are not many left who have the original power. Most of us have died. We, who are neutral elements, were here from the very beginning when everything was created. We were the stabilizing force between positive and negative, between plus and minus. Being a neutral element is hard. You must not act out your own thoughts or take a stand for what is happening around you. It is important that your mind is as clean as water. That you don't get carried away in the heat of battle. That is why most neutral elements withdraw from the world and go to inaccessible places just to be left alone and live their lives in peace and quiet without interference from the surroundings.

"What would happen if you took a stand?" William asked curiously.

"Well, that would be the end of my existence," the tree said, sighing. "I would disintegrate, crumble until nothing was left of me."

"Then the maze would also be destroyed," Iris said.

"Yes, that's right, then the maze would also be destroyed," the tree replied. "If I had not promised my master that I would carry out this mission, I would probably have withdrawn. You see, I'm tired and my joints are aching and it would have felt good to be able to leave this maze and just retire and rest." The tree smothered a yawn.

"Soon you might be able to do it," Iris said hopefully.

"That would have been nice," the tree said, yawning again.

"No, I have to get myself together, it's not over yet. Hold on, I'm going to shake myself up to get a bit more alert."

William grabbed hold of the couch and Iris sat safely in the backpack.

"One, two, three, are you ready?"

"Yes," William and Iris shouted.

The whole tree twisted quickly sideways, first to the left and then to the right, and then the same procedure was repeated a number of times. William almost felt a little dizzy from all the sudden turns.

"Now I can feel my strength coming back," the tree called out. "Wonderful! Let's see, where were we? Yes, right, I had just told you a little about how neutral elements work. I guess you're looking for what's at the end of this maze?" The tree said thoughtfully. "What they have tried to hide from you," the tree said, and fell silent while he took a deep breath. "The truth behind the deaths of two important people. William, may his memory live long in our hearts and the death of the old King Valdemar. What I do know is that both events are connected and that the King's brother is behind both in one way or another. That's what my master believed."

"Who was your master," William asked eagerly.

"He was a very wise scientist. Knowledgeable in many different subjects. He was chairman of the Scientific Council."

"Oh," Iris said.

"What is the Scientific Council?" William asked quickly.

"It's a number of people who possess a great deal of knowledge in different subjects. It's men and women who have researched and come up with new discoveries that have benefited our country. They have done research in a variety of fields of science such as physics, magic, chemistry, psychology, astronomy, mathematics and medicine. It is an independent council that is not subject to anyone. Not the king or the church. My master was an expert in the fields of magic, psychology, and astronomy. He had an apprentice and that was William. That William was his apprentice was only known within the council and no one outside the council knew about it. My master saw great potential in William. The idea was that William would gradually become involved in his various fields of research and when my master eventually became too old and could not continue as chairman, William would take over my master's seat in the Council and become the new chairman."

"Did everyone in the Council know about this?" William asked.

"Yes, of course, my master had informed everyone about it, but he also made sure that they made a vow of silence to keep the information within the Council. Being apprentice to the chairman of the Council is a highly sought-after position. A lot of people want that position. If you are chairman of the Scientific Council, you have a lot of power and thus a great influence in the country. The chairman may attend many different events. For example, all order societies in Thyrridea are open to the chairman, thus he can attend any meeting he wishes. In many ways, the position is more elevated than being king. Being chairman means you have a lot of power. No one can deny the chairman insight into various matters, not even the king. Of course, some can hide their plans and intentions, but no one dares to touch the chairman. He's out of everyone's reach. The chairman has such a deep knowledge of magic that it is frightening to most people. He is a person you choose not to have as your enemy. Therefore, there is often a lot of intrigues and foul play.

The chairman also has the opportunity to exercise their legal role and on his own account bring matters to our Supreme Court. It's something that happens very rarely," the tree said.

"Actually, I cannot recall that this has ever happened. I recall only one time that a case was close to being brought to the Supreme Court but it was resolved just before court. On the other hand, an apprentice has a much more exposed role because he has not yet taken office as chairman and there are many who want that position. You become the hot topic in the eyes of many. Therefore, there is a lot of secrecy around the apprentice. You should know that there have been and still are many power struggles in Thyrridea. There is therefore constant speculation and rumors about who has such a position. Some have been murdered on false grounds and after their death it has

turned out that they were most likely not apprentice to the chairman. An apprentice is usually around 25 years of age and it takes around five years to be schooled into the position. At the age of 30 you're supposed to know yourself good enough and to be mature enough to be able to take over the responsibility as chairman."
"But William was not 25 years old."
"That's right. He was only a teenager but my master saw tremendous potential in him. He would have been the youngest chairman ever. William was unfortunately only apprentice for a few months before he was murdered," the tree said with anger in his voice.
He quickly composed himself and lowered his voice.
"Hmm, I can't get upset. Calm as a slow stream of water," he mumbled to himself. "Calm as a slow stream of water. It's no good if I'm destroyed now," he mumbled.

He took a few deep breaths and then continued.
"My master sensed that a plot was behind the deaths of William and the King. Therefore, he booked a meeting with the king's brother and demanded that I, as a neutral element, would be present if they were going to create a black maze. The king's brother and his magician assured my master that they were not going to create a black maze. That they certainly had nothing to hide. My master accepted what they said and informed them that he would anyway cast a spell that would prevent them from creating a black maze without me being part of it. The

king's brother and his magician tried to convince my master that it was certainly not necessary but he stood by his decision."

"Couldn't they get around it by letting someone else construct the maze instead?" William wondered.

"No, my friend, they couldn't. If you have something that you want to hide, you have to make the maze yourself, otherwise it will not work."

"Ok," William said, "then I understand that the king's brother and his magician were angry."

"You're right about that, but what could they do? They couldn't press the matter too much and they had no way of taking our chairman prisoner or murdering him. They didn't have enough power to do that. My master cast the spell and informed me about it. Shortly thereafter, he died of old age."

"Who took over his chairmanship?" William wondered.

"Yes, that was the problem. His apprentice was murdered, and there was no one on the council whom my master saw as a potential candidate. He eventually chose to appoint his younger brother who never had applied for the position. My master considered it important that whoever would assume the position as chairman was not driven by a desire for power but had pure intentions. My master's brother went through the tests and made it. Everything became ready just days before my master passed away."

CHAPTER 20
FOLLOW THE ROOTS

"Now back to the maze. Where was I? Yes, that's right. The former king's brother and his magician have hidden important evidence at the end of the maze. I know of a shortcut that means you don't have to face all the trials that are in the maze." William listened carefully.

"There's a shortcut through the maze. I've allowed my roots to grow in the direction of the end of the maze. They have grown for centuries and come far through the maze. If you follow my roots, you'll arrive close to the exit."

"Kind of like a rope?" Iris asked.

"No, not at all," the tree said, "my roots are not that small. You will be able to go inside my roots. At first, they're quite big so you'll be able to walk upright and then they'll get smaller. In the end, I'm afraid you're going to have to crawl through. When you can't go any further, you can cut your way out of the root and then you will be near the end of the maze," the tree informed with satisfaction.

He felt proud to have come up with this idea almost by himself, but he remembered that his master had helped him to hatch the idea.

"Amazing," William said.

"We will certainly complete our mission," Iris exclaimed.

"Most likely," the tree chuckled contentedly.

"What, most likely?" Iris wondered.

"I mean, you can never really know for sure. There may be something I don't know about, the tree said."

"Mm," Iris said.

"I'm afraid you'll have to leave soon. Time is running out."

Iris looked at her watch. "You're right, we only have two hours left."

"Yes, after that the whole maze collapses," the tree said.

"What happens to you then?" William asked.

"I'll make it, don't worry about me. When the black maze dissolves or collapses after time has run out, I will be the only thing left. I will take the opportunity to head towards the mountains in the north and stretch out my branches properly and enjoy the tranquility that I have longed for. If you want, please come and visit me."

"Can we, really?" Iris said in wonder. She knew that it was very rare for neutral elements to invite others to their secluded place of existence.

"I mean it," the tree said. "Then we can talk more about the old days, but now you have to hurry."

"How do we find you?" William asked.

"Don't worry about it. I will send you an invitation. Now you really have to hurry."

"Sure," Iris said, "one hour and 58 minutes left."

"Take the door straight ahead and then follow the stairs down. When you get as far down as you can, open the wooden door and then you are in my largest root system. You don't have to think about which path to take. I have only allowed one root to grow, so there is no way you will get lost. Good luck, my friends," the tree said.

"Thank you very much," William replied. "See you!"

"We will," the tree said.

"Good bye and thank you for everything," Iris said.

"Thank you," the tree answered, "and do take care of William."

"I will!" Iris exclaimed.

William opened the wooden door and looked down. It is good to not have a fear of heights here. William looked down on a long, narrow and steep wooden staircase.

"Don't forget to hold on to the handrail," the tree informed.

William looked to his right and saw the wooden railing.

"We promise," he shouted.

"Do you want to travel in the backpack?" he asked Iris.

"Yes, that would be nice."

William picked her up and put her down at the top of his backpack.

"Do you think it'll be okay if I hang around your neck instead? So that I'll see more," Iris asked.

"Of course," William answered and hung Iris around his neck. William grabbed the handrail and started to slowly climb down. The stairs felt very wobbly, almost like an unstable ladder. It crackled and moved when William walked on it.

"I wonder if it holds up?" Iris said quietly when she heard the creaking sound.

"I'm sure it will," William replied. William held tightly to the wooden railing and carefully put his feet on one step at a time. He felt relief when he had reached the last step at the very bottom. Not that he was going to admit it to Iris, but still. At the bottom of the stairs, a warm light shone.

"Now we're down at the root," William said while he took a short jump down.

"Then we just have to open the door and start walking," Iris said.

William put her on the ground and wrapped the necklace around the clockwork and closed the medallion.

"He was surely right," Iris said. "I never would have guessed we're inside a root. It's so big. It feels more like I'm walking in a big, long treehouse." William took a deep breath and felt his lungs fill with a scent of wood and sap.

"It feels good to know that we are safe while we walk in here," Iris said.

"Mm," William replied. There was a pleasant reddish glow inside the root that seemed to come from a tree nerve running in the roof of the root.

"I don't even have to use my flashlight," Iris said, pointing at the ceiling.

"Yes," William said, "he really thought about everything." They walked for a while in silence. William felt relief. All the tensions from before disappeared from his body and he felt how he was filled with a pleasant warmth. At the moment they were protected. He relaxed and for the first time in a long time was able to send a thought to his parents and to grandma and grandpa. It'll be nice when it's all over. He felt how he missed them. It must be the tree's care that makes me think of my loved ones, William thought. When I get home, I'm going to jump into the water from the jetty. Then I'll lay in the sun and listen to the birds flying high up in the air. William walked in his own thoughts and hardly noticed that the root was slowly narrowing. At this moment he felt an intense sense of happiness and he thought of the tree with gratitude. Suddenly he heard a noise. He stopped.

"Cow, cow," he heard. "Where are you, William? We're not dangerous. Cow, cow."

William froze. It must be the black ravens. William and Iris stood completely still and pressed themselves against the wall.

"Cow, cow, where are you? Not much time left, does anyone see him?"

"No," another bird croaked back. "He doesn't seem to be here."

William and Iris heard the sound of a bunch of birds flying just above the root. Then the sound disappeared and it was quiet again. William and Iris stood still a while longer to really make sure the birds were gone.

"They seem to be gone now," William said.

"They're really horrible," Iris said quietly, thinking about how she had almost become their prey.

It's a little strange, William thought. He had felt so safe and secure down here and had finally started to relax and then it turned out that he was not safe at all as the ravens were also here. William continued to walk quietly as he pondered. It must be that if the tree is to be neutral, it must allow both evil and good forces to use it. How hard it must be to be a neutral element and never be able to take a stand. No wonder the tree longs for a peaceful and quiet place.

"What did you say?" Iris wondered.

William didn't really want to explain. "It was nothing," he answered quietly. He felt a little disappointed at the tree. William took a short break and then he continued to talk.

"I think we have to be quiet. We don't know who or what we're going to meet. It is important that we are not discovered."

"You're absolutely right," Iris said, who now understood why William was silent.

The root continued steeply downwards. In fact, it was so steep that William had to use much of his strength to lean sharply backwards so as not to fall forwards.

"It's almost like walking in the downslope of a roller coaster," Iris whispered.

"Mm," William whispered back. It was quite exhausting to walk like this for a long time, but just as William thought he had to take a break, he saw that it wasn't far left of the downhill slope. Hopefully it'll not continue much more downhill after this, William thought. William felt relief. The path downhill was really over. It wasn't a plateau that led to another downhill. William and Iris looked around.

"How strange," Iris whispered. The root seems to end here. It really looked like the root ended here. Both William and Iris were both surprised and confused. What would they do now?

"Wait," Iris said, "I'm receiving a signal. Someone is sending me a message. Wait, I'll check," she said quietly. It took a while before Iris was back. William had almost begun to tire when he heard Iris' happy voice.

"Yes, William, you really have a lovely big brother and a tree on our side," she whispered. "It was the tree that sent me a message. It wanted to make sure we had managed it past the birds. It could not warn us earlier because everything the tree says and does is intercepted. But your big brother did manage to get me a wave frequency that the tree could use to send messages directly to me to help you."

William almost began to cry. Then his initial feeling about the tree was right. Tears of joy, gratitude and love for his big brother and for the tree ran down William's cheeks.

"Oh, it's been a lonely journey," he whispered. Iris didn't mind, she understood what William meant.

"Did the tree say anything else?" William wondered.

"Yes, it did. It told me how to get out of this root system and into another root system and that in the future we didn't have to be afraid because the next root system had been kept secret from the dark side."

William became really excited. "Then it's just for you to lead the way to the secret root system."

Iris flew over his head. She sent some light signals, then it was as if she was targeting a place on the wall of the root system that was almost at William's waist height. There William saw that she was sending out signals of light with a certain frequency. The light signals lit up differently brightly and for different lengths of time. All the time, she worked quietly and focused on her task. Then she pulled away and closed her eyes, almost as if she were quietly praying that it would work. William didn't want to say anything that would disturb her.

Within a few minutes, the wall that Iris had sent signals to quietly slid down. William and Iris walked silently through the opening. It wasn't until the wall had closed behind them that they dared to talk to each other.

"That was absolutely amazing," William said in amazement.

Inside the secret root system, it was not as high and wide as in the previous root system. William and Iris now had to walk slightly crouched, at least William had to as Iris once again hung around his neck. The difference between the two root systems, in addition to the fact that the secret root system was narrower, was also that the secret root system was illuminated by a mild yellow light instead of the reddish light from before. William's favorite color had always been yellow so he felt warm in his heart as he crouched his way through the system. The root became narrower and narrower the further they went. In the end, William almost had to crawl.

"I'll probably have to lie down and crawl soon," William told Iris. They got deeper into the earth and as they got further into the root system, the root became thinner and thinner. William could now sense the earth surrounding the root. It was almost as if he could see through it. He continued to crawl at a brisk pace.

"Wait," Iris said, "I think I've got a message."

William stopped.

"It's from the tree," Iris whispered. William felt his heart begin to pound hard in his chest. I wonder what he wants? It looked like Iris's face turned white.

"It's a matter of life and death. The tree has received important information that he believes can help us get closer to the truth. He tells us to search for something or someone in the catacombs of the maze. Once we get to the end of the root, we should go out of it. The tree said that we will not need a knife because the root will be so thin that we can make a hole in it with our hands. Once we get out of the root, we are no longer protected so we have to be very quiet and stealthy."

"Wait, there's new information coming," Iris fell silent. "The tree tells you to follow your heartbeat, William. When your heartbeat gets louder and you feel an instinctive feeling that you need to run in one direction, you have to go against your fear and do the opposite. It's a big test," Iris said.

"So, I need to face my fear and not run away from it?"

"That's right," Iris replied. "The tree tells us that time is very short if we are to make it. That's all," Iris said.

"We have to hurry," William said and began to crawl the fastest he could. After a while, they reached the end of the root. William reached out with his hands against the wall of the root. It felt a bit slippery, but it was still warm. When his hands made it through, a cold gust of wind came right at his face.

"So cold," William exclaimed, and shivered. He made the hole big enough and made his way through it. Once he and Iris were out, a compact darkness met them. He turned around and looked at the root and saw it shrinking and crumbling before his eyes. The light the root had given was now all gone.

"What do we do now?" William whispered.
"Listen to your heartbeat, it'll lead us," Iris whispered back.
"Yes of course," William mumbled. William listened intensively on his heartbeat. At first it was not easy to find it, but after he had focused on it for a while, he heard it better.
"I think we should go to the right on this stone path." Slowly and carefully, they began to walk on the stone path. It was still very dark around them. William felt carefully with his hands on the walls of the corridor and understood from the cold and damp stones in the walls that they were in the catacombs that the tree had described in its message. We're supposed to go to the far end of the catacombs, William memorized the message from the tree in his head. And when I feel my heartbeat getting louder and I want to escape, then I have to run in the opposite direction. Iris and William continued in the catacombs in silence. When they arrived at a junction, William chose the tunnel where his heartbeat sound was best heard. In this way, he and Iris navigated the cold dark tunnel system. When you go in the dark, it is very difficult to know how long you have gone for or how far you have come. That's why William and Iris had no idea how long they'd been in the tunnels. All the while, William focused

on the sound of his heart while trying to pay attention to other sounds as well. They were no longer protected, so they had to be on guard. William noticed after a while that his heartbeat was getting louder. He whispered to Iris that the heartbeat had begun to get louder so that she would be prepared in case he suddenly started running.

Sometimes it's strange in life because even though you know what's going to happen or what you think is going to happen, you're still not really prepared. All of a sudden William felt his heartbeat thundering in his head and how he became completely dry in his throat. An ice-cold wind swept towards William and he heard the wind whisper
"William oh William are you there?"
William felt how he froze with horror and all of his senses screamed to him to run away as fast as he could. For just a second, William got ready to run away before he composed himself.
Quietly to himself he screamed. "I will go on."
William ran like he never had before in his life. His head kept pounding with his heartbeat and all the while he heard the ice-cold wind, not whispering but instead screaming.
"William, William, don't think you can escape me."
But William just kept running and eventually the voice, wind and heartbeats in William's head subsided. William stopped, bent forward with his head between his legs while feeling the taste of blood in his mouth. He took a

few deep breaths and tried to calm down his breathing. He was completely exhausted and he was breathing very fast. I don't think I've ever run this fast. William was breathing heavily and his mouth was completely dry. He squatted down and searched in his backpack for the water bottle. He took a few sips of water.

"I was almost completely exhausted," he gasped, turning to Iris, who hung around his neck.

"I understand that," she said. "It takes a lot of effort to run for your life."

"Mm," William responded and took another sip of water.

"Look, can you see it?" William asked.

"Where?" Iris asked.

"Over there," William said and pointed with his hand to the ground a little further ahead in the dark. "There's something there."

William walked carefully towards the shadow he saw. He began to feel an eerie sensation in his body. There's something that's not quite right. He slowly moved closer. The shadow did not move. Strange, William thought to himself, has anyone left a jacket here? The closer he got to the shadow, the more he thought it looked like a pile of clothes. He moved closer to it and now he was standing right beside the pile. He bent down to touch the pile of clothes. William flinched.

"What's wrong?" Iris asked quickly.

"I think there's someone here," William answered.

"What!" Iris exclaimed. "Is the person dead?"

"I don't know." William replied. "Can you turn on your light so that I can see better."

Iris quickly turned on her light. She stood a bit away from the body because she thought it was somewhat horrifying. William squatted down and touched the body again.

"Are you awake?" He asked quietly, but received no answer. The body was curled with its head against the wall. William gently turned the body around to be able to see the face.

"No!" He screamed. The face was barely recognizable, but William saw that it was Father Ormund who had mysteriously disappeared after he gave William the map of the catacombs under the church. His face was completely white and haggard. He looked completely dried out. The skin had sunken in at the cheeks and cheekbones where clearly visible. William pulled the body up in his arms and patted Ormund on the forehead.

"What have they done to you? What have they done to you?" He mumbled. William believed that the body weighed barely 20 kilos. He looked closely for any sign of breathing but could not see any. He took his hand and held it about a centimeter above Ormund's mouth, but he could not feel any air coming out of it.

He cannot be dead, William thought. William thought feverishly about what to do. I'll try CPR. William was about to lay Father Ormund down and begin CPR when

Ormund made a sound. William took him up in his arms again. Iris had now ventured forward.

"He's barely alive," William said.

Iris looked at the haggard body.

"Is that you, William?" a weak voice said.

"Yes, it's me," William answered.

"You came and saved me." Ormund looked up briefly and then closed his eyes again. "My prayers were answered. You came."

"I'm going to get you out of here. I promise," William said.

Ormund opened his mouth again to say something but closed it again.

"Water, Iris, can you give me water to Father Ormund." Slowly William brought the water bottle to Ormund's mouth and he took a sip of water. Father Ormund began to speak again.

"William, listen carefully. I don't have much time left and there's a lot you need to know. In your grandfather's order, there is a second vice-master, Mr. Sauluson. He has stolen some books from the order's library and it was he and two other men who sought me out in my room in the cathedral. They demanded that I would show them William's grave and give them the map of the catacombs. I refused," Ormund said in a weak voice.

"Get some rest," William said.

"I can't. I have to tell you what I know, I don't have much time left, William. They knocked me unconscious and then they held me captive in a dungeon here and tried to make me reveal the way to William's grave by starving me, but they didn't succeed. When they realized I was about to die, they dumped me here."

William clenched his fists so that his knuckles whitened with anger.

"You have to watch out, William, promise me that. These men are evil. They kept asking if I had met you and if I knew anything about you and your grandfather. Of course, I refused to tell them. But there's one thing, William. I don't know if you have it, but they asked me several times if I had William's green ring. I don't know what kind of ring it is or what it can do, but there's something important about it."

"I have it," William whispered.

Father Ormund smiled happily.

"Wait and I'll show you William's ring." William gently placed Ormund's head on his jacket on the floor, rummaged around in the backpack and picked up the black box. He put the priest's head on his lap.

"This is my big brother's ring," William whispered. William carefully lifted the lid of the box.

"May I hold it?" Ormund whispered with a strained voice.

"Of course," William answered. Ormund carefully took the ring and held it up in front of his face.

"How beautiful it is," he gasped, "so incredibly beautiful." Then something strange happened because when Father Ormund's breath touched the green stone, it began to sparkle and shine in green. The entire tunnel was lit up and bathed in a green light.

"William, how beautiful," he gasped. "I am extremely happy!" Then Ormund took a deep breath. It sounded more like a sigh and then Ormund's head fell down to his chin.

William understood that Father Ormund had taken his last breath. But instead of feeling sadness and anger, William instead felt a sense of serenity spreading in his body.

"I will miss you," he whispered and closed Ormund's eyes. The whole room bathed in green and when William looked at the wall, he saw a black text appear. *"Rest in peace Father Ormund. You will now meet your loved ones."* Tears rolled down William's cheeks and he sobbed when he suddenly heard Ormund's voice, but this time his voice didn't sound weak, but full of life.

"I have moved on and will soon be with my loved ones. My old body is just a shell and my soul are now with God. I just want to thank you for coming to me and letting me die in peace. Take care of my remains and bury them in the church. Take care of yourself, William, and stop the second vice-master. He belongs to the dark side."

The voice disappeared and it became completely silent.

CHAPTER 21
THE BOOK OF THRUTH

William felt overwhelmed. The tunnel still bathed in a greenish glow. William looked at the ring, still in Ormund's hand. He saw how the green light began to fade and it gradually became darker in the tunnel. William intuitively reached for the green ring and took it into his hands. I wonder why they were looking for the green ring? He thought. There must be something special about it. William put the ring on his right middle finger. Then something strange happened. William felt how his compass mark became hot and it was like the whole stone was filled with life. It was like the stone came alive from his blood. William looked at the stone and in it he could see all sorts of colors, blue, gold, silver, purple, red, yellow. He felt the blood pulsating throughout his arm and out through his hand to his middle finger. William looked fascinated at the stone, which now completely exploded in a multitude of colors.

"Beautiful!" he exclaimed. When his breath touched the stone, something happened that William was not prepared for. The whole stone was filled with a shimmer of gold, and through the shimmer of gold a book appeared. William retrieved a magnifying glass from his backpack. At first, he could not discern what it said on the cover of the book, but the text gradually became clearer. The letters were squiggly and they shone like diamonds in sunlight. William could now see that it said, *"The Book of Truth. A book that can only be opened by someone with a clear conscience and a bright soul. You only have one search. Nothing more. However, the answer to your question will be visible to others and cannot be questioned by anyone. Think carefully about what you want to know and then ask the question out loud."*

William thought long and hard. He felt strongly that he wanted to complete the mission that his older brother had begun.

"Who killed the old King Valdemar?" He asked.

William saw how the book in the stone opened up and a gust of wind flipped through the pages until it stopped and a page lay open. William carefully read the squiggly letters that shone like a diamond. *"The old King Valdemar was murdered by his brother Karl the first and his magician Sir Kanarra. This has had consequences, which means that the wrong king now rules the country. The rightful king is in the family of William the Great. Also known as your big brother and bearer of the compass mark. William was also betrayed and murdered."*

Then he was right, William had time to think before he heard a dark powerful voice.

"You have completed your question and received the true answer, consider it carefully." The voice said and faded away and William saw how the book slammed shut within the stone in the ring while the outlines of the book faded and then disappeared completely from the ring.

William had only time to think for a few seconds when Iris suddenly screamed.

"William, duck!"

Instinctively, William ducked and it was lucky that he did. A razor-sharp dagger flew just above William's head and hit the stone wall. William was quickly on his feet and got hold of the dagger when three men threw themselves at him.

Oh my God, William thought. It's the second vice-master and his two companions.

The compass mark burned hot on his wrist and William fought bravely and struck several strokes with the dagger. I can't give up, he thought. I need to find out the truth about who killed my big brother.

The three men had tremendous strength but William used all his agility to try to escape them. It's me or them, echoed in his head. William fought furiously for his life and for his big brother. Within his mind, he saw the sequence of when his big brother had been murdered. The battle went on for a long time and William felt his strength failing. In the end, he lay pinned down on his stomach against the stone floor with two men holding him.

"Finally, bearer of the compass mark, I have the pleasure of killing you," the second vice-master hissed. "But first I'll take the green ring off your finger so that no one will ever find out the answer to your question."

He crouched down next to William's right hand. William tried to clench his fist to prevent it, but the second vice-master took his right foot and stomped hard on William's hand. William screamed in pain as he heard bones in his hand being broken.

"There, now it shouldn't be so hard to take it off." The second vice-master tore and pulled on the ring, but it refused to let go of William's finger.

"It shouldn't be so damn difficult! Give me the dagger, and I will cut off the finger!"

William shut his eyes and waited for the pain. But instead of pain he heard a thundering scream.

"No! I couldn't save your big brother but I will save you!"

At that moment, the sound of tree roots ripping apart stonewalls was heard and lots of stones were rolling down into the tunnel. William heard a swooshing, cracking sound and after that a loud bang. William quickly crawled up and saw that the second vice-master and his two companions lay dead by the stone wall, crushed by enormous blows from the roots.

"They're dead William," the tree said. "I finally had the opportunity to make a difference. How do you feel, William?"

William felt how his whole body shook. Partly because of the tension from believing that his final moment had come and partly because he had never seen three dead people up close before.

"It's not a pretty sight," the tree said, "but it's a sight that I'd much rather come to terms with than if it would have been you who was dead."

When the tree said those words, William began to cry. He cried so hard that he shook even more.

"My dear friend," the tree whispered softly. "I don't have much time left. I'll carry you and Iris up to me. I want to have time to talk to you before I have to leave this earth as well."

William felt the tree roots gently wrap themselves around him.

"Don't forget Father Ormund," William said.

"Of course not," the tree answered softly. "I'll take him with me."

William closed his eyes and felt the roots of the tree carry him through the stone tunnels and up to the heart of the tree.

When William opened his eyes, he sat in the crown of the tree. The tree held him tenderly and spoke in a calm voice.

"William, I don't have much time left, but I'm extremely

glad I was able to save you. There will be no grove for me. You see that as a neutral element, I'm not really allowed to intervene in the events of life, but I'm incredibly glad I had the opportunity and was able to make a difference. I have been waiting for this moment for a long time! However, it also means that I have to take the consequence of my actions, which in my case means that I will soon die."
William hugged the tree trunk tightly.
"Don't be sad, William. I couldn't save your big brother, but I'm very proud that I was able to save you. As proud as I feel now, I've never felt! William, you have a very special destiny ahead of you and I'm glad I've met you."
The voice of the tree began to become a little weaker.
"You need to know one more thing, my death means that the whole maze will collapse. It is important that you are prepared for it. With my last breaths, I will blow you, Iris and Father Ormund's body back to your grandfather and the boat. But first I need to look at your hand, William?"
William reached out his hand to the tree and the tree took one of its roots and squeezed out some of its sap that dripped down on William's hand.
"Good, now it will soon be healed," the tree said with a satisfied tone. "Now my friend, it's time for you to leave."
William didn't really want to. He wanted to stay with the tree. The tree looked at William.
"I understand, but it's time. I'll see you sometime in the future. You know life doesn't end when you die."

The tree made one final effort and filled its lungs with air and began to blow. William felt a warm breeze take hold of him. He was lifted up by the gentle breeze. Below him he saw the tree shriveling. It kind of dried up and shrank. Root after root, branch after branch blackened. Eventually, the tree crumbled into a grey-white ash. Then he heard something that sounded like a huge avalanche. Stones, walls, everything in the maze collapsed. William saw how a huge hole formed in the ground, much like a crater.
I can't believe we made it. The warm breeze carried William, father Ormund and Iris in the air. When William looked down, he saw how the crater had swallowed half the castle. People were running around in panic.
I hope no one was hurt, William thought. But grandpa, we left him in the castle. I wonder what happened to him, the mirror Wallace and Goblet?

William flew over the forest and out over the sea. The day began to turn to dusk and William saw the sun setting on the horizon. Far out at sea, he saw what looked like a small dot bobbing on the sea. As he got closer, he realized it was a boat. He turned to Iris.
"Isn't that our boat?" Iris shone up.
"It must be. It looks exactly the same."
The dark blue sail glimmered in the evening sun and the foam whirled around the bow. The warm breeze subsided when they were only a few meters above the boat. Softly, the three of them landed on the wooden deck with a

barely audible thud. William stood up and lifted up Father Ormund's body. He put him in a small room in the stern. William wrapped Ormund's coat around him and took off his jacket and put it as a pillow under his head. William reached down and patted Father Ormund's white cheek.

"You have to rest here for a little while until we can bury you in the cathedral," he said softy and then he closed the door carefully.

William immediately began to look for his grandfather. He felt a faint uneasy feeling in his stomach. I hope he's all right.

"They don't seem to be up on deck," William said anxiously.

"Maybe they're down in the cabin," Iris said comfortingly. With quick steps, William was already on his way down the small wooden staircase leading to the lower deck.

"Wait for me," Iris called out breathlessly as she ran on her little legs.

"Hey, we're here!" William shouted. His grandfather sat in a rocking chair and his cheeks were all grey. Fritz quickly stood up and his cheeks began to turn red.

"Oh, William! You made it," he said in a mushy voice. Big tears ran down his face. "I've been so worried, William, you can't imagine." Fritz held William in his arms.

"My good boy," he whispered. "My William."

William and Fritz both cried. William felt that he was slowly starting to relax. Somewhere inside of him, he had had a feeling that he would never see his grandfather again. Relief began to spread inside of him. William didn't know how long they stood and held each other. It was as if time stood still. Finally, when all the feelings had begun to subside, William came to think of the mirror and Goblet.

"Where's Goblet and Wallace?" William asked.

"There's Goblet," Fritz said, pointing. William looked up and now he saw that Goblet was sitting on a chair and watching them. Goblet immediately hoovered up.

"Give me a hug, huh?" Goblet said.

"Of course," William laughed and it wasn't long before Iris joined the hugging party as well.

"Where's Wallace?" Iris wondered.

"He has gone to visit his relatives and friends. With his spell broken, he is now free to do whatever he wants," Fritz explained.

"Ah yes, I remember," William murmured.

"But he promised to be ready if we need his help. I think we both need to get some food, then we have to talk," Fritz said seriously.

"Yes, indeed," William said with a fateful voice.

"Did I hear food," Goblet chuckled, "finally! It's been so gloomy here on the ship since we left Kalvador. I will immediately get some sandwiches and hot chocolate ready and Fritz, you probably need some coffee," Goblet said firmly.

"Let's go to the galley," Fritz said.

It felt homely to sit down at the round table in the ship's kitchen and it wasn't long before Goblet had prepared ham, cheese and liver paste sandwiches, a jug of hot chocolate and a jug of hot coffee.

Goblet and Iris understood that Fritz and William needed to talk undisturbed, so when the table was set with the food and white linen napkins and the five-armed candlestick was lit, they discreetly left the kitchen.

William and Fritz ate in silence.

"I'm certainly hungry", Fritz murmured while he ate his fifth sandwich. William noticed that he too was really hungry, with all the excitement that he'd been through he had not felt how hungry he was. Eventually, they were both full.

"Now William," Fritz said with a serious voice. "You have to tell me everything that has happened to you."

William got a lump in his stomach when he started to think back on the maze. He took a few deep breaths, gathered his thoughts and then began calmly and methodically to tell Fritz everything that he and Iris had been through at the castle. He was very careful not to forget a single detail. William talked for a long time and by the time he was done dawn was approaching. Fritz listened intensely the whole time to William and William noticed how Fritz's facial expression became more and more grim, almost angry. Finally, William was finished.

After a moment of silence Fritz said angrily, "That bastard. If I had known that my order was tainted by such evil, I would have acted a long time ago. The worst thing is that there may be even more evil in the order." Fritz closed his mouth with a grim expression again. He quickly went through the brothers of the order in his thoughts and found that he could not be sure of a single one of them, not even the Grand master. But a plan began to take shape in Fritz's head.

"Hm," he said with a low voice, "if I understand you correctly William, no one knows that the second vice-master Mr. Sauluson and his two companions are dead?" Fritz could quite easily figure out from the description who the companions were, they were also brothers of the order. They had only been in the order a short time and therefore had not advanced high in the hierarchy, but still. The brothers of the order that had been involved will surely get to taste their own medicine. Fritz face was now white from restrained anger.

"I don't know if the news that the maze is destroyed has begun to spread yet," William said lowly. "If the rumor spreads, then it may be that order brothers who knew the assignments of the second vice-master, Mr. Sauluson and his two companions will try to contact them."

"I know, it's an uncertain time we live in," Fritz replied. "It will also have a major impact on the current monarchy."

"I understand," William said. "It is not the rightful king who rules Thyrridea now."

"William, I think we need to split up quite soon. I will deal with my order and you have to find out who murdered your big brother."

"But it may be related," William began to protest.

"It may well be my boy, but we can't be sure of it."

There was another moment of silence.

"How soon will you leave," William wondered thoughtfully?

"As soon as possible." Fritz said, "I will take Father Ormund with me, when I've found the guilty in my order, I can arrange a proper funeral for him. I would also like to bring Goblet with me."

William was heartbroken. He had wanted to spend time with his grandfather, but he understood that they had to act swiftly.

"Yes, take him with you. I'll take Iris. I think I will need her help," William said.

"Let's do it," Fritz said. They went silent. Iris and Goblet who had left them alone could now hear that the conversation had ended. A timid knock on the door awakened William from his thoughts.

"Is it ok if we come in?" Iris asked.

"Of course," William replied.

"We have talked through what has happened," Fritz said, and laid out a rough plan on how they should continue.

"Are there two missions?" Goblet asked thoughtfully. William and Fritz nodded. They quickly went through the plans together with Goblet and Iris who listened carefully while they ate.

"Then we have no time to lose," Goblet said.

"True," Iris filled in. "Let's see, how do we quickly get ashore."

"I need to hurry and go to the order and put Father Ormund in a chapel until he is buried," Fritz said.

"I don't really know what to look for," William said.

Iris frowned, "We need another means of transportation. I wonder how we're going to get it."

"I think we can talk to Axel," Fritz said. "Maybe he has an idea?"

William took out Alexander's magic wand and walked up to the clock. Goblet and Iris knew what to expect and immediately began to clear the table. William hit three times with the wand on the clock. The table turned upside down and the wheel appeared.

"Oh, hello," Axel shouted cheerfully. "Now we're going fast. Old Maran runs at many knots," Axel laughed.

"Axel, my grandpa and I have two missions that we need to complete as soon as possible. Is there any way grandpa and Goblet can get away from here quickly?"

"Hm, it's wise of you, William, that you stay on the ship because it's a safe place for you and I almost feel in the air how evil wants to get to you. It's strong magic that we're dealing with." Axel thought a short time ago. "We have the Frog."

"What is the Frog?" William wondered.

"It's a small submarine that Alexander and I built a long time ago. It's really fast," Axel said happily. "Hold on here," Axel said, "pointing to the helm, and I'll show you how the Frog works."

William and Iris quickly said goodbye to Goblet and Fritz who got up and followed Axel up on deck.

Before Fritz closed the door behind him, he turned around and looked William in the eye. "I love you. Never forget that."

"And I love you," William replied. William saw tears in his grandfather's eyes and he tried hard not to start crying. Fritz walked through the door and then he turned around again. "William, let's get them."

"We will," William answered, feeling the strength return to his body.

William and Iris were alone in the galley. William held the steering wheel tightly and looked at the map that appeared on the window. He saw that they were not far from the coast.

"I wonder where we should go?" William said thoughtfully. I have no idea where to go or who to look for, to find out who betrayed and murdered William. He looked at the map again and saw that now there were two dots flashing. A green dot had been added. It must be the Frog, William thought aloud. I get a feeling that there is something I've forgotten or missed. William began to drum with his fingers on the wheel.

"Are you impatient?" Axel asked, who had just come down the stairs.

"Well," William replied. "I don't really know where to go."

"Ah, you don't have a final destination?" Axel said. "All I know is that I need to find out who betrayed William."

"Mm," Axel replied. "It was something that Alexander thought about a lot."

"I might find a clue amongst Alexander's things," William said aloud.

"It's very possible," Axel said. "I can take over the helm and you can go and have a look."

Where's the chest? Where could grandpa have put it? William's eyes swept across the small kitchen. I'll look in the living room.

When he got out, he saw that the chest was on his bed. He opened it and immediately saw that there was not much sand left in the hourglass. William realized that the hourglass was magical because it didn't matter how he put it. The golden sand constantly flows through it anyway. There's not much time left, he thought. William tried not to panic that the 500 years soon had passed and that the magical objects would lose their powers. He said out loud "Let's see if I can figure it out." Iris jumped up on the bed. In the chest there was a lock of hair, a grayed photo, William's magic book and an ink pen. I wonder if they belong together in any way? William pondered long and hard.

"Don't forget me in the equation. I was in the chest as well," Iris said. Iris jumped into the chest.

"It's good that you reminded me," William said. William looked closely at each object. There must be a reason why they were saved. What could it be? William thought. He began by trying to figure out if there was any common denominator among them but found none.

I think I need something to write on. Sometimes it's easier to think clearly if you write it down.

He opened William's magic book. I wonder if there might be an empty page in it. William flipped through the pages. No, all pages seem to be full. William didn't really know why he did what he did, but he got an impulse. Somehow, they have to belong together.

"Iris, who's in the photo?"

"Oh, it's a picture of Alexander when he was old," Iris answered. William picked up the photo and met Alexander's gaze. Although the picture depicted an old gray-haired man, there was something youthful and a little tricky with his eyes, William thought quietly.

William continued to meet Alexander's gaze. Suddenly it was as if everything around William had disappeared.

"It must be an illusion," William mumbled and rubbed his eyes. He thought the mouth in the photo was moving. Once again, he looked into Alexander's eyes. Now it looked like the whole face began to move and William heard the voice of an old man.

"Take William's magic book, put the lock of hair and the pen in the book. Hang the gold medallion around your neck, hold the magic wand in one hand and place the hourglass against your compass mark."

The face stopped moving and the voice went silent. William gasped for air. It felt like he had really met Alexander. I have no time to lose. He did what Alexander said. When he put the hourglass against the compass mark, something strange happened. William saw how the golden sand began to flow in the opposite direction and everything around William disappeared.

He floated in the dark and suddenly landed hard against cold rocks. William saw his brother and the dark figure who had just murdered his big brother. I must have gone back in time, William thought. It's the moment right after my brother was murdered. He heard the dark figure mumble something. William saw that his brother was lying there injured. What am I supposed to do? William thought feverishly when he heard Alexander's voice.

"You can't save your brother, but you can find out who killed him. Use the magic wand and point it at the traitor and say the words 'Ostende litterae insidiatoris'."

William did what he said. Suddenly a strong wind came into the room and the dark-dressed man's cape fell from his head.

"It's you, Mr. Argilini? How could you?" William heard his older brother whisper. "You've been my magic mentor all these years. How could you betray me?"

William felt how rage filled his body. He lifted his magic wand again and screamed die! A lightning bolt flew from the wand and hit Mr. Argilini in the chest. He looked around in amazement and then he fell to the ground. William ran up to his older brother and sat down by his head. He removed a lock of hair from his forehead.

"You're my little brother. You came!" William the Elder whispered barely audible. "I see you have my magic book, my magic wand and my magic things. I understand that Alexander got my message. He's my true friend. Have you solved the mystery of who murdered the king? Was it the Kings brother?"

William nodded and showed him the ring.

"Thank you, my beloved little brother. Alexander will soon come and take care of my dead body, but do not mourn. There is another afterlife where I will meet my father. Now I can do it in peace and know that my power will live on in you. But there's one thing I want to ask of you. Spin the magic wand five turns around the hourglass and say the words 'Frange animum dulcedine'. Then the spell that my mentor has placed over my magical objects will be broken and they will not lose their magic power after 500 years."

William did as he said, and after he had uttered the words, the objects twitched as if they were regaining their former power.

"Goodbye, my beloved little brother. I can feel the strength in my body drain away from me."

William bent down over him and looked his brother deep into the eyes. "I love you."

"And I love you, our bond will always be there and is stronger than the gap between your world and the world that I will soon be in. Never forget that, our bond is forever. In the future when you die, I will be there waiting for you. Our band is forever. Don't forget that."

"I promise," William answered and noticed that his older brother no longer could speak. William held his hand and met his eyes. His older brother closed his eyes and William heard him draw his last breath. William sat completely still. He didn't want to get up. He felt that he just wanted to sit quietly by his big brother's side. William had no idea how long he had been sitting there when he heard Iris' soft voice.

"I think it's time for us to go home." William looked up. The room was now mostly dark except for a glimmer of light that found its way through the window and shone faintly on his brother's face. It looked peaceful.

"You're right," William said, straightening up.
"Say the words 'volo ire in domum suam', and we'll be home."

William did as she said and the ground around him began to spin and he felt that he once again was lifted up and traveled in the dark. This time he landed on a soft carpet. The room he was in was almost completely dark except for a lit fireplace a little further away. William rubbed his eyes.
"Where are we?" He whispered quietly to Iris.
"I think we're in the house that belongs to your grandfather's order."
"Oh," William said. "Then something isn't quite right. I thought we were going to come home to our house."
"Me too," Iris whispered back. "I see that we're in their library. Come on, let's hide behind a bookshelf."
William heard footsteps and angry voices coming closer. He quickly got up and just managed to threw himself into cover behind one of the wooden bookshelves when the door opened.
"I can't believe the second vice-master is dead."
"And two more members of the order," the Grand master filled in. "We must notify the king immediately. We can't allow this news to go public. The entire monarchy will be overthrown."
"You're absolutely right," the other man said. "All our hard work and secrecy would be for nothing."

"Yes, and think of our ancestors struggle to keep the secret. Our ancestors killed that William and put an end to the speculation."

"You mean Mr. Argilini? He's the one who killed the Compass Bearer. Imagine what the promise of money and power can do to people. He would have become the most powerful black magician ever. Too bad he died in the battle."

"Mm," the other man replied. "Now we just have to eliminate Fritz and everything will return to normal, but we have to be clever. It shouldn't look like a murder."

"I'm already one step ahead of you," the grand master laughed. "I've put a snake that I've enchanted in his bed. When he lays down, the deadly bite will take his life and best of all, the snake and venom will both dissolve within 10 minutes so no one can trace the real cause of death. They'll just think he died of cardiac arrest."

"The old man. I can't believe he thought he could trust you."

"It's not that strange, is it?" the Grand master said. "I've been his best friend for almost 50 years. What is it they usually say? Keep your enemies closer than your best friends," he chuckled to himself.

"All we have to do now is to wait. We'll probably have to wait 20 minutes before we go downstairs and alert the others in the order that Fritz is dead in his bed."

"Yes, he needs at least ten minutes to change and brush his teeth and then the rest goes quickly."

William's heart began to pound hard. We have to warn grandpa. May they leave soon.

"We need to take the emergency exit down to your grandfather's bedroom," Iris whispered barely audibly to William, pointing to a door 20 meters away.

William slowly stood up and they sneaked silently towards the door. I hope the door doesn't squeak, he thought quietly to himself as he pushed down the handle. To his surprise, not a single sound was heard when the door slid open. Phew, William breathed out. He was so eager to hurry and save his grandfather that he forgot to close the door softly behind him and a dull sound was heard when the door slid closed again.

"What was that?" One of the order brothers said to the other.

 "You worry too much," the grand master replied.

"Maybe, but nothing can go wrong. I'll go and take a look between the bookshelves."

"You do that. I'll be sitting in the chair over there."

The other man began to search around in the room. I have a feeling, but of course it might just be my imagination. There's no one here. It's probably just my nerves that plays tricks with me, I hope it'll soon be over.

William and Iris were already on their way down the stairs to the floor where Fritz's bedroom was located. They quietly walked through the dark rooms and hallways.

"Over there," Iris said, pointing to a dark wooden door. William ran fast and opened the door and shouted, "Grandpa, don't lie down in the bed!"

When William entered the room, he looked around in amazement. Grandpa sat in an armchair in the dimly lit room with a grim look.
"William? What a surprise," he said.
"I have to warn you," William said.
"It's not necessary," his grandfather said calmly. "I already know and then he pointed to a mirror that stood by the bed."
"But, it's Wallace, isn't it?" William was surprised.
"Yes," grandpa replied, "he has seen how my best friend, or I must say, my former best friend betrayed me and put a magic snake in my bed." Fritz got an angry look in his face.
"Yes, but he's not alone," William said. "He has several brothers of the order on his side," William said and told Fritz and Wallace what they had seen and heard in the library. Fritz clenched his fist.
"Then we just wait for them to arrive in 20 minutes to see their handywork. I wonder if they have anyone else that supports them?"
"It's hard to say," Wallace said.
"Maybe we should trick them? I lay down in bed and pretend to be dead to look at the reactions of the other members," Fritz said.

"What about the snake?" William asked.

"I'll take care of it," Wallace replied calmly.

"Hmm, I wonder what to do?" Fritz said. "I need to know if there are any others involved in the plans. Maybe there's another way?"

They sat quietly and thought for a moment.

"I can mix a drink that will make you appear dead for a few hours," Goblet said, "but you will hear everything they say."

"Then it's settled," Fritz said and turned to William. "William, you have to be my ears and eyes and sneak around the house and find out the reactions."

William hesitated. He thought the plan was a little too risky, but then he said. "Alright, you know the order better than I do."

"We'll help you," Goblet replied.

"Yes, but I want someone to stay and watch over grandpa so that no one takes the opportunity and really kills him when he lies there seemingly dead."

"You don't have to worry," Wallace said. "My powers and magical skills are strong enough to protect your grandfather."

William felt a little safer.

"Yes, let's go then," Fritz said.

Wallace pronounced a spell and William saw how something started to move in the bed. It must be the snake, he thought shivering. The movement stopped quickly.

"It's dead now," Wallace said. William went over and pulled off the bedspread. There was a 30 centimeters long black snake. After a few minutes, it crumbled in front of his eyes and completely dissolved.

"It's gone now," William said. William pulled his hand over the sheet to make sure there was no trace left of the snake. There was not a grain left.

"Unpleasant," William said quietly to himself.

"Are you okay?" Grandpa came up to William and put his arm around his shoulders.

"Yes," William murmured.

"You know I won't be dead for very long and nothing's going to happen to me. I promise you, but I have to see if there are more traitors in the order or I risk to really be killed when I'm not prepared."

"I understand that," William replied. "I just want it to be over soon so we can relax."

"It'll soon be over," Fritz said, stroking his hair.

"Are you ready?" Goblet asked.

"Yes, I'm ready," Fritz answered. He lay down in the bed and William put the bedspread over him. Goblet sat on the edge of the bed and Fritz drank the mixture.

"Now I'll put a protective spell over him," Wallace explained. For a moment Fritz was surrounded by a light blue glow that disappeared after a little while.

"Right, it's ready now," Wallace said. "You don't have to worry, even if you can no longer see the protection I put over your grandfather I can assure you that it's still there. I put it around his body so that you can sit next to him without being pushed away."

"I'm going to lie under the bed," Goblet said. "Just in case my magical knowledge is needed. Look, William, it's time for you to leave. The traitors will be here in a minute," Goblet said.

William hung Iris around his neck and then he opened the door, turned off the light and closed the door behind him. He snuck on light feet so that no one would hear him.

"I wonder where we should hide?" Iris whispered.

"Let me think," William said. "If we hide in their ceremony room, we'll only find out the official thoughts surrounding grandpa's death. It must be a room where you go to talk undisturbed. Where you are not afraid of being caught."

They heard footsteps approaching from the stairs.

"Quickly, let's hide behind the sofa," Iris said, pointing. William had just time enough to dive behind the sofa when the footsteps got closer. To his surprise, only one of the men showed up in the dark. He stood at grandpa's door and put his ear to the door to listen. It was as if he made sure it was completely silent in the room. Then he gently knocked on the door. First once, then again.

"Fritz, are you awake? It's just me. Let me come in."

There was no response from Fritz's room. The man knocked again, but this time harder.

"Fritz, are you awake?" He grabbed the handle and opened the door. "Fritz are you there?" Still no answer. He turned on the lights and William heard him walk with careful steps towards the bed.

"Quickly," William said. "We have to sneak out now. I think we should go back to the library. It seems to be the place where they usually have their unofficial meetings." William snuck up the stairs and looked for the door to the library. This time he listened carefully before opening the door.

"Wait," Iris said. "What should we say if there is someone there?"

"Then I'll just say that grandpa asked me to pick up a newspaper that he wanted to read before he goes to sleep."

"So, we need to turn on the lights so as not to seem suspicious," Iris said.

"Exactly," William replied. He opened the door and reached for the light switch. The room was illuminated by a soft glow. William noted that they were probably alone because the action did not provoke any reaction. He breathed out and turned off the light switch and the library once again was in darkness. William and Iris sneaked around the bookshelves for a while to make sure they were alone.

"I wonder how long it will take before we know if there are more traitors?" Iris said.

"I have no idea," William whispered back. "We'll probably have to prepare to be here for a while," he said, leaning his back against the bookshelf.

"If you're tired, you can sleep while I keep watch."

William shook his head. "I don't think it's necessary. I feel too tense to be able to sleep."

"Ok," Iris replied, "but I promise to stay awake. You know that I don't need sleep the same way as a human being."

William nodded. They both sat quietly in the dark. Suddenly there was a lot of screaming and through a gap in the door they could see that someone had turned on the light outside the library.

"Is he alive? Do something! Has anyone tried CPR?"

"The doctor is already in there trying to get his heart beating." Someone else answered.

William heard several people running down the stairs. It was really chaotic.

"They have found him," William said quietly. Iris nodded. William heard screams and hysterical crying. The noise went on for a few hours and then it fell silent.

They heard steps approaching the library, but they just passed by.

"It's probably best if we all get some rest and we'll deal with the practicalities and let the family know in the morning."

"And the police," the other man added. "You can never be too sure these days. It's strange that Fritz would die just like that without warning."

"Mm," the first man replied. "We may need to do an investigation, but it will probably be difficult to find out the truth."

"Yes, we don't really know who we can trust?" The other man answered. "But Fritz's closest friend must be our safest bet."

"We'll talk more with the Grand master later. I'm sure it's wise to let him handle the internal investigation."

William felt his pulse rise and how anger flooded through his body.

"That bastard. He seems to have fooled everyone," William hissed.

"He's done a good job at it," Iris filled in.

It became quiet again outside the library and the lights went out. William was deep in his own thoughts. It felt like an eternity passed by. Everything was completely quiet and dark. He tried to listen for different sounds, but not a sound was heard. Suddenly he felt a little nudge in his side. He looked down and saw Iris who pointed at a bookshelf a little further away. Now William saw what Iris wanted to show him. The bookshelf was moving slowly, A few centimeters at a time. William held his breath. A dark shadow became visible. First a head that seemed to look left and right as to make sure there was no one there. A dark, barely audible whisper was heard.

"Is the coast clear?"

"Yes," the man answered quietly.

Out came another four men in dark suits.

"Ugh, they remind me of the two men I met on the boat to Thyrridea," William thought quietly.

The last man closed the bookshelf behind them.

"Should we wait for the others?" A man with a black beard said.

"No," the man who seemed to be in charge answered. William recognized his voice. It was the Grand master. The five men walked quickly towards one side of the library.

"They know where we are so they just have to come after us," the man said. He reached for a book and pulled it out. The bookshelves opened up and a black glossy staircase appeared. The men walked quickly up the stairs.

"We'll probably have to follow them," William whispered to Iris.

"Don't you think it's too dangerous?" Iris asked.

"We have no choice," William whispered back. "I need to hear what they're saying."

"But there will be more people coming," Iris said.

"I know," William replied. His compass mark became hotter.

"I don't have time to talk about it anymore. I have to get in there."

"I'm coming as well," Iris said. The bookshelves were about to close again. William and Iris ran and got there just before the opening to the staircase was completely closed. Further up the stairs, William saw a light shining. William stood by the black staircase and noted that on both sides there were black poles with gold ornaments. One ornament on each pole

"Is it two snakes?" William whispered.

Iris nodded.

"But the snakes are breathing fire," William said a little surprised.

"Yes, they do," Iris answered quietly. "The meaning of the ornament is the snakes of knowledge, but knowledge that kills and extinguishes everything that does not observe what they consider to be the truth."

"I need to get closer to hear what they're saying," William explained.

"I'll stay here and will flash with the flashlight if I hear anyone else approaching. It'll give you some time to hide."

"Good," William replied. He quietly snuck up the stairs. The door to the meeting room was open. On the other side, William saw that there was a large black porcelain urn. I can hide behind it, William thought. He stood completely still and then he took two big steps and then he was on the other side of the door. He heard the Grand master mumble some kind of long and incomprehensible chant. He heard many different hissing sounds. William did not understand what was being said. He looked down the stairs to see if he could see Iris, but he saw nothing. It was all dark. The only light there were came from the room. The sound suddenly stopped and all went completely still. William looked at his watch, it was completely silent for about 60 seconds before Fritz's former best friend begun to talk.

"We have now honored our brave comrades who died fighting for the dark ancient magic."

William stuck out his head so that he could just see through the opening. He saw that the man who was the leader of the group turned to one of the men and raised a golden cup and said, "Lucky that you, brother, saw Fritz bring Father Ormund's body to the cathedral so we had the chance to eliminate him before he could pass on what he knew."

"Can we really be sure he didn't tell anyone?"

"I know Fritz very well," the man replied with a wry smile. "The only thing I would be worried about is that he told his grandson something, but at the same time I am convinced that he wants to keep his family out of this and not put them in any danger. Fritz is a man who thinks he can handle difficulties on his own. Also, he couldn't be sure that those who took Father Ormund had more sympathizers within the order. He couldn't have known that, and if Fritz wasn't sure, he would've kept the information to himself."

"But why did he come here if he knew it could be dangerous for him?" the other man asked.

"He wanted to investigate the situation first. Very unwise of him and at the same time wise," the man said without paus. "You must not forget that Fritz has no evidence that there are more of us involved. I'm sure he could not have imagined that his best friend is involved. Poor Fritz," he said with an artificial sigh. "It's very difficult for old brains to think in new ways. Most often you go for what is familiar and you do not question what you think you know in the same way as you do when you are young and inquisitive. An old man's brain, I would say, usually avoids questioning what's familiar and old habits. It's too challenging and requires too much energy. Don't forget that," the man said with a hiss of a laugh.

William was startled, he rubbed his eyes to make sure he wasn't imagining it. William could almost swear that the man's tongue was like a snake's, long slender and split. William watched in fascination and sure enough, the man had a snake's tongue. William felt uncomfortable. Suddenly, he saw a flash of light from below the stairs. William instantly recognized the signal. He quickly hid behind the black porcelain urn. The wall opened and a man walked briskly up the stairs. He was tall and gangly, taking two steps at a time. From his expression it was obvious that he was stressed.

"Welcome brother," the man who appeared to be the leader said calmly, raising his gold cup again. "Why the rush? What do I usually say? When you've worked hard, you have to rest and we really deserve a break now my friends. Let us just wait for the reward now shall we. This will be our last meeting and over the next few weeks we're going to take it easy and recover. As you know, we will be richly rewarded. Take a moment and think about what kind of reward you want. Think carefully. There is no limitation in what you, or shall I say we, can receive, but first we shall relax. I suggest that we all raise our glasses and toast to an excellently executed mission and that we ease up a little on the pressure for a moment and just being ourselves for a while."

William watched as the men raised their silver cups towards their leader.

"Thank you, my friends, as I said, a big thank you for your loyalty and I am extremely proud of that we have contributed to preserving dark magic's position on the throne, Cheers!"

"Cheers," the men exclaimed and drank from their cups. At that moment the men began to transform. The leader became a huge king cobra. William rubbed his eyes again as if he wasn't sure of what he was seeing. One of the men became one of those nasty black birds that had chased William and Iris in the maze. One of the men became an eagle, another became a wolf. The fifth turned into a large spider, and the sixth became a weasel. On the floor where they had stood were their suits left in different piles.

"And now we shall summon our master, King Victor I," the king cobra hissed. He pressed a button and map of stars that shone of various emeralds, diamonds and precious stones appeared in the ceiling.

Beautiful, William thought. Beautiful and frightening at the same time. William recognized the map because it was similar to the map he had seen with Alexander, but some of the planets stood in other positions. The King Cobra lifted his golden cup with his tail and poured the contents into a gold bowl. The snake began to hiss again and William saw that it sparkled from one of the stars. When the starlight hit the contents of the bowl it began to steam and boil.

Oh, William thought, the king must be deeply involved in this. William had hoped that the current king was not aware of the history behind it all, but now he understood that the king had not only been aware of it, but that he also was actively working to ensure that the truth would not come out. I need to get out of here quickly. The king likely has great magical powers and might be able to sense my presence.

Quickly, he made his way past the door and crept along the wall down the stairs.

"We need to hurry," he whispered barely audibly to Iris. William pushed open the door and then closed the bookshelves behind him.

"You see, Iris, the current king is their master," He said.

"Oops," Iris exclaimed, "that's not good news."

They hurried out of the library.

"What shall we do now?" Iris asked.

"We need to talk to Grandpa," William answered.

"But what if there's still some of the members in the room with him?"

"We'll figure something out," William replied quickly. They ran silently down the stairs. It was dark and quiet everywhere. After a little while they stood outside Grandpa's door. William waited a moment before opening the door. It was completely dark in the room.

"Goblet, Wallace, you must help me," William whispered as he closed the door.

Goblet immediately jumped out from under the bed where he had been hiding.

"We need to wake grandpa up." William quickly told them what had happened.

"Oh my," Goblet exclaimed, "it's terrible that the king is behind everything."

"We have to call the Scientific Council," Wallace said with his dark voice. "That's the only thing we can do."

"Of course," William said, "but how? I have no idea where the council is."

"But I have," Wallace and Goblet said at the same time. "They are the only decision-making body that stands above the king in both might and magic. I can get them," Wallace said, "but I have to leave now while the enemy still is in the room behind the bookshelves."

"I'll stay with Fritz," Goblet said.

CHAPTER 22
THE CHAIRMAN OF THE COUNSIL

William, who realized that they didn't have much time, said, "Iris and I will go back to the library and keep watch. We will follow them in case they leave the room."

"Promise me to be careful," Wallace said with seriousness in his voice. "These people are really dangerous."

William nodded. William and Iris snuck back to the library and hid behind the bookshelves. They sat in silence and watched intently the hidden entrance in the bookshelves. It wasn't long until something happened.

"Do you see the smoke?" Iris whispered.

"Mm," William answered. It had begun to smoke and sparkle in the center of the library. Suddenly half of a gold bridge appeared. Down the gold bridge came seven people, three men and four women dressed in sparkling long gold caftans. It was as if they were star-spangled. The man who walked first had a staff in his hand and at the top of the staff there was a shining stone that was dazzling.

"I feel overwhelmed," William whispered to Iris.

"Me too," Iris replied. "I've never seen anything like it."

"You can really feel the power that they possess," William said, who could barely tear his eyes away from the seven people. On their heads, they wore golden conical hats that was made of the same thick gold fabric as the caftans they wore. On their feet they had glass shoes that gleamed in the light. Wallace brought up the rear. The man who walked first had long white hair and no beard. He turned to the bookshelf where William and Iris were hiding.

"You can come out now William and bring your friend Iris with you," the man said in a loud dark voice that echoed in the room.

William looked at Iris, then they stood up and left their hiding place. William walked up to the man he understood to be the chairman of the council, but he didn't dare to look up and meet his gaze.

"Don't be afraid, I'm not dangerous," the man said. "Come closer so that I can see your face."

William took a few more steps so that he was standing right in front of the chairman. The man took his hand under William's chin and gently brought it upwards so that their eyes met.

"Yes, indeed, you are William's younger brother and bearer of the mark of the compass. The young boy's life that in a cunning and evil way ended far too early. I feel that you have been in contact with your big brother and that his powers have been transferred to you. That's good," the man's voice echoed in the library.

His eyes blackened. "I understand that the king is behind all that has happened." His voice vibrated with anger. "He and his followers will soon receive their punishment", his fingers vibrated and beamed with light and power. "But you my friend will be rewarded for your bravery and above all for your pure heart." The man then gently stroked William's hair. "You're a unique boy. The likes of you are rarely born."

William looked him in the eyes and felt the man's warmth radiating from his ice blue eyes.

"Now, however, it's time for me and my colleagues on the Scientific Council to do our job." His gaze darkened. He turned to face William again.

"If you wish, you can stay here in the library while we destroy them."

William suddenly felt very tired. "I guess I'll do," William answered and sat down in one of the armchairs.

"Good," the chairman of the council said. Then he yelled, "Towards the hidden door!" The entourage walked towards the bookshelves.

William shuddered at the harshness of the chairman's voice. It was like it cut through bone and marrow. William got goosebumps all over his body. William saw how smoothly and easily the white-haired man moved, and how he only lifted his staff slightly, and the bookshelves that concealed the opening were blown to pieces. William ducked as the pieces of wood flew through the room. Then the council plunged up the stairs. William and Iris heard the chairman roar, "You deserve to die. Light magic is stronger than dark magic." After that, screams were heard then everything became quiet. So quiet that William almost found it a little uncomfortable. Minutes later, the council came down the stairs.

"Now they're eliminated," the white-haired man said in a calm voice. He walked up to William. "We'll talk more tomorrow night. Now you should go down to your grandfather and wake him up, and then take it easy for the rest of the day. You've done a fantastic job. Without you, we wouldn't have been able to find the traitors. Thank you, William."

William looked into his bright blue eyes and felt safe. The man raised his hand and the gold bridge appeared in the room. Now that William had the opportunity to take a closer look at it, he saw how the chairman only needed to put his feet at the bottom of it, then the gold bridge carried him all the way up, the other council members did the same. When the chairman of the council was at the top of the bridge, he turned and looked at William and said,

"See you soon."

"Yes, we will and thank you for coming." William replied.

"You're welcome, and we are the ones who should thank you," the man replied with a smile then he turned again and disappeared through the wall.

The Gold Bridge probably continues for a good while longer, William thought.

William stood there for a while after the council had left. It almost felt a little unreal that it was all over.

"My beloved big brother, it's finally over!" he suddenly screamed out in joy.

"Iris, we need to hurry to Grandpa!" William shouted.

They quickly took the shortcut to Grandpa's room. William slammed open the door.

"Grandpa, Grandpa, are you there? Are you ok?" William said worriedly.

Fritz sat lowly up in bed.

"It takes a while for the spell to wear off," Wallace explained. "After a faking death spell, one usually feels quite tired and stiff," Wallace continued.

William only listened with half an ear to Wallace. Instead, he threw himself into Fritz's arms.

"Grandpa, Grandpa it's over!" William bubbled with joy. "The council finished them off so now they don't exist anymore! We have nothing to worry about because the mission is complete!" he laughed happily.

Fritz wasn't quite awake yet. "Do you mean it went well?" he said in a rough sleepy voice.

"More than well, it went excellent!" William laughed.

Fritz began to cry with relief. "How lovely," he snuffled as he held William and rocked him slowly back and forth in his arms. Fritz still felt a little dazed like you can do after you slept very hard and just woke up. When it feels like the brain is not quite keeping up and the thoughts are moving slowly. Fritz cradled William slowly as his own brain slowly began to come to life. Suddenly, he was wide awake and his brain and the stiffness in his body were gone. "What are you saying William?!" Fritz said with a squeal, quickly getting out of bed. "Are they gone? Is everything solved?"

"Yes!" William shouted, "it's true. The Council put an end to them!"

Fritz laughed out. "It's absolutely fantastic! What a victory! What a victory for good and for truth!"

William and Fritz were united in a real howl of joy. And it wasn't long before Goblet, Iris and Wallace with his dark voice also joined in. "We made it! We made it," they yelled at the same time while they danced around on the floor. When they finally got tired, they sat down on the bed. Everything had finally begun to sink in and it was actually Wallace who first took the opportunity to say.

"Think that all this evil that resulted in the death of the king and his son was just to gain power."

"Yes, it's horrible what power can do to people and the worst is that when power hungry have tasted the sweetness of power, they always want more and will do anything to keep it," Fritz said tonelessly.

William shivered. "Yes," he said soberly. "They killed my big brother just because he questioned the death of the king and his son."

"Yes. Indeed, there are many innocents who have lost their lives so that the wrong people could rule Thyrridea.

And it's been going on up until this day," Fritz said grimly.

He thought of his own order and the clean-up that had to take place there to find out who else was involved in supporting the dark side.

"Yes," Wallace said, "a lot will happen in Thyrridea. The council will let the current king have his punishment and then they will have to go back to find out who rightfully should rule Thyrridea."

"It feels pretty good that we don't have to," William said.

"Yes," Fritz said, "you've done quite enough William, and now the history books will be rewritten in Thyrridea and everyone will know what a fine big brother you've had and how he was betrayed by his master of magic."

"Now it will be nice to go home," William said wearily.

"Yes indeed," Fritz replied. "My friends, let's go home!"

William thought it would feel incredibly good to come home to mom, dad, grandma and to his room.

"How I've missed them," he said aloud.